PRAISE FOR THE
Chintz 'n China M

"The perfect book to curl up with." —*The M̲ Reader*

"A truly charismatic, down-to-earth character . . . Don't miss this charming first book in the series. I look forward to the next one." —*Rendezvous*

"A very appealing series with some very scary stuff. Thank goodness there's a charm included!" —Mysterylovers.com

"This paranormal mystery has enough romance in it to keep readers of three genres very happy . . . The audience will adore Emerald, a bright, shining, and caring soul who wants to do right by everybody and use her powers to make the world a better place." —*Midwest Book Review*

"For those who love paranormal mysteries, *Murder Under a Mystic Moon* . . . will not disappoint." —MyShelf.com

Chintz 'n China Mysteries by Yasmine Galenorn

GHOST OF A CHANCE
LEGEND OF THE JADE DRAGON
MURDER UNDER A MYSTIC MOON
A HARVEST OF BONES
ONE HEX OF A WEDDING

One Hex of a Wedding

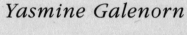

Yasmine Galenorn

BERKLEY PRIME CRIME, NEW YORK

THE BERKLEY PUBLISHING GROUP
Published by the Penguin Group
Penguin Group (USA) Inc.
375 Hudson Street, New York, New York 10014, USA
Penguin Group (Canada), 90 Eglinton Avenue East, Suite 700, Toronto, Ontario M4P 2Y3, Canada
(a division of Pearson Penguin Canada Inc.)
Penguin Books Ltd., 80 Strand, London WC2R 0RL, England
Penguin Group Ireland, 25 St. Stephen's Green, Dublin 2, Ireland (a division of Penguin Books Ltd.)
Penguin Group (Australia), 250 Camberwell Road, Camberwell, Victoria, 3124, Australia
(a division of Pearson Australia Group Pty. Ltd.)
Penguin Books India Pvt. Ltd., 11 Community Centre, Panchsheel Park, New Delhi—110 017, India
Penguin Group (NZ), Cnr. Airborne and Rosedale Roads, Albany, Auckland 1310, New Zealand
(a division of Pearson New Zealand Ltd.)
Penguin Books (South Africa) (Pty.) Ltd., 24 Sturdee Avenue, Rosebank, Johannesburg 2196, South Africa

Penguin Books Ltd., Registered Offices: 80 Strand, London WC2R ORL, England

ONE HEX OF A WEDDING

A Berkley Prime Crime Book / published by arrangement with the author

PRINTING HISTORY
Berkley Prime Crime mass-market edition / August 2006

Copyright © 2006 by Yasmine Galenorn.
Cover art by Robert Goldstrom.
Cover design by Lesley Worrell.
Interior text design by Kristin del Rosario.

ISBN: 0-425-21117-7

BERKLEY® PRIME CRIME
Berkley Prime Crime Books are published by The Berkley Publishing Group,
a division of Penguin Group (USA) Inc.,
375 Hudson Street, New York, New York 10014.
BERKLEY PRIME CRIME and the BERKLEY PRIME CRIME design are trademarks belonging to
Penguin Group (USA) Inc.

PRINTED IN THE UNITED STATES OF AMERICA

10 9 8 7 6 5 4 3 2 1

To Daniela, who was my
matron of honor at my wedding.
You stuck with me through all the crazed planning,
you championed Samwise before
the rest of our friends accepted him,
and you did everything a blood-oath
sister is supposed to do.
Love ya, babe!

ACKNOWLEDGMENTS

As always, love and thanks to my supportive husband, Samwise, and our four cats, who are the joys of my life. Thank you to the usual crew: To Christine Zika, my editor. To Meredith Bernstein, my agent, for believing in me and being there when I need to talk. To my sister, Wanda. To Margie M., Vicki St. C., Siduri, Theresa S., Tiffany M., and Brad R., Lisa DDC, Linda W.—good friends all. To my Witchy Chicks blogging group: You're all warped women and I love you.

Thanks to my readers, old and new. Without you, we authors would be lost. And of course, Mielikki, Tapio, Rauni, and Ukko, my spiritual guardians.

If you wish to contact me, you can via snail mail through my publishers or the address on my website (please enclose a self-addressed stamped envelope for reply), or via e-mail through my website, www.galenorn.com.

Bright Blessings to all,
the Painted Panther
Yasmine Galenorn

Anger and jealousy can no more bear
to lose sight of their objects than love.

—GEORGE ELIOT

One

⁜

THE PARTY WAS in full swing when Harlow grabbed the microphone and motioned for the Barry Boys to take a break from the '80s retro dance numbers they were playing. The strains of "Burning Down the House" fell silent as she stepped up on the stage and clapped her hands for attention, although she needn't have bothered. My ex-supermodel buddy was tall, gorgeous, with golden blond hair braided à la Bo Derek's cornrows, and the mere sight of her standing there in a gold mini-dress and red stilettos stunned the room into silence.

"Welcome, and thank you for coming. As you know, Emerald and Joe will be taking that last leap of faith and making it official. Countdown is T-minus two weeks! And we'll all be right there with them, cheering them on. Until then, let's bring down the house!"

The crowd erupted in a roar and Jimbo, who was standing next to me, swung me up to sit on his shoulder. I grabbed hold of his shirt collar with one hand—I've never been one for high-wire acts—and he braced my legs against his chest and paraded me around the room. I waved as a volley of friendly catcalls rang out from our friends, and then he stopped in front of Joe and tossed me into my fiancé's arms. I gasped as I sailed through the air, but Joe caught me without so much as a grunt. As he set me down on the floor, I looped my arm through his.

Harlow's voice rang out again. "Be careful, Jimbo. Remember she head-butted you to the floor once before. I'm sure she can do it again." Another round of laughter from the crowd. "Okay, let's show these two just what we're made of. Get your butts in gear and bring on the music!"

Joe and I found ourselves unceremoniously pushed into the middle of the dance floor while the band began a frenzied rendition of "Whip It." He grabbed my hand and spun me out to the center, where I let go with a shimmy that brought yet another round of cheers, and then the room was filled with dancers, clapping and head-banging to the beat. As the band segued into "Don't You (Forget About Me)," by Simple Minds, I rested my head on Joe's shoulder, and he wrapped his arms around my waist as we swirled around the floor, lost in the music. Would we still be dancing like this in fifty years? I couldn't see that far ahead, but something inside told me we would.

"Babe, you look gorgeous," he whispered.

And in truth, I felt gorgeous. I had shaped up a lot over the past six months as I advanced my practice of yoga, and while I vowed never to give up my caffeine or chocolate, I had managed to cut back on the sugar. As for my outfit, I'd found the perfect lilac gauze and lace skirt for the party, thanks to Harlow and a trip to Seattle. It floated a couple inches above my knees, and I'd paired it with a plum camisole and a Victoria's Secret demi bra.

I'd also succumbed to vanity at long last, and dyed the silver out of my waist-length mass of curls. When I told Harl I intended to go to Bab's Salon down the street from my teashop, she whisked me away to Seattle. We stopped at the Gene Juarez spa for the works. As an early shower gift, she paid my way through a trim, color job, manicure, pedicure, and massage, and I didn't put up a fight. Then we hit her favorite boutiques, where I found my outfit and the perfect pair of shoes.

As Joe danced me around the floor, I glanced down at the open-toe, sling-back black pumps, still aghast both at how high the heels were and at how much they'd set my credit card back. My toenails, painted a brilliant fuchsia, stood out against the rich fabric. Suddenly overwhelmed by the whimsy of the situation, I pushed aside my worry over their cost and laughed as Joe dipped me. The back of my head almost touching the floor, I raised one leg into the air, toe pointed, in a kick that would have made Catherine Zeta-Jones proud.

After the song ended, the band took a break and everybody headed for the buffet. I rested my head on Harlow's shoulder. "Thank you," I said. "Even with my family here, I'm having so much fun. Thank God, I don't have to entertain them tonight. The buffet will take care of that. It's been crazy since they showed up."

Harl's eyes twinkled. "Relatives can be a bitch, can't they?" She threw her arm around my shoulder and wrinkled her nose. "I'm so glad you let me plan everything. Murray's knee-deep in work right now, and I love playing hostess. You shouldn't have to worry about anything."

I frowned. She'd just touched on a point that had been bothering me all day. "Harl, does Murray seem different to you lately?"

"What do you mean?" Harl cocked her head to one side.

I shook my head. "I don't know. It seems like she's been moody and distant for the past couple of weeks. I know things are okay with Jimbo, so I don't think it's anything to do with their relationship. I'm just a little worried. She doesn't seem herself lately."

Harlow shrugged. "I don't know. Maybe. To be honest, I've been focused on other things. Like this party." She looked around. "Everybody seems to be having fun, don't you think? And the room looks gorgeous."

She was right, on both counts. Everyone—including

my easily offended Grandma McGrady—had a smile on their face. And the banquet room at the Forest End's Diner had been decked out in full glory. A huge photograph of Joe and me blown up to poster proportions graced an easel near the buffet. Roses, both pink and red, filled vases on every table. Streamers in sparkling metallic hues of purple, green, blue, and gold spiraled from the ceiling, and the walls had stick-on hearts plastered on them.

I had a suspicion the latter was Kip's idea. He'd developed a romantic streak ever since he realized that I'd be marrying a man who would be there every day to hang out with him and treat him like his father should have, but never did. Add in the fact that I'd seen the hearts peeking out of my ten-year-old's backpack before he and Miranda headed out to help Harlow get things ready, and I was pretty sure my guess was on track.

"Speaking of Murray, where is she?" Harl asked. "I wanted her to lead the toasts."

Anna Murray, my best friend in the whole world and my maid of honor, was nowhere in sight. I glanced around, wondering where she'd disappeared to. "I don't know. Last I saw she was dancing with Jimbo. Whoever knew he could do the twist? And I'd have lost my shirt betting he wouldn't know the difference between the Hustle and a waltz." Jimbo, it turned out, was not only a biker extraordinaire, but also quite the star on the dance floor.

"You and me both," Harl said. She glanced around and a smile filtered over her face, a smile I recognized instantly. I followed her gaze to find myself staring at her husband, James. He was a lean, muscular, dark-haired man who was a good three inches shorter than Harlow. James carried himself with a quiet dignity. He was holding their daughter, Eileen, who was only a couple months shy of her first birthday. The look on his face said everything was right in his world. Harlow and Eileen were lucky ladies. He was one of the good guys.

"You, my dear, have a beautiful family," I said. "So, what's next on his agenda?" James was a photographer and was often away for several months at a time on photo shoots. A childhood sweetheart of Harl's, they'd reconnected years ago when he was assigned to photograph a layout where she was the star supermodel. They'd rekindled their romance and—aware of the fleeting life expectancy of her career—Harlow decided to get out while she was on top. She had socked away most of her money, after a brief dip into the cokehead-party lifestyle, and they were set for life.

Harl shrugged, her smile fading. "He said he's staying close to home, but I know for a fact he's being talked up by one of the big adventure magazines. Other than that, he's got a three-day shoot coming up at the end of the month for the Seattle tourism board. We're all going and turning it into a minivacation. But that's after your wedding, so don't worry about us skipping out on you."

Just then, I noticed Murray slip back into the room from the double doors leading to the restaurant proper. When she saw us, she motioned with her head. I didn't like the look on her face.

I touched Harl on the arm and she followed my gaze. "She looks upset."

"Yeah, she does, doesn't she? Come on, let's go see what's up."

As we made our way through the crowd, I fielded congratulations from all sides. The party was one last bash before the wedding, for my relatives, my customers, and all of our friends. The ladies who frequented my tea and china shop would have felt slighted if they weren't offered the chance to congratulate their tea-monger. Jimbo and Joe were planning a family-and-friends-only barbecue for tomorrow after my bridal shower, and Harl would be holding a formal dinner a few days before our wedding.

Murray impatiently gestured us over to the doors. "I hate to be the bearer of bad news, but I thought you'd want to know in advance." Her gaze fastened on my face and a shiver ran up my back. Yeah, something bad was coming.

The kids were here, my family was here, and Joe was here, so there couldn't be anything wrong with any of them. A sudden sweep of panic rushed over me. "The cats? The house? Did something happen?"

"No . . . nothing like that," she said.

"Then what? A ghost in the attic? A murderer on the rampage? Don't tell me Cathy Sutton's decided to film my wedding for KLIK-TV?" As far fetched as they sounded, those possibilities were all too real for my comfort.

Mur grimaced. "Worse. Okay, here's the deal—" But before she could tell me, a voice interrupted our conversation and I knew she was right. This was worse than almost anything I could dream up.

"Aren't you going to say hello or are you playing the little snob today?"

Tone on edge, slightly patronizing. Oh yes, I knew that voice only too well. It was one I despised and dreaded every time it winged its way into my ears. I held my breath, hoping that I was wrong, but in my heart I knew I wasn't. I glanced at Mur, swallowing. She gave me a sympathetic smile, and I knew that there was no help for it. I had to face my nightmare come to life.

"So, you're getting married again. My feelings are hurt; you didn't invite me to your little shindig. I had to find out through our son. But then again, you always did specialize in playing the martyr, Emerald."

I slowly turned around, gritting my teeth. Please, oh please let me be wrong. But luck was a fickle mistress. There, in the doorway behind Murray, uninvited and unwanted, stood my ex-husband. Roy. And the smirk on his face told me we were in for a bumpy ride.

WHO AM I? Well, I'm Emerald O'Brien, I'm thirty-seven years old, and I own the Chintz 'n China Tea Room, where we sell china, tea, cookies, jams, and gift baskets, and where the local matrons meet for a quiet cup and scone amidst their busy afternoons.

I'm also the mother of two incredible children—
Kipling, my ten-year-old computer whiz, magic-loving,
tumbling-his-way-onto-the-gymnastics-team son, and Miranda, who's fourteen going on thirty, and who can out-
stargaze any astronomer she meets. She's going to land on
the moon someday. Or Mars. I'm counting on it, and I
have all the confidence in the world that she won't stop
there. No, if there's a warp engine to discover or a new
comet heading our way, Randa will be the first in line for
accolades. To round out our family, we share our house
with four cats—Samantha, a gorgeous calico, and her
now-grown kittens, Nebula, Nigel, and Noël. We almost
lost Samantha last year, so now they are all indoor-onlys,
safe from predators and interdimensional rifts in time.

And then there's Joe. Joseph Ethan Files, to be precise.
My fiancé, who happens to be ten years younger than I am.
We fell in love a little over a year ago, and on Halloween—
my birthday—he knelt down on a dark stormy night when
I was in tears from a tragic and ghostly reunion I'd just witnessed, and he asked me to marry him. I said yes. We're
getting married in a couple of weeks on the summer solstice, under the fading light of the evening sky in the
gazebo flower garden that used to be the haunted, bramble-
infested lot next to my house.

Oh, one more note. A little one, really, all things considered. I'm the village witch here in Chiqetaw, Washington, a small town off Highway 9 in Whatcom County. I no
longer try to deny the claim, because I've finally accepted
my place in the town. When the universe decided to slap
a cosmic badge on me and call me the new sheriff, I resisted at first, but as the Borg say in the Star Trek realm,
"Resistance is futile."

I've accepted my destiny. On the astral realm I fend
off—and sometimes help—otherworldly visitors. And on
the mundane, I've been the downfall of a few murderers
and thieves.

If there's one thing the past couple years have taught
me, it's that when fate comes knocking, you either open

the door or the karma police bash it in. So, when the universe delivers me a new mission, I accept it, even if it seems impossible. As my Nanna taught me, there's usually a solution for every problem. You just have to ask the right question.

HOLY HELL. I closed my eyes, repressing a groan. Roy was out to ruin my evening. I knew it as sure as I knew my own name, and I planned on nipping *that* little prospect in the bud. "What the hell are you doing here?"

He blinked, his expression as guileless as usual. The man had a way of looking naïve and fresh off the turnip truck. Brilliant, he had appeared the epitome of the all-American boy when I first met him, and the look had stood the test of time. Pity his actions didn't follow suit. It wasn't until later that I'd learned the truth hiding behind those wide, innocent eyes.

"Kip invited me, so I thought I'd show up and see who on earth decided to put a ring on your finger."

Damn it. I knew Kip didn't expect—or even want—me to get back together with Roy, but sometimes that little goober did a good job of mucking things up. Kipling wanted his father's approval, a dream seldom realized. I had to hand it to him, though. He persevered. And chances were, Kip didn't think he'd done anything wrong. That was part of the problem with my son. He ran headlong into situations, acting first and only thinking it through later. As a result, Kip had managed to pull off some pretty big blunders for his age.

"Kip made a mistake and you should have known better. You're an adult, so give us all a break and act like one." I leaned in so I wouldn't be overheard. "I know you, Roy. The only reason you're here is to see what havoc you can cause. You're so miserable in your own life that you want everybody else to be miserable with theirs. I'm sorry Tyra left you, but it's your own fault."

Roy's second wife—the woman I caught him cheating

with when we were married—had dumped him a few months ago. She'd mysteriously fallen and had a miscarriage. Having been on the wrong end of Roy's fists a couple of times, I suspected Roy had something to do with her fall, but she wasn't pressing charges. Unlike me, she'd just quietly demanded a sizable alimony. I'd asked for child support, and forced him to pay it, but I'd only asked for a settlement of our property and money on hand when we divorced. I didn't want anything from Roy that might chain him to me any tighter than the bonds forged because of our children.

He blinked. I'd managed a direct hit. "Fine, I'll be on my best behavior," he said. "Congratulations." He pushed past us and into the room before I had a chance to stop him.

I locked eyes with Murray. "This can't end on a good note, not with him here. He drinks, Mur. A lot."

She nodded. "I'll warn Jimmy and a couple of the boys to watch out for him." As she headed off to find Jimbo, I yanked Harlow's sleeve and grimaced.

"Let's go. I've got to reach Grandma McGrady before she sees Roy."

Harl's lip twitched. "What's she going to do? Talk him to death?"

I shook my head. "You don't understand. When I told her that I caught Roy screwing his mistress in Miranda's bedroom, and that Randa walked in on them, Grandma M. swore she'd rip out his heart. And Grandma M. has never threatened to do anything that she wasn't willing to carry through. Nanna was a ripsnorter, but Grandma McGrady's a bull chasing a red cape. And Roy is on her hit list."

Even as I spoke, I could hear Grandma's voice echoing over the crowd. Kip was pleading with her about something. Great, the fireworks had begun. Stifling a snicker, Harl slipped her arm through mine. "I just hope we don't get kicked out of here. Sounds like we're needed. Let's go."

My heart sank as we hurried across the dance floor.

The last thing I wanted was for the party to turn into a brawl, especially in front of my children and customers. I'd managed to keep my prior life with Roy out of the spotlight, and I wanted it to stay that way.

Steeling myself, I waded into the mix only to be greeted by the sight of Grandma McGrady shaking her finger in Roy's face, while Kip tugged on her arm. Grandma M., dressed in a peach polyester pantsuit with her gray hair coiffed into a modern bob slicked to the sides of her head, had backed Roy against the wall next to the buffet.

"Roy William Patrick O'Brien, what in the world are you thinking of, showing up here? I told you before— come near my granddaughter again and I'll throw you out on your butt." Grandma M. didn't mince words, that was for sure, and her opinion of Roy was about as low as it could get.

Roy glared at her. "Grandma McGrady—"

Oops, goof number two. Number one was showing up at all.

"*Don't you call me that.* I am *Mrs. McGrady* to you. You gave up the right to call me Grandma when you decided you couldn't keep it in your pants and went gallivanting around behind Emerald's back. We're no longer related in any manner, and I would think you'd have the decency to mind your business—"

"Great-grandma! Please, he came 'cause I told him about it. I didn't know he wasn't supposed to show up!" Kip tugged harder at her sleeve, and she turned to him, her lips pursed.

"Kipling, you're ten years old. That's old enough to know better—"

"Everybody pipe down!" Taking a deep breath, I entered the fray. Kip was on the verge of tears and whether or not I wanted Roy here didn't matter at this point. "Kip, honey, go with Harl and find your sister. Get something to eat, okay? I want to talk to your father and to your great-grandmother."

Kip sniffed and wiped his nose on his sleeve. He forced

a smile and nodded. "Okay, Mom. I'm sorry. I didn't mean to cause trouble."

I tousled his hair. "Oh, sweetie, I know you didn't. You never do. Now run on. Everything will be fine." At least Roy had the good graces to keep his mouth shut while Harlow led Kip away. After they were gone, I turned back to them. "Listen to me. I want you both to knock it off."

"Emerald! When were you taught that it's all right to speak to your grandmother this way? I can't believe that you've turned into such an ill-mannered—" Grandma looked about ready to pull her smelling salts routine.

I shrugged. "I wouldn't have to if the two of you hadn't decided to ruin my party. Now, let me talk to Roy. Alone."

She seemed to be debating the wisdom of arguing but then stomped off, threading her way through the crowd, no doubt on her way to rein in the cavalry. My mother, father, and sister would be here in full force in a few minutes. I sighed and looked up at Roy.

"Okay, buster. No," I warned him, holding up my hand as he started to speak. "You keep quiet for a change. Kip obviously thought you could behave yourself here. He made the silly mistake of thinking of you as an adult, probably because you're his father and he still wants to believe you have some shred of decency in you. I hate to disappoint our son, but I'm not about to allow you to ramrod your way through my life, including this party. So you have a choice. You can stay and act civilized. Or head for the door right now. Your move, buster. Make it quick."

For the first time that I could remember, Roy hesitated, rather than immediately launching into one of his diatribes. Hmm. What was up? Maybe losing Tyra had been the last blow needed to open his eyes. Maybe her desertion broke down his belief that he was the center of the universe.

After a moment, he shrugged and said, "What the hell. I guess we can be civil one night because of the kids."

The kids. My children. And, unfortunately, his children. Against my better judgment, I assented. "Okay. But if you get out of line, out you go. *Capiche?*"

Roy snorted, his hands jammed in his pockets. "You're a piece of work, all right. Okay, Emerald. Truce for now?"

Still doubting my decision, I slowly nodded. "Truce. Now, mingle, stick to safe topics, and leave unfashionably early, if you would." As I headed over to Joe and Jimbo, who were scowling at us, I had the feeling that my words had thudded against the side of a brick wall.

Grandma McGrady had spilled the beans to Joe about Roy's appearance. She might not approve of our age difference—me being older than Joe the operative problem—but she knew enough to plant the seeds of discord in the right place. And Murray had probably told Jimbo. Whatever the case, both men looked miffed.

"You're letting him stay?" Joe crossed his arms and cocked his head, his way of telling me that I'd slipped into reprehensible territory.

I filled him in on Kip's mistake. "I don't want my son seeing me throw his father out on his ass. I'm going to send the kids home with my mother, or Ida. Whoever I can corral first. Then I'll deal with Roy."

Jimbo grumbled. "I think he needs a lesson in etiquette."

I put my hand on the big guy's arm. "Hold off, okay? Both you and Joe simmer down. If he gets out of hand, then yeah, you two can clean him up, but let me get the kids out of the way first."

Joe rolled his eyes, but then, with a loud sigh, kissed the top of my head. "Whatever you say, babe. Go play Mama."

The Barry Boys were cranking it up again. Irritated, I wondered what it took to have a reasonably uneventful event. I wanted to enjoy myself, not field arguments and bullies and fights. I finally managed to corner Ida in the restroom. "Can you do me a huge favor and take the kids home?"

Ida glanced at the clock. "Of course, dear, but it's early yet. Has anything happened?"

I nodded. "My ex, Roy, showed up and I'm afraid there's going to be a testosterone match before long."

She patted me on the hand. "Don't worry. I'll gather them up and scoot them home. Do you want them to stay at my place?" Ida, a retired schoolteacher who put the *proper* in *prim and proper*, had been the kids' babysitter since I first moved to Chiqetaw. Along with Horvald, she was my closest neighbor. And though Randa no longer needed a lot of supervision, Kip was still a handful.

I shook my head. "We won't be too late, so they can go right home if they want. I'd just feel better with you on call."

As we stepped back into the banquet room, the sheer weight of everybody's emotions, both good and bad, hit me. I felt like bagging it, taking the kids home myself, and curling up on the sofa with a bad movie and a bowl of popcorn. Ida must have picked up on my sudden depression, because within five minutes the kids were not only ready, but willing to go with her. I didn't know how she worked her miracles, but I wasn't going to question them.

"Did you say good-bye to your father?" I asked.

"Yeah, he said he'll call us in the morning, but he wouldn't tell us when. He just said to stick around home until he does."

That was par for the course. Just like Roy to avoid calling, then show up unannounced and expect us to wrap our schedules around him like he was some sort of god.

"We'll talk about it in the morning," I said, then hugged both of them. "Go on now. Joe and I'll be home soon." As Ida and Horvald—our other neighbor, who was courting Ida in every proper sense of the word—headed out with the kids, I breathed a sigh of relief. At least now when the fireworks flew, the kids would be out of the way. And I had an awful feeling we'd soon be witnessing a brilliant show.

I turned to find my sister, Rose, waiting patiently. Rose

was short like me, but fashionably thin and she had a pinched look to her mouth that made her look older than me even though she was a year or so younger.

"Emmy, I know that it's been a long evening, but I wanted to give you this. It's a sister-present." She held out a box.

I hesitated, then accepted the narrow velvet box. Rose and I might be the same height and have the same eyes, but there all resemblances ceased, personality included. She was the good girl, I was the wild child—at least according to Grandma M. Rose was generous, but every gift she gave came with strings attached. I glanced at her and she beamed. Maybe, I thought, maybe she really meant it this time. *A sister-present.*

I flipped the top on the box and gasped. Nestled on a bed of red velvet rested a faceted crystal necklace. The beads were bound together by bronze fasteners, and their surfaces glistened, sparkling with rainbows. Speechless, I lifted it out of the box and held it up to the light.

Rose broke into a wide smile. "Do you like it?"

"I love it!" And I did. It was so much my style that I wondered just how she'd picked it out. Everything she'd ever bought for me had ended up at the thrift store after spending a year in the back of my closet. As I looked at her expectant face, however, I pushed away my ungenerous thoughts. Maybe Rose wanted to mend fences, bridge the gap that had kept us on opposite shores since we were young.

"Here, let me put it on for you," she said, taking the necklace as she motioned for me to turn around. I unfastened the gold chain I was already wearing and slipped it into the box as she encircled my neck with her gift. "It's called the Bride's Circlet," she said. "The owner of the shop where I bought it said he thinks it's about a hundred and fifty years old, but he wasn't positive."

An antique? I didn't dare ask how much the necklace had cost her. Rose was well-to-do, thanks to her ever-absent salesman of a husband, but I still had the feeling this had set her back a little.

"Thank you," I whispered, then impulsively turned to give her a hug. As I did, I suddenly felt dizzy and swayed. She reached for my hand until I could balance myself.

"Are you okay?" she asked, looking worried.

I nodded. "Yeah, I just felt . . . a little weird. Like something shifted." Wonderful—a psychic quake. I wondered what was up, but didn't have time to focus on what had caused my vertigo because she launched into an unexpected monologue.

"I saw that and I thought, that has Emerald written all over it. I know I've been aloof for a while, but I'm so glad you wanted a big wedding with family and everything—we so seldom ever get together. It occurred to me that maybe we should hold a family reunion this autumn and all meet in Seattle or even over on the shoreline, Ocean Shores or Kalaloch or one of those resort areas. So, do you like the necklace?" Without skipping a beat, she fell silent, like a wind-up toy that had suddenly run down.

Still foggy from the vertigo attack and her sudden fountain of words, I nodded and held out my arms. "How about that hug now? I love it, Rosy. I really do. You're a sweetheart."

She stiffened for a moment, then relaxed into the embrace. "Anything for my big sister's wedding. I think this one will last," she added. "I like Joe a lot better than I did Roy. Grandma M.'s having a hissy fit over his age, but she told me—in secret, so don't you say anything—that she likes him. She thinks he's a 'properly mannered young man' and that maybe he can 'tame Emerald into behaving like a proper lady.'"

I sputtered for a moment, then burst out laughing. Rose joined me and for the first time in years, we giggled over a secret. Might we *actually* be able to develop a friendship after all of these years? We'd never had any official falling out, just one hell of a fight when we were young that put an end to our developing bond. After that we were polite, we sent cards and called once in a while, but Rose and I had nothing as strong as my connection with Murray.

I was about to tell her how glad I was that she'd come when a loud shout from the other end of the room caught my attention. I broke a path through the dancers and stepped into an opening near the buffet. Roy, beer in hand, stood nose-to-chin with Joe. By the look of the scattered bottles on the table, I figured Roy had made up for lost time. He was easily three sheets to the wind. The man never could hold his liquor, a problem that had become a serious issue as our marriage had disintegrated.

"Let me tell you a little about her," Roy was saying. "She got fat on me . . . she let her—her—herself go and she got fat on me."

"And let me tell you once again to shut your mouth or get out." Joe hadn't seen me yet. A good four inches taller than Roy, he was glaring down at him, the look in his eyes the closest I'd ever seen to violence.

"What the hell is going on?" I said. "Roy, you dolt! Do you have to cause trouble every time you're around?"

"Where are the kids?" he asked, looking around wildly. "I wanna tell them good night."

Shoving my way between the two men, I jabbed Roy in the chest with my finger. "I sent them home. It's time for you to leave, too. Call them when you're sober." I had no intention of setting him off, but then again, that's how it had always been—never knowing when he was going to blow his stack. Life with Roy had been a series of days spent walking on eggshells. Unfortunately, this turned out to be one of those times.

"Tell me to leave, will you? You're still the same bitch you were when I dumped you years ago! I should have taken the kids, you slut—" And just like that, in front of everyone, Roy took a swing at me. His open hand grazed my cheek before I realized what was happening.

Barely aware of the blow that set my ears ringing, I lost it. "You fucking bastard, you honestly think you can still get away with that? You've got a big lesson to learn, Roy, and one of these days, you're going to learn it the hard way."

Years of repressed anger fueling me, I lunged, shoving him hard. He landed on the main buffet table, right in the center of the two-tier cake shaped like a giant teapot. Before I could do or say another thing, Joe and Jimbo were bearing down on Roy, and they looked ready to kill.

Two

✧

I KNOW THAT a lot of women might find the scenario romantic . . . their fiancé battling their ex-husband to defend their honor, but I was totally mortified. It didn't help that I blamed myself. I'd played right into Roy's machinations by allowing him into the party in the first place.

"I'll teach you to hit my fiancée. Or any woman for that matter!" Joe made a grab for Roy, but stumbled back as Jimbo intervened, hauling Roy off the floor as he lifted him by the collar. Roy's feet dangled a good half-foot from the floor. The look on Jimbo's face was so chiseled it could have cut diamonds.

"We're *both* gonna teach you a lesson," Jimbo said, his voice gruff. His eyes sparkled, and I had the feeling he was enjoying this.

Joe shook his head. "He's mine, man."

Just then, the drunken Roy took it into his head to defend himself and kicked Jimbo square in the balls. Jimbo let out a sharp yelp and dropped Roy back onto the table before doubling over. That was all it took. Joe was on Roy like a wolf on a rabbit. They rolled onto the ground, but Roy was no match for the younger—and stronger—man.

Joe threw a couple of well-aimed punches, connecting with Roy's jaw, and the bone-chilling cracks echoed through the hypnotized circle of guests.

"Stop it! All of you! Knock it off!" My shouts went unheeded. I knew that weddings could bring out the worst in people, but jeez! At least the party at my first marriage hadn't deteriorated into a Jerry Springer scene. Of course, I hadn't had an ex-husband to deal with, either, especially one determined to ruin my happiness. Instead, I'd married him and let him ruin my life that way.

Jimbo was stumbling to his feet, looking determined when Murray leaped up on what was left of the table.

"Freeze, suckers, or I'm running you all in!" Hands on her hips, in her burgundy halter dress with its flirty bow cinching the waist and her high-heeled strappy sandals, she looked ready to spring into the frame of an action T&A movie, but nobody laughed. Nobody ever laughed at Murray when she was upset.

I rushed over and pulled Joe away from Roy. Harlow yanked on Jimbo's arm until he backed away.

Murray glared down at the troublemakers. "You've just ruined Emerald's evening, you've destroyed the cake, and you've made a complete spectacle out of yourselves. Satisfied?"

"Emerald ruined the cake." Roy's voice was slurred, but recognizably whiny. "She pushed me. See what I'm talking about? Pushy broad."

"*You* might want to shut your mouth, Roy. And remember how much better off you'll be by *keeping* it shut. You're on *my* turf now, and I won't hesitate to toss you in jail and forget about you." Murray glanced around the room. "As it is, we're probably going to be banned from the diner. So, what should we do about this situation?"

"I want him out of here. I want him out now," Joe said. He clenched his fists, but kept his arms at his sides. His jaw was bruised. Roy had gotten in one or two punches of his own. "If he's not out of here in five minutes, I'm going to pound him into the ground."

Murray nodded and jumped off the table to kneel by Roy's side. "You are still the same jerk-wad you were when Em left you. Get out of here before I run you in for drunk and disorderly conduct."

Roy wiped away the bloody spittle that rolled down the side of his mouth. He narrowed his eyes. "Still playing the ball-busting bitch I see—" Jimbo took a step forward and Roy made the connection that if he went any further, he was toast. "Fine, I'll leave."

"Show him to the door, boys, but one more punch— from *anyone*—and you're all in trouble. I'm not in any mood to give a second warning, so play it very carefully." Murray supervised as Jimbo and Joe roughly yanked Roy to his feet and led him toward the back exit. He shook them off when he was at the door and turned.

"You won't get away with roughing me up like this— I'll make your life hell," he said, his voice echoing through the room. "You'd better hope your young stud keeps his fists to himself, Emerald. He seems pretty hotheaded to me. Good luck with your wedding. You're gonna need it! I have the feeling it's gonna come crashing down around your shoulders like a house built of cards." And then, my ex-husband plunged out the back door, still drunk and weaving.

Joe stomped over to Murray and tossed her a ring of keys. "He won't be driving anywhere in his condition." And then, with a cold glance my way, he headed for the bathroom.

"WHAT ARE YOU going to tell the kids? This will be all over town by morning, and Ingrid Lindstrom will have a heyday with it." Harlow patted my back as I slumped on the bench in the ladies room.

"Did you have to mention Ingrid?" I moaned. The gossip columnist for the *Chiqetaw Town Crier* would be frothing at the mouth over this one. But she was the least of my worries. "Never mind about the town. What am I going to tell my parents? And Grandma M.? They saw everything and I can just imagine what they'll have to say about all this. Somebody better fire up the smelling salts, because Grandma M.'s sure to threaten a heart attack."

The door opened and Murray peeked in. "You okay, Em?"

"Okay? How can I be okay? You just had to break up a brawl between my fiancé, my ex, and your boyfriend. Not only that, but my entire customer base watched me shove my ex into the party cake. Thank God I sent the kids home early." I straightened up. So far, tears had remained in the background, but I was pissed out of my mind.

"Should I be on the lookout for any more trouble? Do you think Roy will pull any more stupid stunts?" Mur asked, settling down beside me. She looked remarkably pulled together for having just negotiated a brawl. But that was Murray—the head of detectives for Chiqetaw's police force and a beautiful Amazon of a woman. Her eyes flashed, dark chocolate against her caramel skin. Native American, Anna Murray had fought for everything she ever got, and she always came out on top, if a little bruised.

I leaned on the counter, staring in the mirror. My hair was naturally curly so even when it was tousled, it still looked pretty good. But my lipstick had smeared, and I looked altogether too flushed. Otherwise, I'd made it through the fracas unscathed. Harlow handed me a tissue and I cleaned up my face.

"I don't think so, but you never can tell. Roy's volatile. That was one of the problems. Well, one of the warning signs. He's unpredictable and I don't trust him." I'd learned the hard way just how far he would go in his selfish pursuits, but it had taken several years before I'd opened my eyes to the realization that he would never change.

"I'll warn Deacon and Greg to keep their eyes open. Do you know if he's staying in town?"

"God, I hope not. I don't know. He must have called

Kip and found out about the party. Kip's a natural-born diplomat and he's forever trying to smooth things out. He wants Roy and me to be friends. I worry about him."

Murray sighed. "Yeah, the little guy just wants everybody to be happy. I've noticed that for quite a while now. So, is this the first time Joe and Roy have come face-to-face?"

"Yeah, they never met before. I suppose it had to happen sometime, but this wasn't exactly how I envisioned it." I shrugged. To be honest, I'd been hoping that they'd never meet. Unrealistic? Of course. But sometimes the thought of the past intruding on the present was too frightening to entertain. Some events seemed so fraught with potential disaster that I wasn't about to go there unless forced.

Harlow shook her head. "You know, Em, you should have just told Roy to beat it when you first saw him at the door. That's what I would have done." An edge in her voice took me by surprise. I glanced over at her.

"Yeah, well, hindsight gives you twenty-twenty vision, doesn't it? I thought that Mr. Big-Wig Computer Salesman could control himself for once, since the kids were around, but I was wrong."

"I was just saying that next time, you might want to take preventive measures. Maybe tell whoever's watching the door to turn Roy away if he shows up." Harl flashed me a smile, but there was something a little odd about it.

Murray frowned. "Harlow, cut her a little slack. She didn't know this was going to happen. We don't always have control over how others act."

"It wasn't criticism." Harl straightened her dress. The sheath showed every curve and there wasn't an ounce out of place. "I was just making an observation."

"Yeah, right." I glanced in the mirror again to make sure I was pulled back together. I was feeling vulnerable as it was; the last thing I needed was a friend second-guessing me. "I guess I'd better get out there and dive into damage control. I'm surprised that my mother, grand-mother, and sister aren't in here clamoring our ears off."

Murray grinned. "It isn't because they didn't try. I asked them to keep a lookout to make sure that Roy doesn't get back in. And I assigned your father the task of running interference with the manager, who caught the tail end of our little soap opera out there. They were more than happy to be given something to do."

I gave her a grateful smile. "Thank you. I don't need this. Life's been stressful enough, working out all the details for the wedding. I thought it would be easier the second time around, but there are more factors to consider. I want the kids to feel included, my family has expectations, not to mention coming up with a viable explanation for why Joe's parents aren't here. His brother is supposed to be coming in Sunday, though."

Murray shushed me. "Get out there and show them what you're made of, Em. And don't worry about Joe," she said, reading my secret fear. "He was just mad at Roy. You know how guys get. Everything will blow over and your wedding's going to be beautiful."

I took a deep breath, held it to a count of four, then let it out slowly. Another petite wave of dizziness hit me. Too much champagne, probably. "I hope you're right. Okay, let's get this show on the road."

GRANDMA M. SURPRISED me. She was still wear-ing her perpetual frown, but she slipped her arm around my waist and drew me aside. "Finally, you've found a young man willing to stand up for you. He's a good boy, even if he is too young."

I knew she'd never liked Roy. From the very beginning she kept telling me he was going to be trouble. It was one of the few things Nanna and Grandma M. had agreed on. I gave her a quick peck on the cheek. "Thanks, Grandma."

She hemmed and hawed. Having handed me an olive branch, she had to follow it up with a smack. "Of course,

if you'd refrained from getting married to Roy so quickly,
you wouldn't find yourself in this whole mess now."

I didn't bother defending myself, but I knew her buttons by now. "Think of it this way, Grandma M. If I
hadn't met Roy, you wouldn't have two beautiful great-
grandchildren, would you?"

Her lip quivered and I knew that I'd made my point.
She patted me on the shoulder and I made my way over to
my parents. By the time I got there, Joe had already
started reassuring them. I slipped up beside him, slid my
arm through his, and backed up my knight in an EMT uniform.

I MANAGED TO convince my parents to go straight
back to their hotel for the evening, taking Grandma and
my sister with them. My spare bedroom was jammed floor
to ceiling with Joe's stuff. He'd given up the lease on his
apartment the month before and now we were slowly sort-
ing through his things, along with mine, in an attempt to
integrate our households.

The attic—actually a small spare room—on the second floor was filled with boxes awaiting the big garage
sale we were planning for later in the summer, while the
downstairs guest room was filled with boxes still left to
sort through. Secretly, I was relieved. The thought of having family staying with us during the days leading up to
our wedding scared the hell out of me. I could only cope
with so much.

As we pulled into the driveway, I saw Miranda on the
roof, as per usual. When we first moved in, I hired a
handyman to install a reinforced guardrail around a flat
area on the roof directly outside her bedroom. She could
safely crawl out her window at night, dragging her tele-
scope along with her, to watch the stars.

She saw us and waved. I blew her a kiss, dreading
telling her and Kip about their father's latest farce. They'd
seen him drunk a number of times, for which I was in-

finitely sorry. It had taken a couple of years before my hopes that he would turn it around and treat them right crashed to the floor. And I'd long given up on the idea that he might ever treat me with any shred of civility. Since the divorce, he'd been as lousy a father as he had during our marriage. Sometimes I wondered just why he stayed in touch with us at all.

Joe grabbed my hand and pulled me into the backyard, to the trellised opening that divided my lot from the one he'd bought the year before. "Let's sit in the garden for a few minutes and shake off the evening."

"That sounds perfect," I said.

After filling in the foundation that had been the basement for the old Brunswick house, we'd spent every spare moment during the spring decking out the lot with flower and herb gardens. We installed a fountain, several stone benches, and a couple of statues. All hints of the ghostly visitors who had made the lot their home were gone. As we weeded out the thicket of briars and vines, we'd unearthed the past and put it to rest. Now, the land felt clear and happy and whimsical.

Joe and I wandered through the burgeoning flower beds that Horvald had helped us plant. Nasturtiums and poppies colored the new sod, patchwork pretty, and creeping phlox and stonecrop made for a sturdy groundcover. The path forked in two directions. To the right, it led up to a pristine ivory and green gazebo with burgundy trim. To the left, the path wound into a labyrinthine spiral, which coiled its way to a meditation bench.

On warm evenings, we walked the spiral to the center, where Joe would sit and read while I practiced my yoga on a mat under the open sky. Calming, it had become our summer routine, helping us to balance the cares of the day. A month in, I'd begun to notice that my psychic powers were increasing, growing more focused, stronger. Though I had to admit for the past week or so I'd been so distracted I wouldn't have been able to pick up on a ghost if it jumped out in full sheet with chains rattling.

The pebbled tiles reminded me of cobblestones, and the path was lined on both sides by rows of pink rosebushes, interspersed with western maidenhair ferns. Joe loved pink roses, and I'd found myself drawn to them when we went shopping at the plant nursery. The lot was slowly turning into a haven away from the tensions of our mundane routines, a personal sanctuary for our family. Even the kids came out here to read or play. When we were done building the fence that would support the hedge, we'd have full privacy from passersby on the street.

I dropped Joe's hand and set foot on the first tile, breathing slowly. Walking the spiral was a solitary event, yet somehow as I walked, the labyrinthine motion connected me to the world in an integral, grounded manner. I conjured up Roy's face and felt a flash of irritation, but as I took the second step the smell of the roses wafted up to calm me and I found myself letting go of the anger. I thought about why he'd done what he did. Roy was bitter, he was alone again, and he couldn't accept other people being happy. He always had to be the one in the spotlight.

Another step, and another flash of his face. Once, I'd loved him. Once, he'd loved me. But things change. Roy wasn't cut out to be a parent or a husband. Perhaps he'd be forced to find his way, now that his second marriage had fallen apart.

By the fifth step, I'd left Roy behind and found myself drifting in the warm buzz of the evening. I inhaled deeply, exhaled slowly. Step-by-step, I worked my way into the meditation bench, and step-by-step, I reattached myself to the joys that my coming wedding promised, rather than the obstacles.

Behind me, Joe was doing much the same. I felt his irritation drain away, the pain where Roy had hit him was fading. Reaching out, I linked to Joe's energy and blended into the sparkling shimmer that I recognized as his love for me, his devotion. By the time we reached the meditation bench, I turned and he held out his arms. Silently, I slid into his embrace. He held me for a moment, just looking into my face, and then leaned down and rested his lips on my own. I melted into the kiss.

"It wasn't quite the party we wanted, but Harlow's dinner will be better. No outsiders allowed," he said, sitting and leaning against the back of the bench.

I stretched out, resting my head on his lap as I gazed at the flowers surrounding us. "So, are we okay?"

"Of course," he said, caressing my shoulder. "Why wouldn't we be? It's not your fault Roy decided to crash the party. When will you get that through your head? It's not your fault that he was such a jerk during your marriage. He proved that by the way he treated Tyra. But why don't we leave him out of this? Tonight, we relax."

I stared at the sky. We were having a beautiful summer. Spring hadn't been shabby, either, and with the exception of a few minor situations of the ghostly kind, I hadn't stumbled over any dead bodies, had any monsters jump out of the bushes, or faced down any armed-and-dangerous felons for a number of months. Hopefully, the universe would keep it that way.

"So, your bridal shower is on for tomorrow?" Joe asked.

I laughed. "Yeah. I'm so glad they didn't make it a surprise party." I'd never been keen on surprise parties. The last thing I needed was to stumble in on a roomful of friends and family while wearing yesterday's sweats with my hair in a scrunchy. Nope, when there were bound to be cameras present, I wanted to look good.

I leaned on my elbows, letting the evening breeze sweep away my worries. As I sat up, another quick dizzy spell made me frown. Definitely too much champagne— I seldom drank and it went right to my head when I did indulge.

After half an hour, Kip and Randa joined us. Time to face the music and figure out how to tell them that their father had made an ass of himself. They'd hear about it from their friends, and I wanted to give them the facts before the rumor mill hit with a vengeance.

SATURDAY BROUGHT MORE sunshine and a surprise transformation. Randa had gussied up for my bridal shower. She was dressed in a floral sundress, and shock of shocks, she was wearing makeup. A pale sparkle of ivory highlighted her eyes, and a thin sheen of pink gloss shimmered on her lips.

"Honey, you look gorgeous!" I broke into a smile and was suddenly aware that her sundress complemented my own forest green one. I'd decided to go for simple yet elegant, and paired the afternoon frock with jeweled sandals and Rose's crystal necklace, which I'd decided to wear every day until the wedding. Like a good luck charm. As I started to fasten it, I hesitated. Maybe the gold chain would be better? But Rose's feelings would be hurt. I shook my head and finished getting ready.

She blushed. "Well, you know Great-Grandma and Gramms are going to be taking pictures. I thought it might be nice if we matched."

I pulled her to my side and kissed her cheek. "Thank you, sweetie. Let's get moving. Your grandpa is taking Kip out to lunch and then they're going shopping. They'll meet us after the shower, and we'll all drive out to Jimbo's for the barbecue, so make sure you have your swimsuit with you."

We were meeting at Murray's house. As my maid of honor, it was her duty to throw my shower and I trusted her not to embarrass me with anything like a stripper or stupid party games. After the shower the menfolk would meet us, and we'd head out together to the barbecue.

Murray owned a huge old Victorian on Sunrise Avenue, next to the largest park in Chiqetaw. She had taken the fixer-upper from dump to divine over the six years that she'd owned it. The old house now sported a pale pink exterior with gingerbread trim in brilliant white. Flower boxes graced the windows and she'd painted them a brilliant crimson. They were filled with ferns and other perennials that provided a startling contrast to the red and pink.

"What's that?" Randa asked as we climbed the steps to the front porch.

I glanced to where she was pointing. There was a large white envelope with the name ANNA typed on it sitting on one of the benches by the door. I picked it up. "Must be some mail that she dropped or something," I said, though I noticed there was neither a stamp nor an address on the envelope.

As we entered the house, I steeled myself. I loved parties; however, coffee klatches and the like had never been my strong suit, even though I was able to pull off a high tea at the Chintz 'n China without blinking an eye. But I'd never been the guest of honor there, and here all focus would be on me.

I pulled Murray aside and gave her the envelope. "Here, we found this on the front porch. Listen, where are Sid and Nancy? Grandma M. will have a heart attack for real if one of them drops down on her." Sid and Nancy were Murray's boas, and at times they had free run of the house.

She grinned, opening the envelope to pull out a card. "Already thought of. They're locked away in their tanks. But I think you're underestimating her. She was tapping on the glass, talking to Sid a few minutes ago."

I stared at her. "You've got to be kidding." Grandma M. had a fit if she found cobwebs in the attic. But Mur wasn't listening. She was staring at the card and she didn't look happy. "What is it? Bad news?"

Paling, she shook her head and dropped the card on the desk. "Just something I didn't want to see. I'd better go check on the hors d'oeuvres."

As she disappeared into the kitchen, I wrestled with my conscience for all of fifteen seconds, then picked up the card and flipped it open. Something had been bothering

Murray lately, and I didn't like the pall that had come over her face when she read it.

The card itself had a simple but pretty pattern on the front, but inside, in the center, rested a square piece of paper smaller than the card itself. On the piece of paper were five words in block printing: *I know you love me.*

The back of my neck began to tingle and I slowly replaced the card on the desk, sorry I'd snooped. Jimbo hadn't sent the card to her. I knew that without even having to ask. That begged the question: Who did?

And the answer was . . . none of my business, unless and until Murray decided to confide in me. Preoccupied by the thought that Mur had gotten herself into trouble of some sort, I joined the party.

By the time we were halfway through, I was ready to pack it up and go home. First, my mother and grandmother alternately took the opportunity to pass around embarrassing pictures of me from when I was a baby. At least they had the good graces to avoid any mention of my first bridal shower, which had been far more upscale and attended by a number of Roy's friends from college. Even back then, he had exerted an influence over me as to who I should and shouldn't hang out with.

The party theme was lingerie, and I received everything from demure silk pajamas from my Grandma M. to a racy Victoria's Secret teddy from Harlow. Gift baskets of soaps and bath salts also abounded, and I grinned as I held up a crimson baby doll nightie.

"I think some of these gifts are more for Joe than for me," I said.

"Yeah, but you'll reap the benefits of his appreciation," said Cinnamon, one of my employees at the shop. Over the past few years the younger woman and I'd become friends. And with that, we broke for cake and punch.

I'd just finished my second slice of cake when I noticed Rose pouring herself another glass of wine. I'd broken down and accepted a small glass, but after my champagne-induced vertigo from the night before, I was sticking to the fruit punch. Rose, however, looked like she'd tippled more than she could handle. She dropped onto the sofa and stared at the pile of boxes and bows.

"Why aren't there any games? It's not a shower until we dress you up in a toilet paper wedding dress!" She belched, giving me a ladylike "oh" of surprise.

"I don't want any games," I said. "I'm grateful Murray didn't plan any. Can't we just enjoy the afternoon together without any silliness?"

Rose leaned forward, waggling her finger. She tried to whisper but evidently her sense of hearing was as off as her equilibrium because her voice echoed in the large living room and conversation dropped to a dead silence when she said, "Speaking of Anna-banana, why on earth did you choose her to be your maid of honor? I'm your sister. You should have asked me."

Murray glanced at me and I flushed, embarrassed. I bit my lip and made a drinking motion. Mur nodded and headed into the kitchen to make coffee. Everybody in the room had paused, but now they followed Murray's lead and suddenly became busy again, chatting, eating, picking up crumpled paper and ribbons.

I turned to Rose and lowered my voice. "We hardly ever talk. You never come visit, and you never ask me to visit you. I had no idea you wanted to be my matron of honor." I'd asked her, along with Harlow and Randa, to be one of my bridesmaids, never dreaming that she'd be jealous of Murray.

She sniffled—her equivalent of a sob—and placed her hand on her heart. "Well, it hurts."

I glanced around the room and waved my mother and Grandma M. over. "I swear, I had no idea she'd react this way," I said.

Klara, my mother, shook her head. "Rose was always too sensitive—"

"You think it's too sensitive to have your feelings hurt when your own sister doesn't include you in her wedding party?" Leave it to Grandma McGrady to take Rose's part. She always had.

"I'd call being a bridesmaid being *in* the wedding party. She knew perfectly well that Murray was going to be the maid of honor and she never said a word before today," Klara retorted.

Grandma M. glared at her. "Perhaps she'd talk to you more if you hadn't spent her childhood working. Instead, the poor darling had to come to me—"

"Poor darling my ass!" One thing I'd give my mother: she didn't take bull off of anybody. "Nanna looked after both Rose and Emerald without a problem the entire time. The girls didn't suffer a bit. You've just never been able to accept that your son married a German girl while he was overseas—"

"He never even told us he was getting married—"

I'd had enough. The old arguments were making their way to the surface and unless I wanted World War III to erupt in Murray's living room, I had to put a stop to the bickering.

"Will you two give it a rest?" My mother and Grandma M. stared at me as if I'd suddenly grown horns or a beak or something. "I will not have you turning my bridal shower into a battle zone. Last night was bad enough with Roy's antics. I refuse to accept an instant replay from my own relatives."

Klara sighed, loud and deep, while Grandma M. ignored me and focused her attention on Rose, who was sobbing now.

"I'm sorry," Rose said. "It's just so hard, seeing you happy and in love, especially now that Charles is moving out."

Say what? Rose and Charley had been married for fifteen years. I'd never once heard rumors of trouble between the two. I was about to ask what she was talking about when I felt a gentle hand on my arm. White Deer, Murray's aunt—who happened to be a medicine woman in her tribe—nodded me aside.

"Can it wait?" I asked. "My sister—"

"I heard, and I know you need to talk to her, but I have to tell you something." When we were off to one side, she leaned close and cupped her hand around my ear. "Emerald, I sense a lot of chaos around you today. I don't know what it is or where it's coming from, but whatever the source, I'd be careful if I were you. I can't tell if it's in your aura or just hanging around, but I think a psychic leech might have taken up residence."

I frowned. "I've been really dizzy since last night, but I thought it was the champagne. Since I don't usually drink, my system goes into mild shock when I do. I just hope it's not something like Mr. Big & Ugly again. I've been so frantic over wedding arrangements and family squabbles that I haven't even had a chance to check out my aura lately."

"Okay, but don't forget. Whatever it is sure caught my notice."

The doorbell rang and Murray hurried to answer it. My father, Kip, and James were standing there, shopping bags in hand. I glanced at the clock. They were half an hour early, but at this rate, I was just anxious to get the party over with.

Rose had recovered enough to be escorted to the bathroom. I joined her, sitting on the edge of Murray's peach-colored tub while my sister splashed her face with water and redid her makeup.

"Why didn't you tell me you were having problems?" I asked.

She shrugged. "I was hoping it would blow over, I guess. Charles has been fooling around with his secretary, and I gather she's pregnant now. He's going to leave me and marry the little tramp."

That hit a little too close to home. The only differences between my former situation and Rose's were that Tyra hadn't been pregnant when Roy had been screwing around with her. At least Rose didn't have children—that would have made it ten times worse. "I'm so sorry. What are you going to do?"

She shrugged. "Soak him for all I can get, sell the house, move. Maybe I'll go to New York. Maybe I'll travel. I don't know yet. All I do know at this point is that I'm going to make him pay through the pocketbook." She patted her face with a tissue. "Damned laugh lines. Did you know that I'm already four Botox injections into my attempt to halt time?"

Rose was a year and a half younger than I was. That she was already shooting away the wrinkles worried me. "Are you going to be okay, sis?"

She shrugged, then broke into a cheerless smile. "I have to be, don't I? What other option is there? By the way, I'm sorry about that little scene out there. Of course you wouldn't ask me to be your matron of honor. Why should you? I've never bothered to try and be anything more than a distant relation." When I started to protest she stopped me. "Don't bother. It's the truth and I know it. But maybe that can change." She paused in the rearrangement of her hair to turn and clasp my hands. "What do you think? Maybe we can be friends?"

I pulled her in for a hug. "Of course, Rosy. Of course we can. But Murray's still my maid of honor, so will you be okay with that?"

She nodded, giving me a muffled "Uh-huh."

I pushed her back, bracing her by the shoulders. "Now come on. We've got a barbecue to go to. You haven't tasted anything until you've had some of Jimbo's home cooking."

She snickered and I caught a resemblance to myself in her face. "He and Anna make quite the couple, all right. You know, she's come a long way since you two were in college together. Okay, let's go get greasy with some ribs."

Everybody who wasn't going to the barbecue had left their best wishes and been ushered out. Murray raised one eyebrow when Rose walked over to her and apologized for her outburst, but she assured my sister that everything was fine. Grandma M. was fretting about how long it would take to get out to Jimbo's and whether or not he'd have any comfortable chairs, and my mother had enlisted Randa to help her rush around, making sure the gifts and party favors were packed in the car.

We were just about to set out when the doorbell rang. Mur opened it and I heard an exclamation of surprise before she led Deacon into the room. I waved at him, but the smile died on my face. Something was wrong. I could feel it. I slowly approached him, my gaze fastened on his.

Murray rushed up to my side and I knew then that it was bad. "What's going on?" I asked, somehow able to find my voice in the thundering fear that was pounding through me. "Joe? Did something happen to Joe?"

Deacon closed his eyes for a brief second, then said, "You're needed at the hospital, Emerald. Jimbo and Joe were out in the meadow, getting ready for the barbecue, when somebody decided to take a potshot at them. Joe was hit by one of the bullets. I don't know how bad it is, though he was conscious when the ambulance took him away. Jimbo's at the hospital with him now."

Mute, unable to think except for the refrain running through my mind that *Joe's been shot, Joe's been shot*, I felt somebody press my purse into my hands as Deacon and Murray led me to the squad car, where Deacon pulled out all the stops. Sirens screaming, we were on our way to the hospital, where I would find out if Joe—the man who I could no longer imagine living without—was going to be alive for our wedding.

Three

❖

THE AFTERNOON SUN seemed terribly out of place as we sped along to the hospital. It should be raining and stormy, dark as my mood. Deacon tried to reassure me but until I heard word from the doctor that Joe was okay, nothing in the world could help.

"The fact that he was conscious is a good thing, Emerald. It really is," he said, maneuvering down Saddleback Street as cars pulled to the right to get out of our way. "He'll be okay."

"Who shot him?" I asked. "What the hell happened?"

"I don't know. Greg and Sandy were there when I got there. The minute I found out what happened, I took off to let you know." He fell silent, concentrating on the road.

I stared at my hands. My left hand in particular. The brilliant-cut diamond in Black Hills gold weighed heavy on my ring finger, reminding me of just how much I had to lose. Until I met Joe, I never expected to find someone who'd ever love me the way he did. Whom I'd ever love as much as I loved him. Sure, I'd loved Roy in the beginning, but he returned it with anger and taunts, with so many strings attached that I began to believe I wasn't worthy of love. There were a few dalliances after I left him, but nobody really special. Not until the lanky young EMT had serendipitously fallen into my life. I didn't want to lose him. Not now. Not ever.

"He's got to be okay, Deacon. He's got to be okay."

Deacon remained silent, but I could feel his concern reaching out to me, covering me like a soft comforter on a cold night.

I'D BEEN IN the hospital all too often over the past eighteen months, both for my own injuries and those of family and friends. The path of a cosmic crime-fighter didn't run smoothly, and I was weary of the worries that attended the dubious honor.

I bolted from the car and rushed inside the moment Deacon pulled up to the entrance of the ER. As I entered the doors, my feet stopped working and I found myself paralyzed, terrified of what I might hear. Then a firm, familiar presence slipped up behind me and warm arms wrapped themselves around my shoulders. I leaned back against Jimbo's chest, enveloped by the scent of leather and dirt and hickory smoke.

"Tell me he's okay. For God's sake, tell me he's alive." Biting my lip, I held my breath until he spoke.

"He's alive, that much I know. I don't think he's in danger, O'Brien. The doctors will be out as soon as they know what's going on. He caught a bullet in the shoulder; I don't think he got hit any other place." He leaned down and pressed his lips against the top of my head, much like I did when Kip was afraid. For a rough and tumble biker, he could be pretty tender. Jimbo was a good friend and I knew he wouldn't lie to me.

I looked up at him. He looked haggard and was covered with soot and dirt. I pushed myself away, turning to examine him. Reddish splotches stained his shirt. Blood. I reached out, hesitant. "Is that—"

He glanced down. "Joe's. Come on, let's get you to the

front desk." He took my hand and, leading me like a little
girl, he fielded our way through the bustle of nurses and
patients till we stood by the front desk. "This is Joe Files'
fiancée."

The nurse looked up from her chart and her eyes flick-
ered with recognition. It was Wilma Velcox. She'd helped
Kip when I had to bring him in for a broken arm. "Ms.
O'Brien. You're Mr. Files' fiancée?"

"Yeah. Is he going to be okay?"

She closed the file she was holding, set it to one side,
and stood. "You must be frantic. I'll have someone come
talk to you in just a moment. Sir, if you could take her
over to the waiting area—"

Jimbo let out a muffled grunt. "Okay, but don't make it
too long." He steered me over to the all too familiar sofa
in the waiting room and pushed me by the shoulders until
I sat down. I leaned forward, head in my hands, trying to
keep it together. My mind whirled with all sorts of possibilities—most of them bad—but I knew my fear was
overriding my ability to sense how Joe was doing. I tried
to tune in, but couldn't push past the panic.

"Tell me what happened. Talk to me."

Jimbo let out a long sigh. "We were getting ready for
the barbecue, we'd carried the meat down to the lake and
I was working on the grill while Joe was shucking corn. I
turned around . . . I dunno why, but something felt off.
Just then, there was a crack, and the next thing I knew Joe
was on the ground, bleeding. He had his cell phone on him
and I called 911 while trying to pull one of the barrels in
front of us for cover."

I closed my eyes, imagining the scene. The lakeside
area of Jimbo's acreage was overgrown, wild and thick
with cattails and long blades of canary grass. Skunk cab-
bage dappled the area with bright yellow flowers, and a
rickety homemade dock led out over the lake to where he
kept inner tubes and a canoe tied to the moorings. The
meadow had been cleared and we used it for get-togethers
and barbecues. I could see Joe standing there, shucking

corn under the afternoon sun, and then a shot ringing out. Suddenly, the image was all too vivid and my eyes flew open.

"Was he shot more than once?"

Jimbo shook his head. "No. Whoever did it either disappeared or ran out of ammo. One shot, that's all. I couldn't tell if the bullet actually went in or not. I didn't want to mess with the wound too much, so I just applied pressure where it was bleeding, and by the time the ambulance got there, I'd staunched the flow. Joe was awake." He paused, then stumbling over his words, continued, "He told me to tell you that he loves you, O'Brien. That you're the only woman he's ever loved." He stared at the floor.

At that moment, Murray and Deacon appeared at the entrance to the waiting room. Murray rushed over and settled in on my other side. I caught her glance at Jimbo over my head, but she said nothing.

Deacon motioned to Jimbo. "Now that Emerald's here and Joe's with the doctors, I need to get your statement." Jimbo grunted and headed over to the other side of the room, followed by the careworn officer.

Murray took my hands in hers. "White Deer says to tell you not to worry, that Joe will be okay. She took a peek."

Tears sprang to my eyes. "Thank you, I needed to hear that. I trust her. I trust her—really, but . . ."

"But you won't know for sure until the doctors talk to you."

Miserable, I nodded.

She pulled me into her arms and let me rest my head against her shoulder. "Harlow's watching the kids. She convinced your family to go back to the hotel."

Family! Shit, I had to call Joe's family. I grabbed for my purse and frantically began searching for the address book. "Joe's brother is due in tomorrow—I have to call him."

She took my purse from me and set it on the seat beside us. "Wait until you know more about what's

happened. You don't want to alarm them if it's just a surface wound."

I let go of the book and she tucked it back into my
handbag. "You're right. I can't seem to think straight. I'm
so scared, Mur. What if he . . . what if something goes
wrong . . . what if—"

"What if you put those what-ifs on hold? Come on, I'll
bet you haven't had a full breath since Deacon showed up
at the door." She made me turn around and began rubbing
my shoulders. As the tension loosened, I inhaled deeply,
realizing that she was right. As I coughed, I noticed a
movement out of the corner of my eye. A doctor had entered the room and was headed my way. I recognized him,
too, from one of our numerous trips to the ER.

Jumping up, I raced over, scanning his face anxiously.
"Can you tell me about Joe?"

He held out his hand and smiled. "You can relax,
Emerald. He's going to be all right. The bullet winged
him, grazing his shoulder right below his collarbone,
but it didn't go in. Joe must have turned just as the bullet came whizzing by, because it caught him at the perfect
angle—for him, not for whoever it was trying to shoot
him. He'll be fine, though he's going to hurt like hell the
next week or so."

Dizzy with relief, I felt my knees give way, but before
I landed on my butt, strong arms buoyed me up. Jimbo
had rushed to my side, catching me a second before I hit
the floor. He helped me to a chair.

The doctor sat down next to me. "Mr. Files is an ath-
letic young man, and that worked in his favor. He has
abrasions and a lot of bruising, but nothing that won't
heal." He looked at Deacon. "Since the bullet didn't penetrate, your men should find it out at the scene, Officer
Wilson. My guess, from the wound, is that the gun was a
twenty-two. If it had been a shotgun, there would have
been a lot more damage, and the buckshot would have
made a mess of his arm." He consulted the file. "We'll

want to keep him for twenty-four hours for observation, but I think he'll be able to go home tomorrow."

Breathing easier, I asked, "Can I see him?"

The doctor put his hand on mine. "Of course, but give us about fifteen minutes to make him comfortable in a room. A nurse will come get you when he's ready for visitors."

"Is he up to answering a few questions?" Murray asked.

With a shrug, the doctor said, "I think a few questions will be fine, but don't overtire him." And with that, he left the room.

"Thank God he's going to be okay." I slid back in my seat as the panic rushed out like a wave on the ebb. Tears streaked down my cheeks as I silently gave thanks to whatever force had saved my sweetheart. I could easily have been Joe's widow before I'd even been his bride.

Murray pulled out her cell phone. "I'll let Harlow know so she can tell the kids," she said.

Jimbo gave me a thumbs-up. "I told you he's tough. O'Brien, wipe your eyes and blow your nose and fix your makeup. Joe's going to need cheering up and that long face of yours is about as cheerful as a hog on butchering day."

I narrowed my eyes, unable to keep from laughing. "Are you calling me a pig, biker man?"

He grinned. "That's the stuff. You're a tough broad, O'Brien. And *that* is a compliment."

JOE WAS IN bed, propped against pillows, with an IV in his arm and a Telfa bandage covering the space just below his collarbone on his left side. He opened his eyes when we walked through the door. I raced over to his side, dropping into the chair next to his bed.

He winced a little as he shifted to get a better look at me. "Hey, babe, good of you to visit." His voice was groggy; they'd given him pain medication and it had made him tired.

"Joe, don't you ever do this to me again! I was afraid..." My voice trailed off. I couldn't finish my thoughts. Sometimes saying something aloud made it all too real. I clutched his right hand, focusing on the feel of his fingers in mine, the warmth of his flesh against my own.

"I know," he whispered. "I know. I was thinking the same thing myself."

Murray and Jimbo hung back, but Deacon slowly made his way over to the bed. "Hey, Joe, I don't mean to break up the reunion, but are you up to answering a few questions for me?"

Joe cleared his throat. "I can try, man, but I don't remember much. Jimbo had a much clearer view of what went down, considering I was preoccupied with keeping myself alive, rather than looking for whoever shot at me."

Deacon asked him if he'd noticed anything out of the ordinary, if there had been any strange sounds or events before the shot. Joe told him no, he'd just been shucking corn when he heard a loud *crack* and the next thing he knew, his shoulder was on fire in a blaze of pain.

"Can you think of anybody who might be out to get you? You have any enemies, made anyone mad lately? Any threats?" Deacon poised his pen over his notepad.

Joe looked at him sharply. "What do you mean? You think this was deliberate and not an accident? I thought it must be some neighbor kid out shooting birds or something, who didn't look before he pulled the trigger."

As I mulled over Deacon's questions in my mind, an ugly thought crept into the back of my mind. One I didn't want to entertain. I hoped I was wrong. I'd better be wrong. But what if I wasn't?

Joe shook his head. "I can't think of anybody who might be that mad at me. I'm in the business of saving lives, not making them miserable."

I had to speak up. "I know somebody who's mad at you, Joe. I hate to even mention it—but maybe . . ."

"Who?" Deacon looked at me, as Murray and Jimbo moved closer.

I glanced up at Murray. "Roy. He was drunk last night, but he wasn't incoherent. He threatened to ruin our wedding. You all heard him." Once the words were out of my mouth, I wished I could take them back. What if I was right? But surely Roy wasn't capable of murder. Or was he? I didn't want to believe he could possibly pick up a gun and deliberately shoot someone but then again, I'd been on the receiving end of his fist several times and I knew he wasn't above taking his anger out on anybody who happened to be within punching range. Was the leap so far from a fist to a gun?

Murray's eyes grew wide. "Shit, you're right. Deacon, I want you to talk to Greg. I had him find out where Roy is staying. I sent him over to take Roy's car keys back and tell him to watch himself. Ask Greg for the address and if Roy's still there, tell him to stay put. We can't rule him out until we investigate this further." She turned to me. "Would Roy have known about the barbecue?"

I shrugged. "Kip might have told him. He told him about the party. And it's not that hard in this little town to find out what's going on."

Just then, the door opened and a nurse walked in. She was carrying a bag with a bloodstained shirt in it. "The doctor wanted me to ask you if you'll be needing Mr. Files' shirt for evidence?"

Murray glanced at it, then did a double take. "Jimmy," she said to Jimbo, "that's your shirt. I gave that to you for Christmas."

I peered at the Hawaiian print and frowned. "She's right. I don't think you own a shirt like that, do you, Joe?"

Joe shook his head. "No, but when I was mixing up the barbecue sauce, I spilled it all over myself and had to borrow a shirt from Jimbo. My own shirt's sitting on his kitchen counter."

Deacon took the bag. "We'll just keep this as evidence." He jotted down a few more notes, tucked his notepad away, and slipped on his hat. "I think I've got everything I need. Okay, I'm heading out. I'll talk to Greg and Sandy, see if they found the bullet. Then we'll go round up Roy and see what he's been up to."

"Let me know what you find out. I'll be home this evening," Murray told him. He waved and disappeared down the hall. She watched until he was gone, then returned to the room.

I sat beside Joe, parked on the edge of his bed, holding his hand. The thought that he might have died if he hadn't turned to the side—exactly at the precise moment needed—ricocheted through me as surely as any bullet. One fraction of movement, one inch to the right, and it could have been all over. I stared at the snow white sheets, thinking how sterile they looked, and how clinical. I wanted to take him home, to tuck him into bed and take care of him till he was healed. But the hospital was the safest place for him right now, and spending one night alone was a small price to pay for peace of mind.

Joe sighed. I could tell he was getting tired. "Do you want us to leave so you can get some rest?"

He adjusted himself against the pillows and winced again. "No, not really, but I am tired. I just can't figure out why somebody would deliberately shoot me. It had to be an accident. I can't believe that I was the target."

"People are strange," I murmured. "Their actions don't always make sense." But inside, somewhere deep inside, I knew that the shot had been deliberate. For some reason, Joe had ended up with a big fat target sign painted on his chest, and it was only luck that had kept him alive. "You sleep now. I have to go home to the kids, but I'll tell the nurse to call if you need me."

Murray and Jimbo waved and slipped into the hall to give us some privacy. I leaned down and placed a lingering kiss on Joe's lips. He started to reach up, to open his arms, but then stopped and moaned. The nurse entered the room at that point and shooed me toward the door.

"Your young man needs his rest," she said. "If you phone tomorrow around ten, we'll be able to tell you whether or not the doctor will be releasing him."

"What medications is he on?" I asked, watching as she prepared a shot.

"We gave him a broad-spectrum antibiotic to fight any impending infection and a pain reliever. He'll remain on an IV drip through the night, to make sure he's fully hydrated." She held up the syringe. "This is a mild sedative. The doctor wants him to get plenty of sleep and this will put him out for the night."

As she prepared his arm for the injection, I blew him another kiss and then reluctantly slipped out the door to join Jimbo and Murray. We stood in the hall for a moment. "I need a ride home," I said. "I came with Deacon."

"Actually, so do I. I rode in the ambulance with Joe." Jimbo shook his head. "I hope nobody went out to my place expecting dinner. There wasn't exactly time to leave a note."

"Sandy and Greg would have told them what happened," Murray said. "But they wouldn't be able to provide a status on Joe's condition. If anybody showed up, they're likely to be mighty worried by now."

"Can you drop me off at home before you head to the station, Mur?" We headed toward the exit. "I need to make sure the kids are all right and defuse the situation with my folks. This is *so* not going well. They want a nice, quiet life for their grandchildren and so far, I haven't measured up in that regard."

With a laugh, Murray wrapped her arm around my waist. "Don't sweat it, Emerald. Tell them that you get bored with quiet. Tell them that this *is* quiet for you! Tell them that . . . that you're doing the best you can."

*　　　*　　　*

MURRAY AND JIMBO dropped me off, promising to call with any developments as soon as they heard about them. I steeled myself, expecting to find my parents, Grandma M., and Rose all waiting to pounce, and I dreaded the round of questions that was sure to follow. And to top it off, I had to call Joe's brother and let him know what was going down. As I trudged up the porch steps, I let out a long, slow breath. Might as well get it over with.

To my surprise, only Harlow, James, and my children were waiting for me. "Where is everybody?"

Harlow grinned. "I figured you wouldn't be up to facing all those questions so I told everybody to go back to the hotel. They didn't want to, but James and Randa backed me up. We cleared the house out and I brought the kids back here."

I dropped onto the sofa, relieved. "Thank you. Thank you more than I can say." Just then, Kip and Randa rushed in, worried looks creasing their faces. I opened my arms and they dove onto the sofa, curling up on either side of me. I held them for a moment, then explained what had happened.

"So, he's going to be okay?" Kip asked.

"Yep, kiddo, he's going to be okay."

"And they don't know who shot him?" Randa asked.

I shook my head. "No, but they're looking into it. The bullet didn't penetrate—it only grazed him—but that means they have to find it at the scene in order to be certain what kind of gun it came from."

Kip's lip fluttered. "Did Dad shoot him?"

Oh shit, so I wasn't the only one who thought of that possibility. "Who suggested that?" I asked carefully.

"Great-Grandma. She called Dad a bad name and then said she wouldn't put it past him." His eyes were wide and I knew I had to squash the situation before it became part of the rumor mill. Regardless of what I thought about Roy, until the cops excluded or included him in the list of suspects I had no right to tell my children that I secretly thought he might be responsible.

"Grandma M. has a short fuse. She's speculating. That means she doesn't know what happened, but is thinking about possible suspects." I made them both face me. "Listen to me carefully. We don't know who did it. Your father might end up being considered a suspect, but there are a lot of people who could have pulled the trigger. The shot could have been fired by a hunter or a kid out for target practice—it could just be an accident. Until we know more, I don't want you repeating any rumors, okay?"

Kip nodded. Randa frowned, leaning forward. "Did you tell them where Dad's staying?"

I gave her a sharp look. "Do you know where he's staying? I didn't even know he was in town until he showed up at the party last night."

Kip scuffed his foot against the carpet. "Yeah, he's at the Four Seasons Motel. He told me he was coming into town on Wednesday, but he said he wanted it to be a surprise so not to say anything to you. I thought he was coming to see us, but he hasn't called or nothin'." Kip looked hurt, the way he always did when Roy screwed up.

So, good ol' Roy was playing my kids against me. I sighed and picked up the phone. No messages.

"Do you have his number?" As Kip nodded, I grabbed a notebook and jotted it down, along with his room number. Murray said Greg had found out where he was staying, but it wouldn't hurt for me to have the information, since I was planning to light into him myself. If he wasn't already in jail, that is. He had to learn to quit breaking his promises to the kids.

The phone rang and Kip grabbed it, but his face fell as he handed it to me. It was Murray.

"Hey, chica, we found Roy," she said. "He doesn't have much of an alibi for this morning—he says he was sleeping off last night's party. I'm inclined to believe him, but I've ordered him not to leave town until I give him the okay. You never know. Other than that, we found the bullet. The doctor was right, it came from a twenty-two. Joe's just lucky it wasn't a shotgun or he'd be in hurt-heaven by now. I'll talk to you tomorrow, okay?"

I mumbled a quick good-bye and eyed the phone. So, Roy had no alibi for the morning other than a tousled bed. I wanted to believe that he hadn't done it, that he hadn't stooped that low. My gut warned me against jumping to conclusions, but my emotions were running wild. He'd threatened to make my life hell and as good as promised to ruin my wedding. Was this what he meant? Or were his threats merely a drunken stab to make me as miserable as he was?

Either way, I pushed him out of my mind. I had a phone call to make. Joe's brother, Nathan, was due in town tomorrow morning, but if it were me, I'd want to know as soon as possible. I debated ringing his parents, too, but then pushed that thought aside. Joe would have a fit if he found out I'd called them.

He'd refused to invite either of them to the wedding, and I hadn't pressured him. Dexter, his father, had abandoned the family when the boys were young, following the lure of the casinos. As for Terri, Joe's mother, she'd been shacked up with one loser or another for most of Joe's life. He'd long ago given up on expecting support from either his parents.

I flipped through the address book, found Nathan's number, and punched in the keys. After a few rings, Nate answered, sounding so much like Joe that it gave me chills. "Nathan? This is Emerald. Joe's fiancée."

A pause, then an "Oh shit!"

I frowned at the phone. "What?"

"Sorry," came the garbled reply. "Just a minute." Nathan's words were obviously aimed toward somebody in the room with him. After a few blurred syllables that might have been "hold on" or "hang on," he cleared his throat. "Listen, I meant to call Joe tonight. I can't make the wedding."

Great. Could this day *get* any better? "Is everything okay?"

"Yeah, fine," he said, and I could hear the strike of a match. So, he smoked. Well, not in my house he wouldn't. "I've been offered the chance to go to Sweden for a couple of weeks but we have to leave tomorrow morning. I can't pass this up, not when it fell right in my lap. Joe'll understand. Put him on."

I counted to ten, my hackles rising. "I can't put him on. He's in the hospital. That's why I called."

"Oh hell, what'd he go and do now? He been playing hero again? I told him to get out of that business—bad for the health."

"Don't you even want to know how he is?" I said, exasperated.

"Yeah, yeah, don't get your panties in a wad, Sis. I figure if he was dead, you'd be bawling, so he must be okay. What happened?"

Wanting nothing more than to get off the phone and out of this conversation, I forced myself to calm down. "It has nothing to do with his job. Your brother got winged by a bullet from a twenty-two this afternoon. He's going to be fine, but I thought you might like to know before you arrived. Obviously, since you're headed to Sweden, that's no longer an issue. Tell me, were you planning on letting us know about your detour before we were standing at the airport, waiting for your plane?"

"Uh, yeah. I just forgot. Chill, okay?"

Chill my ass. "I'm not in a good mood," I said, biting my tongue to prevent saying anything I'd later regret.

"Okay, okay . . . sheesh." Nathan coughed. "So, old Joe took one on the wing? Tell him to get better and watch his step next time. Was it some redneck yokel out hunting ducks or something?"

I was starting to get a sense for why Joe hesitated when discussing his family. Nathan apparently didn't fall far from Dexter's tree.

"We don't know," I said. "Since you aren't going to make it, I'll just tell Joe you said hello. I have to go now. Bye." I hung up before he could say another word—and before I forever ruined any rapport I might have with my soon-to-be brother-in-law. I stared at the phone in my hand.

Grandma M. might be a pain in the butt sometimes, and my mother and father were bland, if loving, parents. Rose could be a handful, but had somebody called any of them with word that I was shot, they'd be here in a flash. I'd deliberately kept some of my misadventures from them because I didn't want them to worry. In contrast to Nathan, they were as loving and supportive as I could ask for. I glanced at the clock. Time to call Margaret, Joe's aunt. At least *she* would be at the hospital first thing come visiting hours.

My hand poised to dial, I stopped and put the phone down. Aunt Maggie deserved better than hearing the news over the phone. I grabbed my keys and let the kids know I'd be out for a little while. Hell, she might even have some idea as to why Joe had been shot.

MARGARET FILES WAS one of those timeless women. I knew she was in her early seventies, and she looked it, but her spirit was as bright as a one-hundred-watt bulb in a small room. She loved life, and life loved her. A good twenty years older than her brother—Joe's father—she'd been more of a parent to Joe than either Dexter or Terri.

Maggie had worked for the county clerk's office until she retired and now she was always out and about, volunteering at the local hospital, organizing food drives, playing cutthroat pinochle with her friends, and generally keeping herself busy, productive, and happy.

She was also dating Lanford Willis, a retired doctor, and was the scandal of the town's matronly set on two accounts: Lanford was black, and they'd been caught in their robes at the breakfast table by one of Maggie's friends. The race issue would die away quickly. The sex scandal was more problematic.

When she opened the door, I could tell she'd already heard the news. She bustled me in and settled me in the rocking chair with a glass of lemonade before I knew what had happened.

"I know he was shot, I know he's okay, so don't you fret," she said.

I relaxed, thinking again about Nathan and how cavalier he'd been over his brother's injury. With a shake of my head, I launched into what had happened, filling in the missing details for her. As I finished my story, I asked, "Can you think of anybody who might have a grudge against Joe?"

Maggie glanced over at me from the window, where she was studying the last of the evening light that filtered through the lace curtains, casting delicately woven patterns on the walls. After a moment, she turned, a thoughtful look on her face.

"What about that man you were dating before you met Joe? I recall he was pestering you to get back together with him."

"Andrew?" The thought had never occurred to me. To be honest, I'd pretty much pushed Andrew's existence out of my mind. I thought we could be friends but he wouldn't leave me alone. He'd been the one who dumped me, but he couldn't stand the thought I'd moved on. So, I dropped contact with him. "I don't know. I don't even know if he still lives in Chiqetaw."

"You might want to have your detective friend check him out for you," Maggie said, refilling my glass and adding a splash of cherry juice.

As I sipped the concoction, wincing at the tangy combination of sour and sweet tart on my tongue, I thought about what she'd said. Could Andrew possibly still think we had a chance? Was he even aware that I was getting married? The notice had been in the paper, of course, and being a quasi celebrity in Chiqetaw assured me a write-up in Ingrid Lindstrom's column. But even if he knew, would Andrew stoop to shooting Joe? I'd have to call Murray, it was that simple. If there was even a chance it was Andrew, she had to check it out.

The thought crossed my mind that if Joe was in danger, Randa and Kip might be next in line . . . or me. I pulled out my cell phone, excused myself, and punched in Murray's number.

Four

✦

MURRAY DIDN'T ANSWER so I left a message, asking her to call me the next morning. I glanced at the clock. Almost eleven, and I was exhausted. "I'd better be getting home," I said, "but before I go, do you think I should drop by the hospital to tell Joe about Nathan? After all, Joe will expect him to be there when he gets home. I promised to pick up Nate from the airport."

Margaret nixed the idea. "Let him rest." The look on her face spoke volumes. Her brow furrowed, she let out a loud sigh. "Nathan is a carbon copy of Dexter. Dex always has been, and always will be, an irresponsible boy in a man's body. I had hoped that both sons would escape their heritage, but it seems it was too much to ask." She brightened. "At least Joe didn't succumb to the family pattern of addiction. Tell him about Nathan tomorrow, on your way home from the hospital."

She fussed with her tea. "I have to say, Emerald, I consider Joe lucky to have you. You've given him the stability and sense of family he's always craved. And I know he's head over heels in love with you."

"When I asked Joe if he wanted to invite his parents to

the wedding, I thought he was going to raise the roof," I said. "That's the only time I've seen him get angry. He's got a lot of pent-up resentment toward them." I hadn't been afraid of his outburst, but I learned quickly that his family was a subject better left untouched. Apparently, I wouldn't be meeting my in-laws, other than Maggie.

"It's a little chilly this evening," she said, reaching for a lace shawl draped over the arm of the sofa. She wrapped it around her shoulders. "After Dexter left, Terri had no idea what to do. She was young, with two young boys, and her husband abandoned her, taking every cent that he hadn't already gambled away. Terri and the boys' lives became very chaotic after that."

"Did she work?"

"Oh, she managed to land a job in a wineshop and she was good at it. She learned about the business inside out. I gave her a little extra money when I could, and when I came into my part of the inheritance from my father, I set up a small trust fund for each boy. Dex certainly didn't help out. He always said he would, but it never happened. And he worked odd jobs to avoid having his wages garnished. I'll give Terri this—even without child support, she kept food on the table and a roof over their heads."

"It's never easy—even with child support," I said, thinking about the first year I'd struggled to rebuild my family after my divorce. And I'd had a settlement to start my business with and to buy a new house. Most divorced women didn't get a head start. Of course, I'd been angry enough to go after Roy, instead of slinking away meekly to nurse my grievances.

"No, it's not. Unfortunately, the struggle to survive took a toll. Terri ended up resenting the boys for the extra work they caused her. I don't think she ever showed it overtly, but kids are smart. Joe and Nathan knew she wasn't happy. They had a string of 'daddies' who never stuck around. When the boys left home, she moved to California and opened up her own shop, but the steady stream of men and booze never ended."

I gave Margaret a quick kiss on the cheek. "You're right. Joe is a lucky man. He's got *you*. You're one special lady, Aunt Maggie." As I headed out into the night, I felt a flash of gratitude that Margaret Files had become such an integral part of my life. She was a champion supporter, and I adored her.

SUNDAY DAWNED PARTLY cloudy. We weren't due for rain, but the sky was overcast and the temperature mild. So much for sunshine. I just hoped it wouldn't be raining on the solstice. We'd planned to hold the wedding in our garden lot next door, with White Deer acting as our officiate. She had registered at one of those online ordination sites so that she could marry us.

Joe and Jimbo were supposed to build arches over which we would drape ivy and grapevines, and tuck roses into the lattice work. I sighed, making a note to ask Jimbo what kind of help he would need now that Joe wouldn't be able to lift a hammer. Maybe my father could help him slap them together. Or maybe we'd have to buy them ready-made.

Randa came racing down the stairs. In an hour, she was due at the house belonging to the president of her astronomy club. The club was making a field trip to Bellingham to visit the new astronomy museum that had opened up. More of a gallery than a real museum, it was sponsored by the Skies & Scopes shop.

She screeched to a halt in front of the fridge. "Mom, do you know where my backpack is?"

At least some things were running on track. "Try the laundry room. You left it there yesterday. Have you had breakfast yet? And did Kip feed the cats?"

"I'm not hungry, and yeah, Kip fed them," she said, peeking into the pantry where the washer and dryer were located.

"Hold on there, chickie. Make time for breakfast. I want to see something going into your stomach and it better not just be sugar." The light blinked on my espresso machine, indicating that it was ready. I flipped the switch and watched as four shots of pure black gold poured into the glass decanter. I stirred it into a tall glass, along with raspberry and chocolate syrups, milk, and ice. Randa leaned against the counter, a snarky grin on her face.

"And what is that, if not pure sugar?" She pointed to my glass. "Face it, Mom, you're a junkie. You couldn't go a day without caffeine if you tried." A smile tweaked the corner of her lip and I knew she was teasing.

"All right, all right, I'll eat something, too. Let's see, what do we have?" I opened the refrigerator and peered at the food-laden shelves. Since Joe had moved in, we never were without plenty of groceries. He kept the larder stocked a lot better than I had. Feeling just a tinge inadequate, I glanced at the clock. "I have to call the hospital in a few minutes to find out when I can pick up Joe."

"Do you know who shot him yet?" Kip asked, entering the kitchen. "He's gonna be okay, isn't he?"

Kip was lugging a book almost as big as he was. He'd maintained his love of computers from the school year and had progressed to the intermediate class at computer camp, which made me both proud and a little worried. Considering Kip's predilection for getting in trouble, I still had concerns that I might be raising a hacker, but at least he'd found a passion other than the folk magic that Nanna had taught me. I had no problem passing on my magical training, but more than once, Kip had proved himself too emotionally immature to cope with the responsibility. I had told him that we were going to wait until he was thirteen before starting training again.

"Joe's going to be fine, and no, we don't know who shot him," I said. "Okay, I'm making breakfast, and everybody's eating. Got that, Randa?" She nodded. "Good. How about ham and cheese sandwiches? Quick, nutritious, and they won't dirty up any pans." Anything for freedom from dirty dishes.

As I opened the bread, Randa handed me a knife and

three plates, while Kip foraged through the fridge for ham, cheese, mayonnaise, mustard, tomatoes, and lettuce. I spread the bread with the mayo and mustard while Randa sliced cheese and tomatoes, then Kip layered ham and lettuce on the bread.

We worked in silent unison, immersed in the rhythm that ran through our family. Joe had managed to slip into that rhythm, never breaking it. He flowed right into the stream that had become our lives since we first moved to Chiqetaw. The kids accepted him, edging over gently to allow him space next to me. And I'd grown comfortable with sharing my life with another adult. I finally knew what it meant to be *partners* with someone, rather than just "the wife."

When we finished, the kids carried the food over to the table, along with glasses of milk and what was left of my mocha. I picked up the phone. Not quite time to call about Joe, but I needed to touch base with the shop.

It felt odd—being away from the Chintz 'n China for so long. I wouldn't be returning until July—another two weeks—and I was already fussing about how things were going. But I tried to rein in my fretting. My finances would show a crunch, but I wanted to enjoy every moment of my wedding and honeymoon.

"Chintz 'n China Tea Room, how may I help you?"

Cinnamon answered. She'd just graduated with her Associate of Arts degree in accounting. I had the feeling she would be moving on soon; she was a smart girl with children to feed, and I couldn't pay her what she deserved. I was reluctantly awaiting the day when she handed me her resignation and had already informed her that if she needed time off for an interview, she should just ask.

"It's me, Cinnamon. How's it going?"

"Almost ready to open the doors. Lana's going to be a little late, but since it's Sunday, the rush won't come until later. If you have the time, though, you need to sign off on a few checks. Several invoices came in yesterday."

Since Cinnamon had her accounting degree, I figured

she might as well learn the back end of the business and had handed her some of the easier paperwork to deal with. "I'll try to drop by this afternoon. This weekend's been insane—"

"I saw the paper," she said, her voice tentative. "I wasn't sure whether or not you wanted to talk about it, so I wasn't going to bring it up until you did."

A chill ran up my back. Paper? What paper? "Bring what up? What are you talking about?" I asked, knowing full well I wasn't going to want to hear the answer.

She hesitated. I was known for throwing tantrums over the local media, with whom I had tenuous and stressful connections, but I never directed my anger toward the messengers unless they were directly involved.

"Go on. I'm not going to bite you, you know."

"Okay. Ingrid ran a huge article in the *Chiqetaw Town Crier* about Roy being thrown out of the party the other night. She followed it up with an expose on Joe being shot and is linking the two stories by inference. Since the paper said Joe's going to be all right, I decided to wait until you mentioned it."

"Holy hell. If something like this happens again, tell me right away. I haven't been out to pick up the paper— it's still in the yard. So, the shop's fine?"

"Yeah, everything's okay here." I could hear relief in her voice.

"Okay, then. I'm going to go look at that article. I'll drop by a little later today to sign the checks and glance over the invoices."

I dropped the receiver back in the cradle and made a dash out to the front yard. For once, the boy had gotten the newspaper near the porch. Joe was meticulous about keeping the lawn in order, and Kip had taken on a new diligence in his chores, wanting to impress his older buddy. A light film of dew still shimmered on the blades, but a glimpse of sunlight through the clouds promised to burn off the moisture before noon.

I snatched up the paper and returned to the kitchen,

where I slipped into my chair. Randa, almost done with her breakfast, glanced at the paper, then at me, and winced. My fact-oriented daughter had developed a strong distaste for the *Chiqetaw Town Crier*'s cavalier attitude toward the difference between reality and speculation.

"They have something on you in there?" she asked, swallowing the last bite of her sandwich. She drained her milk and wiped her mouth. Kip had already polished off his ham and cheese and was digging through the pastry basket for a doughnut.

I grimaced. "Yeah, so I gather. Don't be surprised if I blow." I shook open the paper and turned to the front page. A grainy picture of Joe and me taken during our party, filled the lower right quarter of the paper. Slow news week, so it seemed.

Next to it was Ingrid's article. EMERALD O'BRIEN WEAVES HER MAGICAL CHARM AGAIN, the headline read. Oh God, just shoot me now.

Emerald O'Brien, Chiqetaw's beloved sorceress and teashop owner, has once again made the front page, but this time not because of some ghostly visitor or murdering marauder come calling. No, Emerald's been plying her charming self into the spotlight via the men in her life.

Reports have it that a brawl broke out between Emerald's ex-husband, Roy O'Brien, of Seattle, and her fiancé, Joseph Files, captain of Chiqetaw's Medic Rescue Unit. Ms. O'Brien must have been brewing up quite a storm of love spells for the tempest that prevailed. Mr. O'Brien was evicted from the premises by Mr. Files and his biker friend, Jimbo Warren. What this reporter wants to know is: Is a reunion in the mix between Emerald and her ex, or was it just wishful thinking on his part?

On a more serious note, yesterday at approximately three-thirty Mr. Files was shot by an unknown assailant out at Miner's Lake while preparing for a barbecue. He was taken to Chiqetaw General Hospital and is due to be released today. Police have no idea of who shot Mr. Files, or why. Considering the goings-on at the engagement party, this reporter can't help but speculate.

Shit! Ingrid as good as accused Roy in print, but there was really nothing he could use to file suit against her. And she made me sound like a scheming cock-tease. Or at the very least, a philanderer. It wasn't like I'd asked Roy to show up at the party. He managed that blunder on his own. I thought about putting in a call to good old Ingrid, but experience had taught me that facing down the media only meant asking for trouble. I sighed and tossed the paper on the table.

"How bad is it?" Randa asked, rinsing the dishes and putting them in the dishwasher. Kip had stuffed half the doughnut in his mouth, and I wandered over and tapped him on the shoulder.

"Take smaller bites. I don't want you choking. Death by junk food is not an acceptable excuse to get out of chores around here," I said. He blinked, then flashed me a brilliant grin.

"It's bad enough. You can read it if you want. You two are probably going to get teased by your friends, so you might as well know why. I apologize in advance." I hated when my actions intruded on the kids' lives, but there was no getting around it. And technically, it had been Roy's fault, not mine.

Randa glanced at the clock, then grabbed the paper and skimmed. Kip finished his pastry and held out his hand. "Mom, I need to get going or I'll be late. Can I have some money for lunch? Our teacher is taking us to Mickey D's."

"Get my purse," I said. I handed him a five as Randa tossed the paper in the garbage.

"Mrs. Lindstrom is an idiot," she said.

I happened to agree, but didn't want to encourage disrespect in my kids. However, in this case, I would happily make an exception.

"You're right, but don't either of you tell anybody I said that or she might just write something worse next time. Okay, let's move it. You'll have to take your bikes. I don't have time to drive you all over town this morning. And Randa, do you have your cell phone?"

I'd recently purchased a cell phone for her with instructions that it wasn't to be used while in school, and that at night it remained downstairs on the table when she went up to bed. Now, anytime she went out of town on a field trip, I had the added security of knowing I could reach her, if necessary, and vice versa.

She nodded. "In my pocket. I'll be careful."

"Okay, hut-two-three-four, on your way out the door!"

Kip and Randa marched out the kitchen door after giving me quick pecks, and I watched them pedal away on their bikes. Only four more years—if that—and Randa would be off to college.

My mother had told me, years before, that time sped up with age. I hadn't believed her, but now I understood what she meant. Only eight more years and Kip would leave home. And then it would just be Joe and me. The prospect of an empty house had made my mouth go dry before I met him, but now it was as if the future had taken on a new life and color. I'd be fine on my own but with Joe by my side, anything seemed possible.

I turned the dial, starting up the load of dishes, when the phone rang. My knee-jerk reaction was to think that something had happened during the night with Joe, but then I caught myself. He was fine. I had to stop being paranoid. He worked a dangerous job and over the years, I'd have to learn to let go and trust that he'd be okay. I picked up the phone to find a frantic Murray on the other end of the line.

"Em, can you come over? I really need somebody here *right now*." Her voice was shaky and she sounded out of breath. Murray seldom ever sounded frantic, so I knew something had happened.

"What's wrong? Are you all right? Jimbo?"

"Somebody broke into my house last night. I stayed

out at Jimmy's and just got home, and the place has been trashed."

"Holy hell! Are you okay? Is the thief still be in the house?"

"No, no . . . Deacon and Greg are on the way and I've already searched the house. I have my gun, so don't worry—"

Oh yeah, the fact that she was packing a weapon made me feel all safe and secure. But then again, Murray knew how to use it, and she followed procedure.

"Okay, I'm on my way. First I have to call the hospital to find out when I can pick up Joe, but I'll be over right after that."

I fished through my purse for the number to the hospital and put in a quick call to reception. The doctor was with Joe, but the nurse told me that I could pick him up any time after two. I grabbed my purse and dashed out of the house. As I sped over to Murray's house, I couldn't help but wonder if there was a connection between Joe being shot and Murray's house being ransacked. The timing was too close. But how could they be related? A slow churning in my gut told me that the universe had just shaken the dice, and once again, we were on the end of a pair of snake eyes.

ALL SIGNS OF my bridal shower had disappeared, and in its place stood a swath of destruction and mayhem. As I stood on the threshold, staring in the front door, it was hard to comprehend that this had been Murray's neat and beautiful living room only yesterday. Mur was talking to Deacon and Greg when I got there and I waited, making sure not to touch anything.

The sofa—a replica of a Victorian-era piece—had been gutted and bits of stuffing covered everything. Knick-knacks were scattered every which way, some broken, some just tossed about. Files from a small cabinet in the corner had been pulled and tossed into the air, and a hailstorm of paper littered the floor. I glanced over at the wall unit that comprised the two snake cages. The glass had been shattered, and Nancy and Sid were no place to be seen. Confusion and anger blackened Murray's expression, but she was keeping it together much better than I had when the Chintz 'n China had been vandalized.

After a few minutes, she joined me. Her eyes were angry, a tinge of fear mixed into those dark depths. I mutely held out my arms and she allowed herself the luxury of a hug.

"White Deer's on her way over," she said. "I'm just glad she wasn't staying here or she might have gotten hurt."

"I thought she always stayed with you." Not once did I remember White Deer staying at a hotel. Of course, with Jimbo around, maybe the equation had changed a little.

"Not this time. She had some business to attend to in Bellingham last evening, and she stayed overnight with a friend. She should be here any minute." Mur looked around helplessly, as if she didn't know where to start. "Deacon and Greg dusted for fingerprints, but there's not much to go on. My back door was pried open, but no prints except for Jimmy's and my own. The kitchen's just as bad. Oh Em, I lost so many of my things. And my clothes—upstairs—some have been slashed."

"Do you have any idea who did this?" The damage was more than superficial; it was going to cost a butt-load of money to repair and replace what had been lost or destroyed. "This doesn't look like standard teen vandalism."

She shook her head. "I have no idea what the hell is going on. Who could do this to me? Who *would* do this?"

"Was anything stolen?"

"No, that's the killer. Nothing that I can figure out. I've trapped Sid and Nancy in the bathroom. Thank God they didn't get out. They could have been hurt, though, when they slithered over the broken glass of their cages. We lucked out on that one. But I'm scared. I can't find Whiplash anywhere, and Sid looks like he just ate."

Shit. That wouldn't go over big. For such a tough man, and a hunter and trapper at that, Jimbo had a surprisingly soft spot in his heart for animals. Snidely and Whiplash had been stray cats, but they were the best of friends now, and he doted on the orange tabbies.

"Where's Snidely?" I asked.

"She's safe. She was hiding under the bed." Murray's voice broke and I instinctively reached out and tried to soothe her, envisioning her cushioned in a circle of golden light. I took her hands in mine and closed my eyes as a golden light radiated out from my fingertips, winding up her arms, wrapping her in a cocoon to heal, to help.

Mur took a shuddering breath and let it out slowly, then dropped to a chair that had emerged unscathed from the onslaught. "Thanks, that helped. Em, can you . . . would you . . ."

"You want me to see if I can find out anything about what happened?"

She nodded, mute.

I patted her hand. "Of course. You know I've got your back, babe. Have you called Jimbo yet?"

"No, he took off out of town this morning to deliver several batches of honey to some of the smaller stores he sells to. I left a message, though."

That was Jimbo, all right. He hived bees, trapped for fur, cut deadwood for kindling bundles, anything to keep out of the clutches of a regular job. And he'd done quite well for himself over the years. I knew that his land was paid off, and he didn't owe a dime to anybody.

"Tell you what. Let's find Whiplash first, then I'll do some scrying and see what I can pick up. I wish I had my crystal ball with me, but I can make do, or if we can find your cards, I can throw you a reading."

As we waded into the mess, we decided to start upstairs in Murray's bedroom, since that's where Snidely had been hiding. Her clothes looked like they'd been through a shredder, but that was the least of our concerns.

"I think my favorite bra and panty set is missing," she

said, piling the lingerie and panties that remained intact onto the bed. The oak finish on the four-poster bed had been marred by a few dents, but it could be repaired.

"What? Are you sure they aren't around here somewhere in this mess?"

She glanced around, a puzzled expression on her face. "I suppose so, but they should have been with all of the others." As she sorted through what had survived and what was now worthless, I rummaged through the closets, looking for any sign of the missing cat. Nada.

"Mur, hon, what are you doing?"

Murray was dumping every piece of underwear into a big plastic garbage bag, even the ones that had survived the onslaught. "I can't wear these. Someone's touched them, ripped some of them up. How can I even think of wearing them again? My credit cards are going to get a workout this week." She shuddered, holding up a lace bra of the sort that I didn't even know she owned. It had been slit in all too obvious places.

My stomach lurched and I quickly glanced around the room. A feeling that we were being watched niggled at the back of my brain. The air thickened as the sensation grew stronger and, shaking, I backed away to the door. Someone had crept through this room, someone with a careful eye, prying, touching, thinking thoughts better left unspoken.

"Shit, Mur . . . I just . . . there's something really creepy going on. Somebody left a strong signature imprinted here. I think that you need to stay somewhere else for a few days. You can come to my place, if you want."

She swallowed hard. "No. I'm not letting anybody push me out of my home. But I will buy new locks today and we'll install them by nightfall."

I slowly turned around, feeling out the energy of the room. "You need to cleanse this place and cleanse it good."

"I can ask White Deer to help. I know you've got way too much on your mind to worry over this mess."

We sifted through the room, calling for Whiplash, but to no avail. The heavy wood furniture had survived, but the mattress had been gouged in several places, big holes exuding stuffing all over the place. I couldn't ignore the sense of hatred surrounding the room. Hatred and . . . something else.

"Mur, something's seriously warped. Whoever did this was mad as hell at you."

She blinked. "But why? Unless it's somebody I locked up. That could be, you know. A lot of cops get collars from the past out for revenge." As she looked around the room, she let out a long sigh, exasperation, fear, and anger warring for dominance. "Whiplash isn't here. Let's go check in the spare room. Sometimes the cats sleep in there." As we headed down the hall, she turned to me. "I almost forgot. What was the message you left? I'm so frazzled I can't even think straight."

"Oh, yeah, I meant to ask you about something Aunt Margaret mentioned last night. It's a long shot, but you never know." As she led me into the spare bedroom, I noticed that this room had just been tumbled, not destroyed. Everything was relatively intact. "Looks like whoever did this either ran out of time or energy."

"Well, at least the universe gave me one little break. I just wish that I'd been here—I would have put a stop to whoever did this," Mur said.

I shook my head. "I never will understand people. Don't know if I want to, either. Okay, so the deal is this: Do you think Andrew might have been the person who shot Joe? He was sniffing around me quite a bit over the winter and even tried to convince me to break up with Joe and go back to him."

Mur paused, distracted from her own worries for a moment. Then she shook her head. "I don't think so. No, Em, it couldn't be Andrew. Not unless he moved back to town."

"Moved back?" I hadn't known he'd left. "What are you talking about?"

Shifting uncomfortably, she frowned and then said, "Harl thought it better we didn't bother you with this, but I knew you'd find out eventually."

Feeling a little irritated, I said, "Since when have you and Harl been keeping secrets from me? I'll be the judge of what I can—or cannot—handle. Now tell me, what's up with Andrew?" I didn't care much for anybody, even Joe, playing thought police around me.

She cleared her throat and sat down on an untouched ottoman. "Andrew moved to Hollywood. He told James, who told Harlow, that he thought he'd have a better chance of selling a screenplay there. After the aborted attempt with his book option, he got bit by the screenwriting bug and I guess he fancies himself an undiscovered genius. I think he wants to try to hook up with Zia again. Andrew doesn't like rejection."

"Oh really?" I snorted. "Then maybe he should stop acting like a jerk. Whatever. I wish him the best of luck. I have my doubts whether he'll make it, but hey, hell could freeze over."

She gave me a sheepish grin. "You upset we didn't say anything?"

I shook my head. "Nah . . . I don't care what he does. At least we know he's not to blame for shooting Joe. That puts that idea to rest."

"You okay?"

I snorted. "Okay? I'm fine, for someone whose fiancé was shot at, and whose ex-husband is being a pain in the butt. The fact that my ex-boyfriend has delusions of grandeur just seems par for the course."

Mur broke into a smile, laughing. "Oh, Em, I needed that. So, I guess that we're back to Roy as the prime suspect, though I'm telling you, I don't know if we'll ever find out who did it."

"Actually, we're back to finding Whiplash. We have to find that cat before Jimbo comes home." I was about to pull back the comforter so I could peek under the bed when a streak raced out from beneath the dresser, leaped, and landed on the middle of the mattress.

Murray let out a grateful shout. "Whiplash! You nutjob! You had me scared out of my mind," she said, grabbing the tabby and carrying him into a second spare bedroom that had barely been touched. "You stay in here for now." She closed the door and leaned her head against the wall. "Okay, so he's safe, and the snakes are in the bathroom, safely locked away. I need to replace the glass in their cages tonight."

"Call Marvin Eyrland. God knows, he did a lot of work for me when all that crap was going down with the jade dragon, and he's available for emergency jobs." We headed down to the living room. As Murray broke a path through the mess, I glanced over at one of the end tables at the bottom of the stairs. A small box sat atop what appeared to be a card on the wooden table, exquisitely wrapped and looking terribly out of place. "Mur, what's that?"

She glanced at the box, furrowing her brow. "I have no idea." She walked over and picked it up. "This is odd. I don't remember seeing it last night."

Alarm bells began to ring as she unwrapped it. "Mur, I have a bad feeling about this."

She ripped off the shiny purple paper and opened the box, gasping as a brilliant golden ring flashed into view. "Oh hell, who left this here? I wonder if Deacon bought it for his wife and forgot to take it with him?"

"Murray, that's a wedding ring. Could it be from Jimbo?" I asked, even though I knew in my gut it wasn't.

With an absent shake of the head, she opened the card and her face drained of color. "Em, look at this."

I gingerly took the card. There was a picture of an old bridge on the front that I recognized leading to Icicle Lake Falls, a campground on the way to Mount Baker. I opened the card and silently read the typed poem that had been glued inside. It was simple, six lines, but chilled me to the core.

*Every time I think of you, I lose another night of
      sleep,
I pray that you will come to me and be my own to
      keep.
I would bring you to my home, to my side to stay,
In the mountains by a lake, we will find our way.
I wish on every falling star, though my heart, it
      breaks,
I will have you for my own, or life itself forsake.*

"Murray, there's a big freakin' alarm going off in my
gut. You have to show this to Deacon. This looks bad,
very bad." In fact, the damned thing practically sizzled in
my hands. I tossed it on the table. "Does this have anything to do with that card on your doorstep on Saturday?"

"You read that?" she said. I nodded and she let out a
long shuddering breath. "Em, something's been going on.
Phone calls in the middle of the night—but whoever it is
always hangs up. Twice now, I've had the feeling that
somebody was in my house, but couldn't find anything to
prove it. Flowers delivered to work with no card, and
Jimmy didn't send them."

"I thought something was going on with you. How
long has this been happening? I take it you have no idea
who's behind all of this?"

"The first time I got a hang-up call was . . . oh . . . two
weeks ago? Maybe three. I didn't think anything of it at
the time, of course." She rubbed her forehead. "I haven't
got a clue who's doing this." She picked up the card and
read the verse again. "Whatever prints were on the card
are probably toast thanks to the way we handled it. Em, I
don't mind telling you, I'm a little scared. But I don't
want Jimmy knowing about the ring. Not yet. I don't want
him going out and doing something stupid that could get
him hurt."

"What could he do? You don't know who sent it."

"Precisely. He might take it into his head to pin the
blame on somebody innocent. I don't want him hurting

somebody just because he's gone off half-cocked. Promise me you'll keep this a secret?"

I sighed. "Only if you promise me that you'll talk to Deacon."

With a shrug, she tucked the box into her purse. "No worries there—this is the sort of thing I'm always warning women about."

"Okay then, but I don't like it. You shouldn't keep secrets like this," I started to say, but then stopped. She was a cop, she knew her job. If she wanted to keep Jimbo out of the loop for a little bit, she had her reasons. And speak of the devil, the sound of a chopper pulling up told us he'd arrived. I took that as my cue to leave. "Your sweetie's here, and I have to get to the hospital to collect Joe. You going to be okay with this mess? I can come back and help you clean if you like."

She threw her arm around my shoulder. "Thanks, Em, but don't bother. White Deer's on her way. She'll help me sort out this mess. Between her and Jimmy, I'll be fine. You tell Joe we love him and that he'd better get well in time for the wedding or I'm getting out the shotgun."

I humored her, forcing a laugh, but inside I was worried. Worried about Joe, worried about Murray. It was bad enough when things happened to me, but far worse when events turned nasty on my friends and loved ones.

I headed out the door, giving Jimbo a quick peck on the cheek as he entered the room. As I clattered down the stairs, I heard his cry of surprise, and Murray's quick voice. Wishing I could stay to help, I slipped into my SUV and aimed myself toward the hospital, stopping at Starbucks on the way. Caffeine was the best attack against stress, I'd found. As long as it was spiked with plenty of chocolate and flavored syrup.

Five

❦

WHEN I REACHED the hospital, Joe was waiting for me, his shoulder bandaged with a light dressing that barely covered the bruising. I gathered that being grazed by a bullet hurt a tad more than a skinned knee. He fussed as the nurse pushed him in the wheelchair toward the entrance.

"I can walk—"

"Hush! We've been through this already. It's protocol." The nurse gave me a harried look. "Is he this much trouble at home?"

I grinned at her. "Only when he's awake."

Joe snorted. "Trouble? She's the troublemaker in the family."

"Be good or I may rethink marrying you, Files."

His eyes glittered at me, a little curl giving his lip a seductive turn. "Yes, ma'am. I'll sit still until we hit the doors." I'd brought him a loose shirt that wouldn't pull at his bandage and his favorite jeans. He cleaned up pretty good, though he hadn't let them shave him. Joe was trying to grow a beard, a proposition I found appealing, as long as he didn't try to outdo Jimbo. ZZ Top wasn't my idea of sexy.

We finished the paperwork, maneuvered him into the car with only a couple of groans, and headed for home. I stared at the road as it passed beneath our wheels. Time to spill the beans about his brother, as much as I dreaded approaching the subject. Might as well get it over with now, because he'd be expecting to find Nathan at home.

"Babe, I have some bad news."

"What now? You find a dead body in the shed or something?" He was joking, but I detected a tinge of worry behind his smiling face.

"Jeez, give me a break. I did not find a dead body."

"Well, it wouldn't be the first time, now would it?" He snickered. "You know I'm forever going to be on the lookout for corpses, ghouls, skeletons, and ghosts. Somehow I don't think that Brigit was your last. Face it, you're hooked."

"Stop it! If I swerve off the road it's all your fault," I said, trying to keep a straight face. "I'm being serious."

He raised one eyebrow, then cocked his head. "Yes, Ms. O'Brien?" he said with mock solemnity.

"Joe! You make me feel like Mrs. Robinson when you call me that." I took a deep breath. "Okay, so here goes. I called Nathan last night to tell him about you and he—"

"He flaked out, didn't he? He's not going to show." He said it so flatly that I realized this wasn't the first time Nate had screwed over his brother.

"Yeah," I said softly. "I'm sorry, babe. He's on his way to Sweden with a friend." Joe stared out the side window, mute. As I turned onto Hyacinth Street, he let out a long sigh.

"Nate's a fuckup, just like Dexter." Joe never called his father by anything except his first name or "the old man." "He doesn't give a damn about anybody but himself. Ten to one, he's been playing up to some sugar mama just to get a free trip, and when he's over there, he's going to find some snow bunny just out of high school to screw around

with. That's it, I'm done with the whole family, except
Aunt Maggie. She's the only one who has any common
sense. She's been more a mother to me than my own
mother."

I turned into the driveway and switched off the ignition. "Joe, there's not much I can say. I can't make it better. I can't make them into what you wish they would be.
But you have family. You have your aunt, you have me
and the kids, and you have our friends. Harlow and Murray adore you; count them as your sisters and Jimbo and
James as your brothers. Sometimes, we have to create the
family we need."

Even though I'd been happy as a child, at a young age
I'd realized that Nanna was better suited to raise me than
my mother. Klara was a career woman at heart, but I always knew she loved me, and with Nanna by my side, I
felt complete. Rose, on the other hand, had turned to
Grandma M. out of anger. She and Klara were still dancing around each other in a waltz of guilt and resentment.

Joe shrugged, wincing. "I guess you're right. Well,
Nate can go to hell. I'm just grateful to be alive, to be marrying you." He edged himself out of the car and we went
inside.

"Speaking of getting married, do you want to postpone
the wedding? Your brother can't make it and you were just
shot—"

The look on his face was answer enough. "Are you
crazy? Even if I'd taken the bullet smack in the shoulder,
I'd have White Deer over at the hospital to marry us. Even
if she had to dress like a nurse and sneak into my room.
I'm not letting you slip through my fingers, Emerald. And
incidentally, I'm okay with you keeping your last name,
so tell Grandma M. to back off. She waxed long and hard
on that subject during the party, trying to sympathize with
me. I know she thinks I mind, but I don't. It may be Roy's
name, but you should have the same last name as your
kids."

"And *this* is one of the many reasons I love you," I

said, settling him in on the sofa with the remote, a six-pack of Coke, a bag of pretzels, and the phone. "I've got errands to run," I said. "You rest. And if any of my family calls, tell them I'll talk to them tonight."

He looked at me, suspicion clouding his eyes. "You aren't trying to find out who shot me, are you?"

I gave him a long look. "Joe, you know perfectly well that I'm not about to let this go. The cops aren't going to find much, that we can be sure of, unless the dude dropped a calling card out there and that's pretty unlikely. But right now, I'm thinking about something else. Murray found her house trashed when she got home this morning."

"What?" Joe straightened up.

"Her place was trashed, and I do mean ransacked. Thing is, nothing but a few pieces of lingerie were missing. And . . . we found a gift there." I told him about the ring. "She doesn't want Jimbo to know about it yet. She's afraid he'll lose it and hurt somebody."

"Did she report it?"

"She promised me she would. But Joe, her whole place felt slimy. Icky, like something had crept in and nested." I dropped into the recliner. "I'm worried about her. What if she'd been in the house?"

Joe shook his head. "Murray has a gun, Em, and she knows how to use it. She probably would have blown their head off. You can be sure she's a lot better marksman than whoever took a potshot at me."

Another thought had crossed my mind. "At the party, Mur got into it with Roy, too. Remember how rude he was to her? I wonder . . ."

"Don't. Don't wonder. Don't even think about it." He leaned back and I could tell he was sleepy. "Besides, Roy wouldn't give her a present, would he? Let alone a wedding ring."

"You're right, I guess." It didn't make sense, now that I thought about it. And Roy almost always made sense, even if it was of the wrong kind.

"I think I'm going to take a nap, babe. See you when

you get back. Let me know if they find out who broke into her house."

I kissed him, gently at first, then a passionate, full, tongue-meets-tongue kiss. "What do you want for dinner, Files?"

He reached around and cupped my ass. "You, but Italian will do as an appetizer."

A shiver of anticipation running through me, I gave his hand a gentle slap, grabbed my keys, and headed for the shop. That man could push my buttons like nobody else in this world. I thanked my lucky stars that he felt the same way about me.

AFTER A QUICK stop at Starbucks for another mocha, I pulled into a parking space near the Chintz 'n China.

Cinnamon was waiting on Farrah Warnoff, who'd been one of my regular customers since I'd first opened the shop. As I looked around, I realized that—as much as I was anticipating my wedding—I could hardly wait for it to be over and for things to be back to normal. I missed coming in every day, arranging the teapots and tea, greeting the gentle ladies of Chiqetaw who accepted my quirks and eccentricities with a mere blink of the eye. I'd become somewhat of a local legend to them, a status to which I'd never aspired, but sometimes fate propelled us into positions we weren't comfortable with at first to make us stretch and grow.

And grown I had. My shop was thriving. I was in love with, and beloved by, a good man. My children were growing and evolving along their own paths. What more could I ask for? And if ghost-busting and falling over dead bodies was part of the process, then who was I to say the universe had it wrong? I'd finally given in, accepted my place in the scheme of things, and was over and done with freak-out city. Well, in the long run. In the short run, I was still at the mercy of caffeine and panic.

Cinnamon motioned to my office. "The invoices are in there, as well as the new shipment from Amberlane China. I think you're going to go nuts over it. I doubt the pieces will sit on the shelf for more than a day."

I settled into my chair. It felt good to be back, even if it was just for an hour or so. As I cautiously opened the first box from Amberlane, my pulse quickened. Their teapots and cups were made by hand and, as such, were terribly expensive. But the glaze shone with an opalescence that reminded me of the full moon on a summer's night, and the delicate attention to detail was obvious in every curve of the pot. I'd ordered four of the teapots, knowing full well that if they were as beautiful as I thought they might be, I'd be buying one myself. Thank heavens I'd planned ahead.

I picked out my favorite, then jotted a note for Cinnamon to display the others, making sure they were on one of the protected shelves. I had four shelves specifically glassed in for the extremely expensive pieces. Though not foolproof, it at least lessened the chance some bull might come into my china shop and break them.

After turning my attention to the bills and assorted admin work, I leaned back, staring at the phone, a plan formulating in my mind. I had no doubt that Murray and her crew would do their best to find whoever had taken aim at Joe, but I knew the odds and they weren't good. However, with my abilities, I might be able to ferret something out. I grabbed the phone and put in a call to Jimbo.

"Yeah?" His usual greeting, but I was used to it.

"Yo, dude, I want to come out and walk your property like I did when I was looking for Scar. I thought I might be able to pick up something on the frootloop who took a crack at Joe. You up for visitors?"

Jimbo cracked out a laugh. "You take the cake, O'Brien. But I owe you one. You just won me twenty bucks."

I rubbed my forehead. "Say what?"

"I bet Anna twenty bucks that you'd be asking to come out here before the week was over. She said you'd be too preoccupied."

With a snort, I said, "Uh-huh. By the way, how's she doing?"

His voice dropped into scary mode. "If I ever catch whoever ripped up her house, he's dead meat. O'Brien, I'm worried about her, but she won't even think about leaving for a few days. White Deer's staying with her, but neither one of them are strong enough to KO some pervert. I'm going to camp out there for the next few days. I'll be at home tomorrow though. Eleven A.M. work for you?"

I jotted a note to myself. "Sounds good to me."

"Cool beans. I think I'll call in some of my buddies from the enclave to search the property for me. Make sure no psycho's hiding out in the back forty." Jimbo's buddies from the Klickavail Valley bikers' enclave were a formidable crew. I wouldn't want to be any trespasser they might catch.

"Good thinking. Okay, well, I'm outta here for now. See you tomorrow." As I hung up, I turned over several thoughts in my head. One was flashing a neon red alarm, and I had to put it to rest, one way or another. Might as well grit my teeth and get it over with. I grabbed my purse, stuck a Post-it on the teapot I'd chosen for myself, and headed out. With a wave to everybody and a slew of good wishes following me out the door, I jumped in my SUV and pointed myself in the direction of the Four Seasons Motel where Roy was staying.

THE LOOK ON Roy's face when he opened the door was priceless. Made me wish I had a camera. Before he could ask what I was doing there, I pushed my way into the room, tossed my purse on a chair, and perched my ass on the desk.

"Okay, let's get this over and done with. I'm ready to

hash it out once and for all. And I'm sure you want to go home." I'd be able to tell whether Roy had been the one who shot Joe. He wasn't good at hiding his feelings, even though he'd been an excellent liar during our marriage. I'd been in such denial, I'd ignored every warning sign until I couldn't turn away anymore. After the last blow up, ending with me starting a fire using his clothes as fuel, and him giving me a black eye, I knew it was over. From then on, I never had a problem pinpointing his lies.

Roy stared at me, uncertainty clouding his face. "Fine. What exactly are we hashing out?"

"First—what the hell were you thinking when you showed up at the party? You're lucky that I sent the kids home early, but they sure got an eyeful when the paper came out with Ingrid's article in it. They—and everybody else in town—now knows what a drunken buffoon you are. Not only that, probably half the town thinks you shot Joe."

His eyes narrowed and he let out an exasperated sigh. Typical. The martyr rode again. *Oh poor me, my ex-wife just won't quit ragging on me.* "I didn't intend on losing it."

"Then why did you show up? You know you aren't going to control yourself. What on earth possessed you to open your mouth when you know it always gets you into trouble?" I shook my head. Maybe this wasn't the best idea, but we'd been round and round for the past five years, and I was tired of it.

Roy leaned against the wall. He was still a handsome man, that I'd give him, but his arrogance had grown to outshine the charm that had snared me in when we first met. Five-ten, with a curly mass of strawberry blond hair the same as Kip's, he'd kept himself trim. For just a moment, I flashed back to the good days, before the kids and I'd become burdens to him rather than joys. We'd had some good times, a fact that I conveniently tended to forget.

"Emerald—oh never mind." He suddenly slumped. "You wouldn't understand."

"Try me," I said softly. "Talk to me like a human being for once and maybe I'd surprise you. Surprise *me*, Roy. Be a man instead of a spoiled brat who throws a temper tantrum when he can't get his own way."

And to my shock, he took me up on the dare. He slid down to the floor, hands clasped between his knees as he stared at the floor. "What can I say? What do you want me to say? You want me to be happy for you? Well, I am. So there. All better now?"

I decided to take a chance and sat on the floor next to him. "No, not all better. Yes, I want you to be happy for me, just like I'd like to think you're moving on with your life and not holding the kids' feelings hostage. Why are you so mad at me? I'm not the one who—"

"Who cheated. I know—you never let me forget. Will I ever be forgiven for that slip?"

I stared at him, aghast. "Slip? You call it a slip? Roy, think for a moment. Put yourself in my place. Your slip ended our marriage and you traumatized Randa. Why the hell did you decide to fuck Tyra in our daughter's bed? I've never understood. The day I burned that bed on the front lawn, along with your suits and everything else I could find of yours, I burned up any chance of forgiving you. You don't deserve it."

Roy blinked—one long, slow blink that drew me in. A whirl of sorrow, a vortex of tangled feelings slid over me and I realized that he would never have an answer. That *he* didn't even know why he'd done what he did.

"You have no idea why, do you?" I asked.

He slowly shook his head. "No, I've never been able to figure out why I acted like such an idiot. You think I wanted to hurt you? To hurt Randa? I didn't." A pause. "Maybe I did, but I don't know why. There's something you don't know about that time. I never told you because I knew you'd use it in court."

My stomach lurched. Had he hurt one of our children?

Surely he wouldn't admit it to me now if he had. "What? What were you doing?"

"At that time . . ." He paused, and for the first time since I'd known him, I saw fear on his face. "Emerald, I was strung out. I was hooked on cocaine. That's where the money was going that you thought I spent on Tyra." He wouldn't—or couldn't—look me in the eye.

I turned away, staring at the bed, at the dresser, at anything but him. So, that's what had been going on. "And when you hit me that night? The last time?"

"Higher than a kite. I never said I was sorry. I know it won't do any good, but I want to say it now. I'm sorry, Emerald. I'm sorry I hurt you. I'm sorry I hurt the kids. I know I can't ever make up for it."

He caught my gaze and held it. I blinked and looked away, a flurry of confusion raced through me. I'd spent so many years hating him, hating what he'd done to us, that I didn't know how to handle his confession, nor his apology.

"Roy, I don't know what to say," I stammered out.

"I didn't expect you to say much of anything, actually. In fact, I thought you'd laugh in my face." He bit his lip and I saw a few drops of blood dribble down the corner of his mouth.

"Are you clean now? You know I can't let you see the kids if you're still using." I focused on practicalities, trying to navigate the mine-filled territory into which I'd just been thrust.

He rubbed his chin, a stubble of growth caught my notice. "Yeah, I've been going to NA for two years, though I still have a hard time with alcohol when I get upset. I backslide a lot with booze. Tyra said she would leave me unless I joined NA, so I gave it a shot."

And then it dawned on me—why we were having this conversation. Why he was here. "You're going through the steps aren't you? You came here to apologize?"

He shrugged. "Maybe. I don't know. All I know is that when Kip told me you were getting married again, that you were marrying a man ten years younger than you and that you were happy . . . something cracked. After Tyra left, all I could think about was how bad I blew it. Both times." He hesitantly held out his hand. "I don't know what happened. But I'm tired of fighting. I'm tired of being enemies. I'm tired of blaming you for my own screwups."

It was what I'd waited years to hear, what I'd hoped for. So, why did I feel so cold? So aloof and alienated? I stared at his hand, at the fingers that had once caressed me, then bruised and blackened my skin. And I knew deep in my core that I'd never be able to believe Roy about anything. He'd broken my trust so painfully that I couldn't take the chance.

I swallowed the lump that had risen in my throat. "I don't want to fight, either. The kids need you in their lives, and I want them to find this part of you—the part of you that won't rag on Kip and deride Randa. Do you understand? They're the ones you need to focus on. Not the broken remains of our marriage."

Roy dropped his hand. For a second, I saw a look I knew only too well flash in his eyes and then he let out a rough laugh. "I should be grateful you're even still speaking to me. Okay, I'll try to be a better father to the kids, and I promise I won't turn them against this guy you're marrying." He gave me a long once-over. "Joe's a lucky man. I know I've said a lot of rotten things to you, but you've still got it going on."

I didn't want Roy looking at me that way ever again. "Joe loves me, and he loves the kids. So, you'd better not do anything to destroy the rapport they've built up. But you'll always be their father, Roy, and even though I've wished you'd burn in hell, I've never done anything to make them hate you."

I unfolded my legs and pushed myself to my feet. After dusting off my jeans, I added, "However, and you had better listen to me—if Kip or Miranda ever come back from a visit and tell me you were drunk, or acting

weird, that's it. I'll take you to court for full custody.
Got it?"

He stood up and stretched. "Got it."

As I headed for the door, I stopped and turned. "Answer me one thing, Roy. And look me in the eye when
you speak."

He tilted his head, waiting.

"Did you try to shoot Joe? And did you ransack Murray's house?"

Without missing a beat, he shook his head. "No, I
don't even own a gun. I'm bad, but not that bad and you
know it. And as for Murray—no, not interested in anything to do with her."

I knew he meant it. I opened the door, pausing. "Roy,"
I said, not looking at him. "Thank you for apologizing."

His voice echoed over my shoulder. "Yeah, well, I
guess it was time." As I left, I wondered just how long it
was going to be before he was back to his old antics. But
for a moment at least, I'd seen a glimmer of the old Roy
and hoped with all my heart that he'd be able to retain a
hold on the man who had at one time made me the happiest girl in the world.

ON MY WAY home, I stopped at the station to talk to
Murray. Chiqetaw's police department was small, but this
wasn't Mayberry, and Tad Bonner didn't allow any Barney Fifes on the force. Oh, some of the guys were pretty
stuffy, but for the most part, the cops in Chiqetaw deserved the respect they commanded.

A clerk I didn't recognize sat behind the counter. I
smiled at her and gave her my name. "You new here?"

She nodded. "My name's Tansy. Detective Murray
will see you now. You know the way?"

I nodded and headed back to Mur's office. She was sitting behind a large stainless-steel desk, staring at the pile
of folders in front of her. They looked in danger of top-

pling over and burying her. Had Chiqetaw been besieged by a crime wave in the past few days?

"Good God, what is this? *Cops Gone Wild?*"

She set down her pen and closed the file she was perusing. "You'd think so, huh? Maybe I should flash my boobs and they'll go away?"

I slid into the chair across from her desk and let out a little snort. "Just make sure there aren't any hidden cameras in your office. What's all this?"

"We're going through some cold cases, seeing if there's anything that's begging to be reexamined."

"I see you have a new clerk out front."

Mur nodded, frowning. "We finally hired someone to replace Rusty—remember that creep?" The last clerk had tried to sabotage Murray's job when she didn't respond to him the way he thought she should have.

A lightbulb popped on in my head. "Mur, you don't think he could be your stalker, do you? He had a thing for you, if I remember."

"No," she said, moving a stack of files to the other side of her desk. "At least, I doubt it. From what I heard through the grapevine, he moved to Seattle. And I haven't heard a word from him since he left his job. Good idea, though, but I think it's probably somebody I busted, trying to get back at me. Now, why are you here? I know it's not for the ambiance. What's up?"

I told her about my morning with Roy. "I had no idea he was addicted to cocaine when we were together. No wonder he had such erratic mood swings. Now I'm a little afraid to let him near the kids. I know he says he's quit, but he's obviously still boozing it up. What do you think I should do?"

Murray frowned. "Em, I hate to tell you, but chances are he's not going to stay clean until he gets clean all the way. I'd insist on supervised visitations. He may hate you for it, but you owe it to the kids. Tell him you want to be there when he's got them, or you'll go to court to demand he be supervised."

I groaned. "But I don't want to be there. I don't want to be anywhere around him. Honestly, it was almost creepier with him apologizing than when he yells." I sighed. "But you're right. I'll talk to him after the wedding. Maybe, if he's sincere about changing, he'll understand."

"And if not, you'll know you'd better get the law on your side. Coke, huh? That's an expensive trip."

"No wonder we were short every month. At first I thought he might have a gambling problem, but after I found out about Tyra, I thought it was all going to her. Anyway, I no longer believe Roy had anything to do with shooting Joe. That much I'm sure of." And, when I searched the depths of my heart, I knew it was true. For all of his faults, he wasn't a murderer.

Mur shrugged. "I might as well tell him he can leave. There's no evidence pointing to him other than the fight, and that's certainly not enough to take someone to court on." She held up one finger before I could respond and punched a button on her phone. "Deacon, head over to Roy O'Brien's room at the hotel, tell him he can go home. Strongly suggest that it would be best if he did so today." She grinned at me and I snickered.

"So, any leads on who trashed your place? White Deer have anything to say about it?"

Murray's smile disappeared. "No and yes. And worse. To say that White Deer was upset is an understatement. She refuses to stay at my house until I do a thorough cleansing. Em, she did a little scrying and she got sick afterward. Sick as in throwing-up sick. Said she felt like she'd just eaten snails. Whatever energy this perv is running has an oily feel to it. I tossed every stitch of underwear I had and tomorrow we're going shopping in Bellingham for new clothes."

White Deer knew her way around a crystal ball, that was for sure. "Sounds like she's picking up on the same thing I was. If it's strong enough to make her lose her lunch, then you'd better pay attention. I don't like it." I tossed a few thoughts around. "Have you warded your place lately?" I thought of Nanna's trunk at home. "I could come over and help you later on today."

Mur contemplated the offer. "Thanks. Normally I'd say no, considering how frantic you must be with wedding plans, but my aunt scared the hell out of me. She's gone out to Miner's Lake to gather some willow branches from the shore. I think she's planning on making me some sort of protection charm."

"Willow's good. And we can plunder the oak in my backyard. So, you said no, yes, and worse. What's the 'worse'? Or do I want to know?" Ten to one she was under-exaggerating.

She reached in her desk and pulled out a sheet of paper, pushing it across the desk to me. I unfolded it, glancing at the writing. Printed in big bold letters, obviously via computer or typewriter, were the words I'M WAITING FOR YOU. As I held the paper, a spark raced through my fingers and I dropped it on the floor, my fingers tingling. I tried to wipe the feeling off on my pants.

"Shit!" I said as she reached down to pick it up. "The damned thing shocked me! Where'd you get this?"

"I found it in my in-box this morning. No return address, but it was mailed from the post office, looks like. I had the boys run it through dusting, but no prints. I'm scared, Em. First my house, then the ring, now this? I think I've got a stalker." She stared at her hands helplessly.

"I think you're right. Did you tell Deacon about the ring?"

"I told my boss. Tad's going to have all my mail that's delivered here at the office diverted to fingerprinting, before I even get hold of it. I've given him permission." She tried to sound nonchalant, but I could tell she was freaked out. The nervousness was rippling off her like honey down a bee-tree.

"Good, but you need to think further than that. Remember what you told me when I got the security system for my house? That I had to think of the kids? Well, what about your animals? And Jimbo? Mur, you need to have an alarm installed at home, like I've got. I hated it at first, but now it gives me peace of mind. And I wasn't worried about someone stalking me, just stealing my stuff."

The brief thought of "why all of this right before my wedding" raced through my mind, but I booted it out the door. Murray was my best friend, and if she needed me, I'd be there, wedding or not.

"I'll call Marvin Eyrland after we finish talking and then I'll call the home security company," she said and I knew that she was spooked. She wouldn't have given in so easily otherwise.

"Did you tell Jimbo about the ring and this note yet?"

She shook her head. "No, and he's going to hit the roof. I think I'll wait, though, if you're coming over today. I'm beat and the last thing I need is to get into it with him tonight. He won't let this rest, not if he thinks I'm in danger. Providing I call the security company before I tell him about the letter and the ring and card, then he can't say I'm not doing anything about it."

"Yeah, I guess." I had the burning desire to grab the phone and spill everything to Jimbo. I wanted him to protect her, and he couldn't do that if he remained blissfully ignorant. At least he'd be staying in town for a while. There would be somebody with her at night. I glanced at the clock on the wall. Almost four-thirty. "I'd better get on home and see how Joe's doing. I'll be over at your place around eight. That okay?"

"That's great. Jimmy has a meeting out at the enclave until nine." She waved as I headed out the door.

As I swept my hair back, my fingers brushed against my bare neck. Shoot—I meant to put on the crystal necklace Rose had bought me. Oh hell! At the thought of my sister, I suddenly remembered that my family was coming over to dinner. Now what? No way would I go back on my promise to Murray. She needed me. I sighed. Well, they'd just have to settle for takeout. We'd eat early and then Joe could entertain them while I was out. Not for the first time, I wished that we'd eloped. Sometimes, the whole damned process of getting married seemed more trouble than it was worth.

Six

AS I STARTED to fasten my necklace before dinner, my fingers began to tingle. I paused as once again a wave of dizziness threatened to sweep over me. Could I be pregnant? We'd been so careful. More children just weren't in the equation right now, if ever. But if not that, then what was throwing me off balance? I didn't feel sick.

I turned the necklace over in my hand, trying to sense anything that might be coming off of it. There it was. An energy hovering just below the shining and brilliantly faceted crystals. I tried to zero in on its nature but whatever it was darted like fish in a mountain stream. The moment I caught a glimpse of the energy, it disappeared again.

If there was truly danger around, surely I'd know. Or would I? The past couple of weeks had left me scattered and frantic. Unsure of what to do, I dropped the necklace into a velvet bag and put it in my purse. Maybe Murray or White Deer would have an idea.

A glance at the clock told me that my family should be here any minute. Resigned to a strained meal fending off

Grandma M.'s nosy questions and my sister's worry, I swept my hair into place and headed downstairs.

AFTER SPENDING A stressful hour trying to reassure everybody that Joe and I were fine and that we didn't need to move back to Seattle, I left for Murray's house, over a multitude of protests. I felt bad for putting Joe in this situation, but inwardly, couldn't resist a sigh of relief. As much as I loved my family, a few days of being around them—especially Grandma M.—was almost more than I could bear. Now, if it had been Nanna, I would have invited her to move in.

I turned onto Sunrise Avenue and pulled into Murray's driveway. She waved at me from the porch as I dashed up the steps. "Hey, Em, you bring your magic bag of tricks?"

Holding up the travel bag in which I kept a few choice items like sage smudge sticks, Florida water, a couple of quartz crystals, and other assorted goodies, I nodded. "Right here. I left Joe in charge of my family, by the way. I can't stay too long. He's too sweet to leave because of the machinations of Grandma M."

White Deer was waiting for us in the living room. A striking woman, she was more beautiful every time I saw her. Not cover-model beauty, but the same regalness that I saw blossoming in Murray as she came into her own. White Deer was dressed in a pair of dark jeans and a plain black tank top, and her salt-and-pepper hair was held back in a single braid that touched her butt, but she might as well have been wearing a purple cloak and crown, for the strength that radiated out from her.

The scattered mess of clutter and debris had been cleared away, although gaping spaces on all of the shelves stood as a silent reminder that somebody had plundered Murray's home. The sofa had been carted away, as well as several other pieces of furniture. She'd managed to get Eyrland out on an emergency call—the glass covering the snake cages against the wall had already been replaced, and the wooden frames surrounding it looked all but untouched from their original state.

"You guys have been busy," I said, turning around to take it all in, amazed that they'd been able to clear it out in one afternoon.

"Jimmy and White Deer worked on it while I was at the station. Jimmy brought a couple of his buddies over from the enclave and they kicked ass before going back out for their meeting. I owe those guys a big one." She dropped into one of the accent chairs that had remained untouched. "That note scared the hell out of me. It looks like it was mailed Friday, from the postmark, but didn't show on my desk until this morning."

I settled down next to her. "Bonner's taking this seriously, right?" The last thing she needed was her boss to blow off what was happening, as was often the case when women were harassed in a predominately male occupation.

"Yeah, he is. As I said, they dusted the note for prints but nada, and they're going to check every piece of mail that comes addressed to my desk at work." She sighed, then shook her head. "I'm so sorry. I forgot to ask how Joe's doing. He get home okay?"

I grimaced. "He'll be fine. Unless my family scares him off. Let's get busy, shall we? I don't want to be too late tonight, in case he decides to do them all in and stuff them in the shed out back."

We decided to work our way through the house, from the kitchen up to her bedroom. Murray put on a CD and as a rhythmic drumbeat filled the air, I grounded myself. Holding a crystal in either hand, I locked my energy with that of the deep earth mana that rose up through the floorboards. White Deer took out her rattle, while Murray lit the smudge stick and picked up a red hawk's feather. As the swirling scent of sage rose to encompass the room, I began to slip into trance.

We started slow, circling the perimeter of the room. As I slid deeper into the music, I sensed the same disturbance that I'd picked up on that morning—as if someone had broken through the charms of protection Murray had created. The presence violated the warnings to beware and tread gently.

Step by step, we traversed the boundaries of the kitchen, the smoke from the sage rising to clear negativity from the air, the sound of White Deer's rattle shaking up whatever had gotten tangled in Murray's space, the light shining from my crystals reaching out to push back the invasive tide that had rolled through in the wake of the intruder.

We carried the wave before us, building it, charging it, amplifying it as we entered the living room. The snakes, coiled in their cages, harkened to attention, tongues flickering as we passed by. The cats, Snidely and Whiplash, curled on one of the large overstuffed chairs. They blinked but stayed where they were, content to let us do our work.

Up the stairs we worked our way, eating away at the edge of the etheric trail Murray's unwelcome visitor had left behind. As we progressed, I knew with total assuredness that the intruder was a man and with equal certainty that he wasn't through bothering her, but I held my tongue. We'd discuss our impressions after we were done, and I didn't want to interrupt the flow that we'd built. But as we came to Murray's bedroom, a cold sweat broke out on my forehead and a sudden fear swept over me that whoever it was, was still here—hiding in the dark shadows of her attic.

White Deer glanced at me, her eyes luminous and deep. She inclined her head ever so slightly and I knew that she felt the same thing as me.

We entered the bedroom and I immediately felt eyes on my back. Eyes watching, eyes staring, ears listening. And then, *bam*—a blast—right between *my* eyes and I heard a voice in my head shouting, "Pay attention to me!" I stumbled and landed on the bed. White Deer was by my side instantly, and Murray shoved the censer holding the smudge stick onto the dresser and joined us. I shook my head.

"Holy hell, I didn't expect that," I said, rubbing my head. I'd been zapped like this once before, but the energy behind that incident had been of a far different sort. I felt like I'd just taken a nosedive into a vortex of slimy, voyeuristic energy.

"Are you all right?" White Deer pushed back my bangs and examined my forehead. "You're broadcasting like a high-powered radio station." She motioned to Mur. "Get her a cool washcloth, Anna."

Murray rushed to the bathroom and brought back a damp cloth, which she'd sprinkled with a little peppermint oil. The icy scent helped revive me, shaking me out of the fugue into which I'd been unceremoniously dumped. As I shook the cobwebs out of my brain, I realized that the feeling of being watched had grown stronger.

"Mur, does your window look out on another house?"

"Why?" She took the cloth and put it in the laundry basket. "How's your head?" She sat on one side of me, White Deer on the other.

"Better. No permanent damage, I think. But listen, whatever the energy was, it's still hanging around."

"Oh great. You mean I've got a ghost?"

"No," I said, trying to articulate my thoughts. Finding the right words wasn't easy. Feelings, hunches, intuition don't always lend themselves to verbalization. "I think somebody's spying on you. It feels like he's here, in this room." I closed my eyes trying to zero in on the direction from which the energy was coming.

White Deer frowned. "Here," she said, putting her hands on my shoulders. Her calming nature streamed through me, anchoring me so that I could focus with a clear mind.

Within seconds, I turned toward the lamp on the night-stand, walked over, and yanked off the shade. I gazed at the base, trying to figure out what I was doing. I tipped it upside down and found myself staring at a small, black button. "What the hell is this?"

Murray slowly took the lamp in hand, eyeing the device. She held her finger to her lips, then cautiously set the lamp down. "I don't know—looks like a hairball the cats coughed up," she said.

Confused, I opened my mouth but she shook her head and then motioned for us to follow her out of the room. She led us downstairs and out on the porch. "A bug. That damned thing is a bug. I didn't want whoever it is that put it there to know we'd found it."

White Deer paled. "A bug? You mean somebody's been listening to you?"

Murray closed her eyes and leaned against the railing. "Me . . . and Jimmy." Grimacing, she dashed down the stairs where she promptly threw up in the bushes. She turned on the hose and rinsed out her mouth, then stared bleakly at her house. "Who's doing this? I can't believe that somebody's been in my bedroom—listening to us. Jimmy's going to go ballistic, and there's nobody for him to take it out on."

White Deer ran down the stairs and took her arm, leading her back to the porch. "Breathe deep. Come on. In. Out . . . that's right. Another breath."

"We can't clear the house until we know if we've found all of them," I said. "Have Deacon and Greg help you go through every closet, every cupboard. Where there's one, there might be more."

Murray nodded. "Yeah, I'll call them now and have them come over with one of the chiphead gurus in the office."

I had to leave, but as I looked back at the beautiful Victorian that Mur had worked so hard to renovate, I wanted to cry. I knew what it was like to feel at risk in my own home. That Murray had to go through the same thing galled me. Angry, wanting to go smash the device attached to her lamp, all I could do was reassure her that I was her friend. And I knew that wasn't enough.

*   *   *

AS I WALKED through the door to my house, I realized that I'd forgotten to ask them about my necklace. Considering what we'd found, however, my worries over some fuzzy energy on a string of crystal beads were insignificant.

I was greeted by a quiet and peaceful house. My mother and father were gone, along with Grandma M. Rose had stayed, talking to the kids. Joe was in bed, fast asleep. I watched his chest gently rise and fall for a few moments and leaned over and kissed him on the forehead, then dropped the velvet bag with the necklace in my jewelry box and went downstairs.

Rose had made a pot of Orange Spice tea and added honey. As I joined her, she poured it over ice and we went into the living room. Kip had been showing his aunt a few of his projects from computer camp. He looked up as we entered the room.

"Time for bed, Kip. I'll be upstairs to check on you after a while." He ran over and gave me a peck on the cheek, then took off upstairs.

Rose grinned, watching him leave. "Miranda's on the roof. I swear, I don't know how you manage it. Aren't you afraid she'll fall off?"

"Only if she decides she can fly and crawls over the guardrail," I said, curling up on the sofa next to her. "So, was Grandma mad at me?"

Rose smiled. "She's always mad at you. Remember? I'm her favorite, just like you were Nanna's. But I think she's equally pissed at me, now that she knows Charles and I are breaking up. She can't understand why."

"I wondered about that myself. We really haven't had a chance to talk since the party. What happened?"

She shrugged. "What usually happens? Charley met a younger woman. And another one. And another. And then he found out about my affair. So, he got his secretary pregnant and decided to ditch me."

"*Your* affair? You cheated on him?" I couldn't believe what I was hearing. My sister had to be one of the most straitlaced women I knew. How could she, of all people, have fallen into an affair?

Coloring, she hung her head. "Not until after I found out about the first few he had. I thought I could do it, Emmy. I thought I could handle it. You know, the rich-bitch life, with him leading his life and me leading mine, and we go on, appearing the perfect couple. Our friends didn't have to know. But I couldn't."

I knew all too well about keeping up appearances. I'd done it through Roy's increasing anger and abuse for several years, until he set the bar so high even I couldn't leap over it. "Who did you get involved with?"

She grinned, a little sheepish. "You're going to laugh. He was my Pilates trainer. I started going to the gym every day. You know the routine. *If I can just make myself pretty enough, he'll quit seeing those other women.* Josh and I started talking after my workouts, then we went out to coffee. One thing led to another. But even though I liked him, I always felt like such a loser."

"What happened? You said Charley found out?"

"Yeah, and I guess he believes in the double standard, because he blew up. I thought he was going to have a stroke, he was so mad. He threatened to kick me out with just the clothes on my back until I pointed out his many indiscretions and asked him just what he thought our friends would say if I told them how long it had been going on. And I had proof."

I stared at her. "Oh Rosy, not a private detective?"

She blushed. "Yes, I hired a PI to follow him. I kept asking if something was wrong and he kept telling me I was just imagining things, that I needed help because I was so jealous. So, I finally decided to find out once and for all. I've got the pictures, and he knows it. I showed him a couple of them. That put an end to his threats to kick me out."

"Hold on," I said. We needed something a little stronger than iced tea for this discussion. I went in the kitchen and foraged through the cupboards until I found a package of mint Oreos.

As I arranged them on a plate, I thought about what Rose had done. I'd always prided myself on never snooping on Roy. For some reason, it had been a point of honor, but now I began to understand just why a woman might hire a PI. Roy had pulled the old "you're imagining things" spiel on me, and I'd spent an extra year in the marriage trying to convince myself that if I just tried hard enough, everything would be okay. Now, it seemed like a clear case of self-delusion. I hadn't been willing to find out what I'd probably known in my gut.

I carried the plate back into the living room and settled down on the sofa. "Eat. Sugar soothes the spirit."

She grinned, fingering one of the cookies. "Some things never change, Emmy. So, after I showed him the pictures, we agreed to part ways, to divide the estate equally, and to keep mudslinging out of the papers." She sniffled. "We've been oh-so-civil about it. Our divorce will be final in November."

I stared at her for a moment, then slid over and wrapped my arm around her shoulder. We hadn't sat like this since childhood, snuggled together on a sofa. "You aren't losing anybody who's worth keeping, Rosy. You're going to be okay. Look at me. I made it back after a divorce, and I have kids. You're going to receive a good settlement. You'll be okay."

Rose gave me a long look, then shook her head. "You don't get it, do you? Of course you made it. You're strong. Stronger than I could ever hope to be. Nanna taught you to trust in yourself, a gift that Grandma M. never gave to me. And Mother never thought to teach us self-confidence. She just assumed it should come naturally. I don't know if I can do it. I don't know if I can lose my husband and home and still hold my head up. That's all I've got, Emmy."

"Bullshit. You're a McGrady, and we McGradys always survive. You just have to find out what you love and follow your passion, and I'm not talking about a man. I love Joe more than I thought I ever could love anyone again, but if I hadn't met him, I'd be okay because I have my shop. And I love my life."

"Do you realize how much I admire you, Emmy?" Rose said, smiling shyly. "I've always been jealous of you. You're courageous and you had the guts to stand up and say 'I won't take it anymore' when Roy hurt you. You didn't play games behind his back. You had the guts to start a business, to make it work. And now you're getting married again. You're incredible!"

I blinked, totally unprepared for the way the evening had turned out. Rose and I hadn't talked like this for years. "I've got a secret to tell you, Rose," I said, debating on whether or not to say anything. Very few people knew about a part of my past that I kept hidden. "Do you remember a few years back, before I moved here, how the folks took the kids for a week?"

She shook her head. "Barely. I was too busy with . . . whatever it was I was doing. Chairing some party or fundraiser or something."

"When I left Roy, before Murray convinced me to move to Chiqetaw, I fell into a deep depression. It was hard for me to think, hard for me to see my way through the darkness. One night, I swallowed a handful of pills. I was hurting so bad that I couldn't see any other option."

"Oh my God, do Mom and Dad know about this?"

"No. They still think I had a horrible case of the flu. Randa found me throwing up in the bathroom, and she didn't know what to do so she called Murray, who called a mutual friend to come over and make sure I wasn't going to die. Apparently, I hadn't taken enough to do myself in, but I'd still made the attempt. An hour later, Mur showed up. She must have driven like a bat out of hell to get to Seattle that quickly. When she arrived, she packed the kids off to our folks', and spent a week helping me sort myself out. That's when she convinced me to move to Chiqetaw. I owe her my life."

I closed my eyes. Even the kids had never known about the pills. They'd thought I'd been sick because that's what Murray told them. In fact, Mur was the only person who knew what really happened until now. I'd always intended to keep it that way, but Rose needed shoring up. She needed to know that I wasn't invincible, that I'd pulled back from that terrifying edge, just like she would.

Rose sighed. "I didn't know any of that. I was too wrapped up in my own world to pay much attention to what was going on with the family. I regret it now. I'm sorry I wasn't there for you when you needed me."

I shrugged. "Past is past. It's over, and I'm happy now, and the kids have turned out relatively well-adjusted, regardless of Roy's poor parenting and my breakdown." I glanced up at the clock. "I'm beat. I need to go to bed. Hey, you want to stay over? I can make up the sofa for you."

She shook her head. "No, I'll go back to the hotel. But Emmy . . . thanks. Thanks for being here—and thanks for not giving up on me. I miss doing sister stuff. From now on, I promise to keep in touch."

As I waited on the porch until she made it safely to her car, I realized that I loved her. All these years I'd felt rather indifferent, but now it seemed like we'd forged a reconnection. One I was determined to keep alive.

I WAS DRESSED and ready to head out to Jimbo's by ten the next morning. Joe was healing up, though he wisely decided to spend the day puttering around the house.

"I'm a medic," he said. "I'm not stupid. I want to be able to go back to work after our wedding. The graze wasn't bad, but the bruise is horrible." He submitted when I insisted on putting a comfrey poultice on his shoulder.

"You promise me you'll take it easy?"

"All right, all right. What are you going to do?"

I bit my lip. I didn't want to tell him I was going out to

Jimbo's. He'd only insist on coming along. "Wedding stuff," I said, figuring that I'd stop at the florists on the way home and see how the flowers were coming along. That way I wouldn't be lying. "I'll be out for a while, so don't worry. I'm taking my cell phone, though."

I drove the winding road to Miner's Lake mulling over all the chaos that had happened. The brief thought that it might be connected to the fuzzy energy around my necklace crossed my mind, but that seemed too far-fetched. For one thing, Murray's problems had been going on for quite a bit longer than I'd owned the choker.

Usually when things went down, I felt like the prime target, but this time the events swirled around me, touching the lives of my friends and loved ones. Joe's shoulder, of course, impacted me directly, but it still hadn't been me out on that meadow taking the bullet. Murray was my best friend, but I wasn't the one facing a stalker. And I'd already been through my divorce, so I wasn't in that frantic, confused phase that Rose was going through as she mourned her lost relationship.

Instead of relief, all I felt was a sense of helpless unease. I wanted things to run smoothly. Selfishly, that meant my wedding. But on a deeper level, I hated watching from the sidelines, unable to stop the parade of nightmares going on in the lives of my friends and loved ones.

As I turned onto the dusty lane leading to Jimbo's house, I slowed the car. Wildlife roamed this area, as well as cats and dogs and chickens and the occasional odd turkey or cow making a jailbreak for the open road. Another few minutes saw me to the edge of Jimbo's acreage, and I eased into the driveway, turning off the ignition and listening to the lively sounds of the wooded lake. It was so peaceful that I leaned my head against the headrest for just a moment.

"Hey, O'Brien, get your ass out here." Jimbo, followed by his beloved three-legged Roo, a little dog that he'd rescued from the side of the road, were headed my way. She ran as fast as any normal dog and had adapted to the loss of a limb with ease.

I climbed out of my car. Jimbo's house sprawled across the front of the lot. He'd built onto it, one room at a time, until it resembled a jigsaw puzzle, with rooms sticking out every which way. He never bothered with building permits, and since he lived in an unincorporated area, nobody had bothered him. A garage sat off to one side; to the other, a shed where he skinned his furs and slaughtered chickens for dinner and took care of all the messy business with which a trapper and hunter had to cope.

I glanced up at the sky. The clouds had failed to put in an appearance, it looked like our hot spell was back. The smell of freshly cut grass assailed my senses, along with the heavy summer scent of blossoming flowers and warm lake water lapping the shore.

Jimbo slid his arm around my shoulder as we wandered toward his house. "So, Anna told me about the bug," he said, and he didn't have to say another word. I knew that if he ever caught the culprit, he'd pound the living crap out of him. "She and White Deer stayed out here last night, and today, they went into Bellingham to buy outfits for your shindig. How's Joe?"

"Joe will be just fine," I said, leaning against him. I'd always wanted a big brother; now it seemed that I had one. "I'm just worried about it happening again. Occasionally they lose people, you know. EMTs aren't miracle workers, and there are times when somebody dies on them. I wonder if maybe the relative of somebody that he couldn't save went a little nuts and blamed Joe?"

Since I'd dismissed Roy as my primary suspect, I'd been forced to look in other directions. Murray told me they hadn't found any evidence pointing to a suspect. She seemed to think it was some kid who was target shooting, who happened to point his gun in the wrong direction. Perhaps she was right, but I wanted some sort of assurance that it wasn't going to happen again.

"Let's head down to the meadow," I said, turning in

that direction. "I want to get a feel for where Joe was standing. Then you can take me over to where the sniper was hiding."

As we pushed through the overgrown path leading to the lakeside, I petted Roo, who bounced along beside me. It might be nice to have a place out in this neck of the woods. The kids would have room to play, although Randa would cry foul over not being able to run to the library on a whim. At least we owned the lot next door, and I was thinking about buying the two on the other side of my house—both lots were wooded ravines with no houses. I'd leave them wild, untouched.

Jimbo pointed to the open swath next to the lake. He kept it under control with a weed whacker and a mower. "That's where we set up the grill."

Miner's Lake was bigger than a large pond, but you could still see the other shore, covered with the upscale housing developments that were starting to infiltrate the area. In time Jimbo's land would be worth a small fortune, and I hoped he'd keep it pristine as long as he could and not sell out to the corporations.

"Joe was to the right of the grill. I was over at the table getting the meat ready to throw on the charcoal."

The grill was a hunkin' old broiler, not propane like the modern ones, but using old-fashioned briquettes and wood charcoal. Jimbo refused to grill over gas, saying the fumes tainted the taste of the food. It was just one of the quirks that made him all that more loveable.

I parked myself on a long log that had been barked and sanded to make a bench. The sound of gentle ripples cresting against the shore broke rhythmically as they kissed the land. I shaded my eyes and stared at the water. The breeze ruffled it into concentric rings that radiated out, and the sun beat down on the indigo surface. Everything felt in order, nothing out of place.

"Where did the bullet come from?" I asked after a moment.

Jimbo pointed down the path, across to a patch of tall

huckleberry and ferns. Shaded by a stand of oak and Douglas fir, the foliage glistened green under the sun, and as I stared at it, I began to feel a chill creep up my spine.

"Okay, let's go take a look. Lead the way."

He led me along the path, which had recently been pruned back, probably for the barbecue. Wistfully, I thought of how much fun we would have had, and for a moment, a flare of anger rose up. Why were all our special events marred in one way or another? The week leading up to my birthday had been a nightmare. Even Christmas this past year had felt a little off—with Joe having to work, and with my kids once again angry at their father who had run off on a trip to the Caribbean after Tyra dumped him.

Jimbo pointed to a large bushy vine maple, which was partially obscured by a thriving patch of Scotch broom. "There, that's where they said he must have been hiding. I meant to cut down the broom two weeks ago, but got distracted. If I had, maybe he wouldn't have been able to sneak back in there."

"It's not your fault," I murmured, suddenly aware that Jimbo felt some responsibility for Joe's predicament. "You weren't the one who was holding the gun, and you didn't pull the trigger." I crept forward into the blind. As I stood there, turning so my gaze traveled along the path, I felt a shift in the air and found myself staring at Jimbo and Joe, standing near the grill. But Joe was out of phase, almost invisible. Jimbo stood out loud and clear, but he was superimposed over Joe, like a bad double exposure.

"Huh?" I said, shaking my head. Jimbo kept silent. He'd been around me long enough by now to recognize when I was out on the astral, exploring. I blinked, then looked again, allowing my senses to reach out, to cross time and see just what the shooter had been seeing.

Once again, Jimbo came into view, superimposed over Joe. Joe might as well have been a ghost. I frowned, then remembered something. "Hey, you said that Joe was wearing your shirt, right?"

"Yeah, one of my favorites, too. Anna gave it to me."

"How often did you wear this shirt? Did a lot of people around town see you in it?" A suspicion was beginning to form in my mind; one that made all too much sense.

He thought for a moment. "I guess I wore it a lot, though it's a goner now. It got pretty banged up from that bullet, not to mention that the medics cut it off of Joe to see what was going on with his shoulder. Why?"

I turned the words over in my head. "Because when I look at the meadow, the person who stands out is you, not Joe, but you're standing right where you said Joe was. It's a fair distance to see a lot of detail. If somebody saw Joe wearing that shirt, they might have thought—"

"That Joe was me," he said slowly. "Shit, then they might have been taking aim at me?"

I nodded, certain that we were on the right track. "I think that's what happened. The more we talk about it, the stronger my hunch is. Jimbo, you were the target. Which makes what's happening with Murray all the more frightening. Whoever's stalking her might want to get rid of you. So much so that . . ."

"That he took a chance on killing me, but missed." Jimbo grunted, stabbing at the ground with his boot. "That puts a whole new spin on things, doesn't it?"

I nodded. "Yeah, and it means that Joe just got in the way, so you'd better be damned careful out here. Our pervert just might try again." No matter which way I turned it over in my mind, I came back to the same thought: Jimbo, not Joe, had been the target. Which meant my sweetie wasn't in any further danger, but it left a big red target on the biker's forehead.

We headed back to the house where I sprawled on the front step, playing with Roo, while Jimbo silently fiddled with his chopper. After a few minutes, I asked, "Are you going to tell Murray about this?"

He glanced up at me, his eyes dark. "I don't know," he said gruffly. "I don't want to worry her with all that's gone down the past few days."

"Yeah, but even you have to admit that the more information she has, the safer you both are." It occurred to me that Mur hadn't been all too forthcoming with Jimbo, either—she still hadn't told him about the ring or the note. At least there'd been no way for her to avoid talking about the bug under her lamp.

He shrugged, then climbed on the chopper. Sugar, as he called her, roared to life. Jimbo leaned back and took her for a spin around the yard while Roo and I watched. All of a sudden, the bike went out of control, and it looked like he was fighting to keep upright. I jumped up, watching in horror as he wrenched the chopper sideways as it raced in a mad frenzy. It skidded, roared again, and tipped, pinning him beneath it. As I dashed over to him, the engine sputtered and died.

"Jimbo, are you all right?" I struggled to push the heavy machine off of him, and after a moment, he shook his head and managed to lever it from below. Another moment and I was bracing it with my weight, holding it upright as he stumbled to his feet, coughing.

"Shit," he croaked. "Motherfu—" Stopping abruptly, he glanced at me. "Here, let me take that." He locked the kickstand into place, then stood back, eyeing the bike suspiciously.

"Jimbo—" I fussed, noting the torn jeans and the patch of rough skin where his elbow and upper arm had slid along the driveway. Tiny pebbles were embedded into the skin, and blood dripped in a slow trickle.

"I'm okay—don't sweat it. I'm fine," he said, squatting to examine the front of the bike. He moved to the back and looked at another wire. After a moment he whistled. "Well, looky here."

"What?" I closed my eyes. Whatever it was wasn't good, and that same creepy energy that I'd felt in Murray's house now pervaded the yard.

"Somebody's been screwing with my chain. It's been loosened. If I'd been on the freeway . . ." His voice drifted off, leaving the rest unsaid, but both of us knew exactly what would have happened. He would have stood a damned good chance of being killed.

He strode inside and I followed, watching as he grabbed the phone. Punching in a number, he paused, then said, "Trigger, this is Jimbo. Yeah, fine. Listen, can you round up five or six of the boys and bring them down to my place? Remember what I was telling you guys at the meeting last night? Well, it's for real. I want to do a walk-through, make sure nobody's camped out around here." Another pause. Then: "Yeah, like that Bear dude. Half an hour? Sounds good. Thanks."

As he replaced the receiver, I made a decision. Murray would probably be pissed at me, but things were getting out of hand. "Jimbo, there's something else that you don't know. When I was at Murray's . . ." I told him about the ring, and the note she'd received at work.

No longer worried about Joe, now I was nose-deep in concern for my friends. My wedding plans paled in the face of what was going on, and I knew that I couldn't in good conscience just turn and walk away from this to go on my honeymoon. I knew Joe would feel the same way. Until we had some idea of what was going on, our wedding plans would have to wait.

Seven

THE MINUTE HE heard about the ring and the note, I had no problem convincing Jimbo to call Deacon. While we were waiting, the roar of bikes thundered from down the road and six burly men came riding into the driveway, all in jeans, leather, and dark shades. My heart flipped for a moment, and I had the sudden urge to slip into a halter top and a pair of Daisy Dukes. Oh, yeah. That was me, all right.

The guys waved at me as they fanned out around the yard. By now, I'd been around the enclave enough to know a few of their names, and they'd dubbed me the "weird tea chick." I wasn't suburban enough to rate the word "lady," for which I was grateful—the word conjuring up images of soccer moms, soft pop radio stations, and minivans. I was proud to be Kip and Randa's mother, but I preferred grunge and my SUV.

Terry-T strode up to Jimbo. They clasped hands. "What's shakin', my man?" he said. Terry-T had long wheat-colored hair and facial hair that lingered on the verge of *Beards Gone Wild*.

Jimbo was about to fill them in when Deacon and Greg

pulled into the yard. The boys stared, not unfriendly but solemn and silent. I sidled up to Jimbo's side and we went over our respective stories. Normally, I didn't bother telling the cops—other than Murray—when I had a psychic hunch because I knew they couldn't act on it, but this time it made sense. Common, logical sense. I had the feeling they'd actually consider the idea that Jimbo might have been the target, given everything else that had been happening.

By the time we finished, Deacon was shaking his head. "I don't mind telling you, I'm worried. We haven't had someone on the force with a creeper in a long time," he said.

"Creeper?"

"That's what the Chief calls it. Occasionally you get a cop who attracts a wacko. A lot of times, it's somebody they've busted; once in a while it's your everyday, average neurotic who fancies the officer to be their own personal savior. Hero worship bordering on fantasy. But whoever this is, this dude's escalated the pattern. He's skipped a few steps."

"Like what?" I asked. If he was upping the ante, there had to be a reason.

"He's invaded her house and she still doesn't know who he is." Deacon glanced at me. "You might just be right about the shooter. We'll look into it."

They inspected the chopper and noted down the damage, then checked out the rest of Jimbo's vehicles, but could find nothing else out of place. As they headed to their patrol car, they left Jimbo with a caveat to be careful and make sure to lock up his vehicles in the garage.

"You might want to give them a once-over before you ease out on the road, too," Greg said. "Just to make sure there's nothing wrong. I don't want you paranoid, but if somebody's been tampering with your bike, next time you use your truck, you might want to look under the hood."

Jimbo frowned. "Why?"

An image flashed in my mind and I knew I'd picked up

on what Greg was thinking. As softly as I could, I said, "Explosives. You don't want to get in a booby-trapped car. Isn't that right, Greg?"

Greg's gaze flickered to me and he nodded. "Yeah. Pretty much." On that note, they pulled out of the driveway.

I sighed. There was nothing more I could do out here, and I had an appointment with the seamstress who was altering Nanna's wedding dress. My mother had found it in the attic, and it was a vision in ivory lace and satin. It was too big for me—Nanna had been a stout woman—and I wanted a lower neckline, but Janette Armor, who owned the Bridal Veil, had promised that she would work her magic. I only hoped that I hadn't gained any weight. I'd been stressing a lot the past few days and eating everything in sight.

I gave Jimbo a hug and he swept me up in his arms. "Thanks, O'Brien. You may have just saved my can. If you're right, at least now I can be on the alert. And I'll keep a close eye on Anna, so don't worry your scrawny little butt over that."

As I headed toward my Mountaineer, escorted by none other than Terry-T himself, I heard Jimbo briefing the guys on what he wanted them to do while patrolling his property.

Terry-T held my door open for me as I scrambled in. I blinked in surprise. "Why thank you, Terry. Keep an eye on him for me, will you?" I nodded Jimbo's way.

The big galoot grinned. "Sure thing, sweet cheeks. He's the Man, all right. So, you're getting married to the paramedic."

I nodded. "Yeah, supposed to be, if things ever calm down. Why?"

He hemmed and hawed for a moment, then said, "The boys and I wanted to do something to thank you for catching that S.O.B. who killed Clyde and Scar last year, and for what you did for Traci. We've been talking about it for a while now, and we've come up with a gift for you. But

I don't want to spoil the surprise. When we heard you were coming up here today, I figured why wait. So, a couple of the boys delivered it to your house. By the time you get home, it should be there."

I blinked again. A present? For me? From the Klick-avail bikers' enclave? Shades of surreal. "I have no idea what to say. You didn't have to do anything—I'm just glad I could help out." I broke into a wide grin. "But I do love presents, so thanks, Terry-T. And tell the boys that, whatever it is, I'm sure I'll love it."

He slapped the side of my door as he shut it for me. "Yeah, we think you will, too. Okay, gonna go help Jimbo here. Can't have the Man in trouble, you know?" As he sauntered away from my car, I couldn't help but think about first impressions, and how very wrong they could be. I'd learned a lot from Jimbo and his buddies, and I hoped I never forgot the lesson.

On the drive home, I wondered what on earth a bunch of bikers could have settled on for a wedding gift. As I pulled into the driveway, the answer became abundantly clear. There stood Joe, Randa, and Kip, big goofy grins on their faces. They were gathered around a beauty of a chopper. A Harley with a passenger seat, painted brilliant emerald green. Oh my God, the boys had given us a motorcycle!

I leaped out of the Mountaineer and raced over, laughing. Joe caught my gaze, his eyes twinkling as he pointed to the side of the chopper. Instead of flames, the words CHINTZ 'N CHINA EXPRESS had been painted in lemon yellow and outlined in black, a perfect contrast against the green. When I could control my laughter, I told them what Terry-T had said.

Joe nodded toward the house. "There's more."

"More? That thing is worth a good ten or twenty grand, or would be if it was new." I knew the boys had refurbished an older bike, which was just fine—a new one would be way too expensive for me to feel comfortable accepting. I also knew that Joe would have a blast with it, and I fully intended to be right there, behind him on the passenger seat.

We trooped up the steps to the porch where I saw two black leather jackets, one in my size, one that would fit Joe. On the back was the enclave's sigil, and beneath it, the words HONORARY MEMBER.

Grinning like a hyena, I decided that maybe our wedding would go off without a snag after all. And if it didn't, we could hop aboard the bike and elope.

AS I TOOK a shower, Joe sat on the toilet, talking to me. I told him what I'd figured out. "I don't think you were the target," I shouted over the running water, as I lathered rose-scented shampoo into a thick foam. I wasn't about to go to a fitting for my wedding dress with anything but powder-fresh skin and clean hair.

"You know, that makes sense," he shouted back. "I can't imagine who would want me dead. Not even Roy."

Roy. Yeah, my suspicions about Roy had been alleviated by our talk, but I wasn't ready to tell Joe about my visit. As it was, I had my doubts that Roy would ever really shape up. Oh, he might actually stick by his word and try to be a better father, but until he could take full responsibility for his addictions, he'd always be blaming someone or something else for his problems.

I rinsed my hair and turned off the water, stepping out of the shower as Joe handed me a towel. "Thanks. I'm worried sick, though. Who could be stalking Murray, and why? And if this psycho's taking potshots at Jimbo, then he's serious."

"How do you know it's a he?" Joe asked.

"What?" The thought that the stalker might be a woman hadn't occurred to me. "Usually women stalk men, don't they? If a woman was stalking Jimbo, wouldn't she have sent presents to him and shot at Murray?"

"I'm just saying, don't make any broad generalizations until you know for sure. Who knows? Maybe some woman has fallen for Murray and is angry that she's with a man? It happens." Joe smacked me soundly on the butt as I padded over to the vanity and peered at myself in the mirror. I turned around, eyeing him, and he raised one eyebrow. "Ms. O'Brien, would you like to retire to the bedroom?"

"I would indeed, however, I'm going to be late for the fitting of my wedding dress so you'll have to hold that thought for later. We don't want to aggravate your injury, either, so maybe we'd better hold off for a day." I returned to the bedroom, searching for the corset and panties I'd be wearing under the dress. You could never be too careful with special-occasion outfits. Always best to wear the foundation garments you were planning to wear with the dress when you went to have it altered. The wrong bra—especially for someone with boobs my size—could make or break a look.

Joe followed me, stretching out on the bed. "My shoulder's not what I was planning on using," he grumbled, but gave me a good-natured grin. "Wow, that's hot," he added, as I cinched the ivory bustier a little tighter.

I grinned at him as I shook Rose's gift out of the velvet bag into my hand. Once again, I had the feeling something was off and, as I reached up to fasten the necklace around my throat, I couldn't go through with it.

"Damn it!" I dropped to the vanity bench and stared at the chain of crystal beads. This was getting ridiculous.

"What's wrong, sweetie?" Joe slowly pushed himself to a sitting position. "Everything okay?"

"No," I said, frustrated. "There's something weird about this necklace Rose gave me. I love it, but every time I wear it, I get dizzy, and now I'm nervous about putting it on at all. I guess I'll have to wait until I have more time for scrying. I was going to ask Murray and White Deer to look it over for me, too. I've been so preoccupied that I'm finding it hard to focus on the crystals when I try to tune into the energy."

He frowned. "Just leave it home, then. You don't really need to wear it today, do you?"

I slowly slid the necklace back into the velvet bag and put it in my jewelry box. "I guess not. I wanted to make sure it worked with the outfit, but I can do that later."

As I reached for my peach chiffon skirt and a tan tank top, I glanced in the full-length mirror. Even though I was comfortable with my looks, I never thought of myself as particularly sexy or beautiful. But this time, I felt like I was looking in the pages of a lingerie magazine. The corset was embossed, tone-on-tone ivory, with a delicate floral design. The panties matched. Thanks to my yoga, I'd toned up a little and, while I'd never be a size six, I didn't really care. I looked better than I had in years. And part of it, I knew, was directly thanks to being in love and happy again. Turning away slowly, it occurred to me that, for once, I knew what it was like to *feel* beautiful. Really beautiful.

AFTER I'D DRIED my hair and grabbed my purse, I headed down to the dress shop. The title for the bike was in my purse. As much as I appreciated the guys' good-will, I was planning on having Murray run a background check on it first to make sure everything was on the up-and-up. The last thing I needed was a hot chopper in my possession.

I turned onto Hawthorn Boulevard five blocks north of the Chintz 'n China and managed to find a parking spot just around the corner from the Bridal Veil. As I approached the shop, a nagging feeling tapped at the back of my brain. I tried to shake it away; usually that feeling meant trouble, and more trouble was the last thing I needed. But when I rounded the corner and pushed on the door, I knew the universe had once again dropped a speed bump in my path.

The shop was closed. Not just closed, but the window displays had been torn apart. Anxiously, I cupped my hands around my eyes and peered inside. From what I could see, the place looked in total disarray, and the racks of gowns were nowhere to be seen.

Shit! What the hell? I forced myself to remain calm and set my purse on the sidewalk, flipping through my Day-Timer till I found Janette's home number. I pulled out my cell phone and punched the keys, trying to keep my cool. A loud beep sounded, then a voice announced, "This number has been disconnected. If you think you dialed in error, please hang up and try again."

Cripes. Maybe I'd punched in the wrong number? It couldn't hurt to try again. I dialed Janette once more, making sure I hit each key correctly. Again the beep and the voice. Oh, hell. Bloody freakin' hell. I dialed the Bridal Veil's number and again, the same message. *Now* it was time to panic. I dropped my phone back in my purse and pounded on the door.

"My dress is in there!" I shouted. And then I saw Tilda, the shop cat, pacing back and forth in front of the door, meowing. Had Janette abandoned her cat? Anger welled up as I thought of Nanna's dress being held hostage. It increased with the thought of the little gray ragamuffin being left to fend for herself in a locked building. I grabbed my phone again and dialed Murray. The minute she came on the line, I started shouting.

"Calm down! Calm down!" She cleared her throat and waited for me to shut up. "Em, now start again and tell me what's going on."

"Janette's disappeared, and my wedding dress is still in her shop. And her cat's in there. I can't get her at home—both her home number and her shop number have been disconnected. What am I going to do?" I swallowed the rising swell of panic.

Mur let out a sigh of exasperation. "Well, that frosts it. Okay, I'll be down there in a few minutes and pick you up. We'll check out her home address, see if she's there. If she's not, we'll decide what to do next. Hold on, and please calm down. We'll get your dress."

While waiting, I tapped on the window, watching as Tilda reached up, trying to touch me through the glass. If Janette had just dumped her, locking her in the shop, I hoped to hell they caught the woman and hauled her ass into court for animal abuse. I couldn't watch an episode of *Animal Cops* on the Animal Planet station without bursting into tears, and neither could Kip. Randa, either, bless her hard-hearted shell that protected a very vulnerable and gentle nature.

Ten minutes later, Murray pulled up. I'd settled myself on one of the sidewalk benches, staring at the shop as if by focusing my attention, I could make Janette somehow magically appear. Unfortunately, even though I'd seen things resembling miracles, this wasn't one of those times.

Murray looked through the window, then tried the door. "Come on, let's go check out her apartment. I found the address. We have to do that before I can make the call to go in. If she's not there and it looks like she's disappeared, I can always say that we were worried something might have happened to her, so I had to break into the shop. Bonner wouldn't give me flak for that."

I climbed in her car—as head of detectives, she drove one of the unmarked vehicles the station owned—and we zoomed off in the direction of Janette's home. Located on Brookline Drive, the Wilkenshire Arms was probably the most expensive apartment complex in Chiqetaw. Stately, the building stood four stories high and had recently been painted with a cream-colored fresco faux finish. It reminded me of some old building in southern California, with a clock tower rising a level above the roof.

Mur found a parking space near the entrance and we headed inside, where she contacted Doreen Jenks, the manager. I recognized Doreen right away; she was a lovely old woman who frequented my tearoom. When we told her we were worried about Janette, she quickly led us up to the apartment. After knocking several times, she produced a master key and unlocked the door. Murray cautiously entered, motioning for us to stay behind. After a minute, she called for both Doreen and me to join her.

The apartment was a disaster. While nothing appeared to have been damaged as far as walls or counters, there were scattered newspapers and junk all over the place. The furniture was there, but all personal mementos were gone, as were the TV, microwave, and any other small appliances Janette might have owned. No photos, no pictures or paintings on the walls, no knickknacks, no personal items of any kind left behind.

Murray checked the bedroom. "Closet and dresser are both empty. Okay, I'm going to call in an officer to search the apartment. She probably just ditched town, but we'd better make sure."

Doreen shook her head. "I can't believe she ran off like this."

"Was she a good tenant?" Murray asked.

Doreen hesitated, then said, "Not the best. To be honest, Janette was behind on her rent, and I'd given her three weeks to pay in full. I warned her last week that if she didn't produce the money by the deadline, I'd start eviction proceedings."

Mur glanced at a calendar that was hanging askew on the wall. "How far in arrears was she?"

Doreen frowned, concentrating. "Well, on April first, she couldn't make rent, but I wasn't too worried. People have problems, they come to me and talk it out, and usually they're caught up in a month or two. I try to be understanding. Janette told me that somebody had stolen her ATM card and managed to wipe out her bank account."

"It should be easy to find out if she reported a theft." Murray tapped her notepad with her pen. "My guess is that it never happened."

"That's what I think, too, now. But I believed her at first. She'd never given me any reason to doubt her," Doreen said. "At the beginning of May, she claimed that the bank was slow about replacing her money that had been stolen. She said she'd sent out invoices to her clients and should be able to pay me everything by the first of June. So, even though I was starting to get suspicious, I decided to give her a break. Sometimes a spate of bad luck happens to the best of folks."

I glanced around. "Looks like she left in a hurry."

"I'm not surprised," Doreen said. "When June first came and went, Janette did everything in her power to avoid me. I left a notice on her door."

"What did it say?" Murray asked.

"That she had until June twenty-first to pay all three months' back rent or I'd turn her out." Doreen wrung her hands. "And now, it's coming up on the twenty-first and she's obviously skipped town. But I couldn't just let her walk over me like that. Three months' rent comes out to twenty-four hundred dollars. I hope that she's all right, though. I don't wish her any harm."

Murray muttered something under her breath. I patted Doreen on the arm. "You did the right thing." Inside, I was boiling. If Janette had ditched Chiqetaw, then where was my dress?

After Mur called for one of the boys to come assess the apartment, we returned to the car. "You okay?" she asked. "We'll go check the shop as soon as Sandy gets here. I want to fill him in on everything before we head out."

Five minutes later, she was doing just that while I waited, white-knuckled, in the car. Before we headed out, Murray phoned the superintendent who owned the building that Janette's store was in, and she put in a call to Deacon. He was waiting for us as we pulled up in front of the shop and parked, holding a search warrant.

"Got it, boss," he said, grinning at Murray.

I was out of the car like a light. Murray followed more slowly. We only had to wait for a moment before the building superintendent showed up. He rolled his eyes as Murray explained what was going on.

"Wouldn't surprise me if she lit out of here," he said, pulling out a huge ring of keys.

"Why?" Murray asked.

"Because that little girl was two months behind on rent and I told her to either give me my money or be prepared to find another place for her shop. She's a repeat offender. Two times in the past, she'd been a month late with rent and I warned her one more time and she was out." He pushed open the door and we slipped inside. Tilda ran over to us, meowing, and the owner caught her up in his arms. "Hey, pumpkin," he said. "Let's see if we can find you something to eat."

While he looked around for cat food, Murray and I walked through the shop. The racks of new gowns were gone, a few left scattered on the floor like they'd been dropped in a rush. They were crushed and dirty. My heart in my throat, I headed into the back room where we'd done the earlier fittings. No sign of Janette anywhere, but there—in pieces on the floor—lay the remains of Nanna's wedding dress.

"Damn it!" I dropped to my knees, gathering them up in my arms.

Murray rushed in. She looked at the pieces of material. "Oh no," she said, putting her hand on my shoulder.

"She said she'd have it ready. She had to take it apart to fix the waist band and the neckline, but she said she'd have it done by my wedding. Why did she do this? Why didn't she just tell me she couldn't alter it?" I was seriously in danger of losing it. Not only was I out one wedding dress, but it had been Nanna's, special to me in a way that no new gown would ever be.

Murray knelt down beside me. "Em, did you already pay her?" I nodded, too choked up to speak. "Then she's defrauded you. We'll put out an APB on her. There are probably other women she did the same thing to. I found her appointment book," she said, holding up a black planner. "It looks like last week was pretty sparse. Before that she had an appointment scheduled with a Lavyrl McKenzie. If Janette kept that, then we have a time frame for her disappearance."

I glanced over her shoulder. "Look." I pointed to this

week's schedule. "There are five women due to come in for fittings this week. I guess I'm not the only one who's going to be in tears."

She nodded. "I'd better have Deacon get a team down here to sift through what's left. We're dealing with a scam artist at this point, and we need to contact these other women and find out everything we can."

I stared at the ivory lace pieces in my hands. "Can I take these home? There's no way I can fix them before the wedding, but they belonged to Nanna."

"I'm sorry, Em." Murray gently shook her head. "They're part of our investigation, and we'll have to keep them as evidence for now. But I'll make sure they're treated gently, and you'll get them back as soon as we can."

That was it then. I had no wedding dress, and Nanna's dress had been ruined. Distraught, I slumped against the wall.

Murray held out her hand. "Get up, Em. You'll get your skirt all dusty. Come on, now. Don't worry. We'll find you a dress. I promise."

I blinked back tears. "But I wanted Nanna's dress. Why is everything so screwed up? What's happening?"

She sighed. "I wish I could give you an answer, but I can't."

As I stared at her, bereft, I realized that I hadn't told her what I'd came up with that morning. The lack of a wedding dress was enough to make me cry, but it didn't compare to the worry over Jimbo's life being in danger.

"Let's put my problem aside for a moment," I said. "I have something to tell you. I went out to see Jimbo today. I wanted to get a feel for the meadow and the energy out there."

"I know," she said, holding up her hand. "He called me and told me everything, and I'm plenty spooked. I'm also not thrilled that you told him about the ring and the note, but I understand why you did. It's okay."

"Have you come up with any leads?" I asked. If I was

right, nobody had tried to kill Joe. It had been a case of misidentification.

She shook her head. "No, but seeing that Jimmy might actually have been the target, I'm going to get a security system like you suggested. I've already made an appointment for them to come over and install it."

A commotion at the front of the shop told us that her team of investigators had arrived. I recognized their faces, but couldn't remember their names. While she gave them the rundown on the situation, I wandered over to the building superintendent, who had managed to find a can of cat food stuck away in a cupboard somewhere. Tilda was gobbling the food, purring away.

"I wonder what will happen to her," I said, reaching out to scritch her behind the ears. "I wish I could take her, but that's not an option at this point."

He gave me a quick smile. "Don't worry. The detective said that she'd have to call Animal Control. They need to check whether the cat's underweight or if she's been mistreated. That way they can add a charge of animal neglect or abuse to whatever Janette's gotten herself into. I'm going to adopt her after she's been checked out. She's a nice cat, and our old Tommy died recently. He was fifteen. My daughter misses him and Tilda would be good for her, I think."

At least I wouldn't be lying awake at night, worrying about the cat. I told him he was doing a good thing, and then turned to find Murray headed my way. "Come on. I've asked them to be careful with your grandmother's dress, by the way. They know that I'll have their heads if anything happens to it. Let's go get some caffeine. I think we both need it."

As we left the shop, I glanced back, ruing the day I'd picked the Bridal Veil's name out of the phone book.

STARBUCKS WAS ALMOST empty—odd on a hot summer's day, but good for us. I ordered an iced quad-shot Venti raspberry mocha, no whip, while Murray opted for a triple-caramel Frappuccino. We helped ourselves to gooey chocolate brownies, too. As we settled at a window table, more than ready for our sugar rush, it occurred to me that over the years Mur had walked through hell and high water with me. I just hoped I could return the favor.

"So, here we are again," she said after a moment. "Seems like this is our 'I need my hand held' spot." She raised her drink. "Here's to holding hands and friendship."

Mur seemed a bit wistful. I gazed at her, wondering if something other than the obvious was wrong. "Mur," I said gently. "Is something bothering you? Is everything going okay with Jimbo?"

She glanced out the window for a moment, then turned back to me. "Jimmy and I are fine, actually. Even with all this crap going down. But there's been a lot of other stress lately. Stuff I didn't want to bother you with because I know you've been so frantic with the wedding plans."

I stared at my cup. "Yeah, I have been frantic, I admit it. But I want to know what's going on. We're best buddies, Murray. We've been like this since college." I held up crossed fingers. "So, talk to me."

She cleared her throat. "I had a pregnancy scare last month." Before I could say a word, she held up her hand. "It turned out negative, thank God, but it made me think. And Jimmy and I've had several long talks. Neither one of us sees ourselves as parents. We love our nieces and nephews and so on, but we just aren't interested in having any of our own. So, I was talking to him about getting a vasectomy."

I nodded. Made sense. Both of them were established in their lives, they weren't kids who changed their minds depending on the way the wind was blowing. "What's the problem?"

She shrugged. "My mother. You know that we don't see eye-to-eye, but it's gotten worse. When I told her that we weren't going to settle down and raise a passel of kids, she got upset at me. She wants grandchildren. My brother's probably fathered a few, but if he has, the women haven't come forth and aren't likely to. He's such a loser. White Deer's going to talk to her for me, though. Try to smooth things over."

I winced. Even though I loved my kids, I didn't see motherhood as life's crowning achievement. It was an integral part of life for some women, but not the be-all and end-all for *every* woman. "I don't know what it's like to think of life without my kids, and I'm not going to pretend I do, but I am sorry she's giving you trouble."

"I just hate knowing that my mother thinks I'm a failure because I don't have kids. I've climbed my way up a very difficult ladder to the job I have now. I'm in a responsible, important position. I own my own home, I'm in a stable relationship, and all she can say is 'When are you going to get married and give me a grandchild?'" She sucked hard on her straw.

I was searching for something to say that might help when my cell phone went off. As I opened the phone and looked at the caller ID, my stomach dropped. It was Rose. Something was wrong, I just knew it.

"Oh shit," I said, flipping it open and pressing the phone to my ear. "What's wrong?"

Rose wasted no time with small talk. "Grandma M. had a heart attack," she said. "For real this time. We're at the hotel. You'd better come soon. They don't know if she's going to make it, and they've already sent her to Seattle. We're leaving in fifteen minutes."

Eight

MURRAY DROVE ME back to my car immediately. "Are you going to be okay? Do you want me to go with you? I can drive you there."

"I'll need my car later," I said, shaking my head. "And there's really nothing you can do. You know that Grandma M. and I aren't that close." In fact, I was feeling numb. A little too numb. I cared about Grandma M., probably even loved her. I just didn't like her.

As Murray headed off in the other direction, I put in a quick call to Joe to tell him what happened, then pulled out into traffic. As I sped along toward the hotel I thought over everything that would likely happen and, once again, shoved my wedding to the backburner.

Rose and Dad would need me. They were both prone to hysteria and were the designated basket cases in our family, while Mom and I shored everybody up. That was how it usually worked out in our household. My mother anchored the boat for everybody involved. Just like Nanna always did. Just like me.

My mother had never liked Grandma M. and the feeling was mutual. By now they'd learned how to coexist, but no love was lost between the two. The trouble being that Grandma M. and my mother were engaged in a long-standing rivalry over my father, who conveniently played the part of Switzerland, refusing time and again to choose sides. I'd never understood his hesitance. In fact, through my childhood I'd been repeatedly angry at him for not standing up to Grandma more. I always felt he owed his allegiance to his wife, not his mother, and that he should stand by her side when the battles raged. And rage they had.

I swung into the parking lot, made sure I had keys in hand before locking the car, then ran along the outside of the motel until I came to Rose's room. The door was wide open. As I rushed inside, I saw her throwing clothes in a suitcase. Our parents were standing there. By the looks of things, they'd already packed.

"How's Grandma M.?" I leaned against the wall, panting a little from the heat. I was in better shape than I'd ever been, but I still wasn't cut out for jogging, especially while wearing a tightly laced corset under my clothes.

Klara pressed her lips together and wrapped her arm around me. "Not too good, honey."

"Is she going to make it?" I asked, resting my head on her shoulder.

My mother gave me a gentle hug. "We don't know. They're transferring her to Seattle. She needs better care than she can get here. The ambulance left the hospital about twenty minutes ago."

I let go of my mother and wrapped my arms around my father. He held me tight, his cheek grazing the top of my head. For a moment, I flashed back to when Nanna died, and how he'd just held me, never saying a word, rocking me gently as I cried. Now, it was my turn. I glanced past his shoulder at my mother, who gave me a tight smile, her face creased with worry lines. Gently, I broke away from my father.

"Transferring her to Seattle means she had a major heart attack. Why didn't you call me from the hospital?"

Rose shook her head. "Everything happened so fast. By the time you could get there, they'd already have her on the road. I called you on the way back to the hotel."

"When did it happen?" I asked, feeling like I'd been cut out of a vital family event. I knew that Rose was right, but once again, I felt alienated, as if my life were set in a world apart from theirs.

Klara glanced at her watch. "Only about an hour ago. We were eating breakfast and she said she wasn't feeling well. Since she's always saying that, we didn't really pay any attention. I didn't . . ." Her voice drifted off and I could see the conflicting emotions play across her face.

Rose surprised me. She put her hand on our mother's shoulder and, with a shake of the head, said, "Grandma M. is always complaining. I didn't take her seriously, either, so don't blame yourself, Mother. I thought she was playing wolf again until she started talking about her arm hurting and her chest feeling tight."

"We all thought that," my father broke in. "Never mind about it now. We have to focus on treatment rather than on what happened."

I slid onto the bed next to my sister and pulled her down to sit next to me, taking her hand in mine. "Rosy, I'm so sorry." She blinked and ducked her head, tears collecting in the corners of her eyes.

My father cleared his throat. "We have to leave, Emerald. I want to be there as soon as we can. They're taking her to the University of Washington hospital and I want to get there as soon as possible."

I stared at them bleakly. "Do you need a ride? I can take you down if you aren't up to driving—"

"I'll drive," Klara said. "Your father will ride with me. Rose will take her car. She's a good driver and will be just fine, won't you darling?" My mother's voice was steady, soothing almost, and it was during times like this that I could hear a little bit of Nanna in her.

Rose shrugged. "I don't have a choice. I'll be fine."

She looked around the room. "Everything's packed. We just need to put the suitcases in the cars."

"Have you checked out yet?" I asked, feeling a little guilty and desperate to help. I couldn't run off to Seattle and leave Joe and the kids alone, but surely there was something I could do.

Mother shook her head. "Not yet."

I cleared my throat. "Give me your room keys. I'll check out for you."

"Thank you, darling," she said, giving me a distracted kiss on the cheek. "I'm sorry we won't be here for your wedding—"

"Oh, your wedding!" Rose let out a little gasp. "I'd forgotten all about it. We won't be here—"

"I can postpone it for a few days," I said grimly. It wasn't like I had a dress for it, after all. I didn't have the heart to tell them that Nanna's dress had been ruined by that butcher of a seamstress.

"Nonsense." My father's voice was firm, the same voice he'd used to end all arguments when we were children. "Even if my mother survives, she's going to require a lot of care. She'll stay with us once she's ready to leave the hospital. I doubt we'll have a chance to get away for the rest of the summer."

I sighed. No doubt Rose would feel the same and while I understood, a slightly selfish, tiny little voice inside wanted to protest. One of the happiest events of my life, and my family wouldn't be able to share it with me. As much as I'd dreaded facing Grandma M., the fact that she'd wanted to come and participate had made me happy.

I bit back my disappointment. "You're right. Are you sure you don't want me to go with you? For a day or so?"

Klara hoisted her suitcases. "Honey, you have Kip and Miranda to watch over, and your fine young man to nurse back to health. I want you to be happy and safe and healthy. We know you and Grandma M. never really clicked. No one is going to think less of you for not going with us."

I gathered their key cards as my father wrote me a check for what he estimated the hotel had cost them. I fingered it, looking at his spidery signature. He was getting older. Both he and Klara. My parents had always seemed young to me until now. As I folded the check and slid it into my purse, they stowed the luggage in the trunk.

I cornered my mother, away from Rose and my father. "What are her chances? Really?"

Klara scanned my face. "Honestly? The doctor gives her fifty-fifty odds. She could be a lot worse, but she's not out of the woods yet. The heart is such a resilient organ, but push it too far, and it's going to fail."

"But she was so trim," I said. "And she walked a lot. She didn't drink."

"That's not all there is to it," Klara said. "At her last checkup, we found out that her triglycerides were sky-high, over five hundred. Her cholesterol was two-fifty. She's always so stressed out that it affected her body." She shrugged. "I'm afraid it may be touch-and-go for a while. Your father and Rose aren't going to be much use over the next week or so."

I took her hand in mine and we walked over to where Rose was standing.

"We'd better get moving," she said. "I don't want . . ."

Her voice trailed off, but I knew what she was thinking. If Grandma M. didn't make it, she wanted to be there for the end. And my father would want to say a proper good-bye. Tears sprang to my eyes.

"Go," I whispered. "Go and be safe on the drive, and call me when you know anything more. I love you."

"We love you, too, honey," my mother said. "Don't you forget it, and don't go getting into anymore trouble."

I watched their cars ease out into traffic, waving as they sped down the street. Once they were out of sight, I stopped by the reservations desk to check them out. Afterward, I'd stop at the bank, then go directly home. I had to tell Kip and Randa about their great-grandma, and then

I needed a bubble bath. Our wedding plans were turning from a dream into a nightmare.

IT TOOK ME a total of thirty minutes to place an ungodly amount on my credit card and to deposit my father's check in the ATM. Dad had underestimated the bill by a hundred dollars, but I wasn't going to tell him. They had enough to worry about as it was. By the time I pulled into our driveway, I was exhausted, both physically and emotionally.

Joe heard the car and was waiting on the porch for me, wincing a little as he leaned against the wall. He stopped me before I could go inside and guided me over to the porch swing, settling down beside me.

"Murray called me. Tell me about it. Talk to me before you have to go tell Kip and Randa."

I leaned my head against his shoulder—the one that didn't have a big white bandage covering it—and told him about Grandma M. "It's not that I don't love her. I do. But I just don't have the same connection with her that Rose and my father do."

"But seeing them hurting, hurts you," he murmured.

I nodded, relieved that he understood. I hoped and prayed she would recover, but I wasn't going to be a hypocrite and suddenly become her favorite granddaughter. I took a deep breath. "There's more."

"More? What else?"

"I have no wedding dress." I straightened my shoulders and rubbed my forehead. Big headache looming and I was right in its path.

Joe gaped. "What?"

"I said, I have no wedding dress. Janette skipped town, leaving my dress in pieces that will take a seamstress weeks to restore, if it's even possible. And I can't even get my hands on them because they're being held as evidence. I have a feeling there are going to be a number of unhappy brides-to-be crying their eyes out today."

"I take it you've already cried?" He tipped my chin up and gazed into my eyes. All I could see was love.

"Yeah," I said, slumping. "Anyway, I'm too tired to cry. But the upshot is that I'm out both a wedding dress and a family for our wedding." I started to add, "I'm beginning to wonder if we should call it off for now," but one look at his soulful eyes put a stop to my words before they could even escape my lips.

Joe let out a low sigh and brushed my bangs away from my eyes. "Well, you've got the groom. That's one thing you can count on."

True, I had my groom, all right, though if the sniper had taken better aim, I'd be attending a funeral rather than getting married. The thought made me shiver. I stood up.

"I'd better tell the kids," I said. I wasn't sure how they were going to take it; they'd never been a big fan of their great-grandmother, but then again, kids could surprise you with their attachments. Finding no further excuse to keep me outside, I headed through the door to deliver the news.

MIRANDA AND KIP were both solemn, but I had the feeling it was because they felt they should be, rather than a gut reaction. Kip awkwardly patted me on the back. He had such a sweet look on his face that I just wanted to wrap him in a bear hug and tousle his hair.

"Don't be sad, Mom," he said. "The doctor said that she might get better, right?"

I nodded, thinking this was a good time to show by example. "Listen, kids, I want to explain something to you. I love your great-grandma, but this is harder on your Aunt Rose than on me. She's a lot closer to Great-Grandma M. They get along really good. She's Great-Grandma's favorite, just like I was Nanna's favorite. Do you understand? What I'm trying to say is that while I'm sad about this, I'll be okay."

"Do you feel bad about the way you feel?" Kip asked, and I could see him struggling. I knew exactly what he

was feeling. Was it okay that he didn't cry? That he
wanted to go play? Or should he sit with me, pretending
to be more upset than he really was in order to make me
feel better?

I was struggling to pick the right words when Randa
spoke up.

"Of course she feels bad, but she's being honest and
that's more important. It's like when Andrea dumped
Gunner right after they started going out. I felt kind of
guilty about being happy, but he hurt my feelings and the
truth was that I was glad she dumped him."

I nodded. "It's important to be diplomatic at times like
this, Kip, but you shouldn't pretend to feel any other way
than you do. In other words, don't gloat, don't be callous,
but don't force yourself to cry if you don't feel like crying. Understand?"

He nodded, digesting the information. "Okay, then. I'm
gonna go play. Call me as soon as dinner's ready. I'm hungry."

As he hit the stairs, Randa looked at me. "You're such
a cool mom. You know that, don't you?"

I grinned at her. Compliments from my impatient and
temperamental fourteen-year-old daughter were few and
far between now, but occasionally she surprised me.

"Thanks, hon. Backatchya."

The phone rang and she grabbed it, mumbled a few
words, then handed it to me, mouthing "Murray." As she
disappeared into the living room, I wondered what life
would be like in four years, when she'd be vanishing out
the door to college. I didn't even want to think about it.

"'Lo?" I eyed the espresso maker, longing for a pick-
me-up. Just a couple shots to see me through the evening.
I maneuvered over to the counter while balancing the
receiver between my ear and my shoulder. My neck
twinged, but caffeine was worth a few strained muscles.

Murray's voice was a welcome embrace. "Hey, Em,
how's your grandma?"

I told her what had gone down, while trickling beans

into the grinder. "Hold on, if I don't get caffeine, I'm going to collapse."

"Go ahead, you caffeine freak," she said, laughing.

I put the phone down, quickly ground the beans, and tapped the grounds into the mesh cup, fitting it firmly in place under the nozzle. As the water began heating, I grabbed the milk, the cocoa, a bottle of raspberry syrup, and a tall glass, then fetched a tray of ice cubes. I turned the knob and watched the black liquid drizzle into the shot glass. Two . . . three . . . yep, that should do it.

"Let me just finish this and I'll be right with you," I shouted at the receiver as I poured the espresso into the glass, added three spoonfuls of cocoa, a shot of syrup, then milk and ice, stirring with the straw. Carrying the phone and mocha over to the table, I settled into a chair, relaxing for the first time since morning.

"Back," I said.

"Good. I'm sorry about your grandma. Keep me posted, okay? Listen, Jimmy and I were thinking we might come over for dinner, if you haven't eaten yet. We'll bring the pizza this time. What do you say?"

I could tell she wanted to keep my mind off my grandmother and my dress, and the offer was just what I needed. I glanced at the clock. Six-thirty.

"Sounds good," I said. The thought of Rose's wan expression at the hotel haunted me. It was as if her own mother, not her grandmother, was speeding toward Seattle in that ambulance.

"I'm at work. Jimmy's meeting me here in a few minutes. We'll stop by the house to check on the animals, then pick up the pizza and be over in about forty-five minutes." She signed off and I wearily set the phone on the table, staring at it. Suddenly fearing that I might have missed a message from my family, I grabbed it and listened for the *beep-beep* of the dial tone announcing a voice message, but nada. With a sigh, I held up my mocha, toasted nothing in particular, and tried to chill out.

Joe wandered into the kitchen a few minutes later. "I

forgot to tell you something. Well, I didn't forget but it didn't seem the right moment when you first got home."

Oh God, now what? My expression must have mirrored my fear because Joe held up his hand. "Don't worry, it's nothing bad. Remember that photo shoot I mentioned a couple months back? The calendar featuring the heroes of Whatcom County?"

I stared at him. "You were serious?" Joe had come home one morning from the station with the news that his picture might end up in a hunk-filled, eye-candy, hot-to-trot calendar. Sponsored by the Chiqetaw Women's Auxiliary Group, the sales would benefit various local charities. I'd thought the idea fizzled since he hadn't mentioned it again. Apparently, I'd been wrong.

Joe ducked his head, blushing. "Yeah, I'm serious. The shoot's been moved up to tomorrow. That's the only day the photographer will donate his time. Want to go?"

Uncertain whether to congratulate him or laugh, I chugged down the remainder of my mocha. "So, you gonna have pants on, or does every woman in town get to see why I walk around with such a big smile on my face?"

One thing was for certain, if this was a full frontal, I'd make damned sure that DON'T TOUCH was tattooed on his thigh. Joe was more than adequately endowed, and he knew exactly what to do with every inch of what he'd been blessed with. What I'd been blessed with, now that I thought of it. And thinking about that particular blessing brought a wide smile to my face.

He grinned. "I'm glad you're smiling again. I hate seeing you sad. As far as showing my goodies, pants yes, shirt no. They'll shoot with the bruise. They said it would make me look more heroic. I told them I wasn't wounded while on duty, but they don't care. So, you want to go along or you going to leave me at the mercy of a bunch of horny women?"

I coughed. "I'll go, I'll go." I wanted to be the only horny woman there with an actual claim to the stake.

* * *

BY THE TIME Murray and Jimbo rang the doorbell, my mother had called from Seattle. Grandma M. was holding on, and that was a good sign. Every hour that passed with her still alive increased her chances. I felt better as I hung up the phone.

As Murray entered the living room, however, that good feeling dissipated. She looked like Bambi in headlights, and Jimbo's scowl set me back a few steps. I motioned toward the kitchen. Jimbo deposited the pizzas on the counter, then pulled me aside.

"We need to talk. Do you think the kiddos could eat outside? I don't want them to overhear what's going on."

"No problem," I said, calling the kids down to the kitchen. I fixed their plates and asked them to eat on the porch. Unusually cooperative—maybe it was because of Grandma M. or maybe they were just mellow from the summer heat—they complied without an argument. I made sure they had everything they needed before Jimbo, Murray, Joe, and I gathered around the table.

"So, what the hell happened? You both looked ready to pitch a fit when you came in." I bit into a Hawaiian special, closing my eyes at the delicious merger of melted cheese, pineapple, and ham.

Murray shuddered and Jimbo put his arm around her shoulder. "The perv's been at it again," he said. "I find him and he's dead. That simple."

I glanced at Mur. She gave me a surreptitious look that told me she was a lot more frightened than she was letting on. "What did he do?"

She pulled out a box from the bag she'd been carrying. "This was on the porch when we got home." Shoving it across the table, she seemed reluctant to even touch it.

I reached for it. A spark leaped from the lid to my hand, a bright flash illuminating the table. "Damn! It happened *again*!" I yanked my hand back and examined my fingers. Nothing. No marks, no burns. "I sure am tuning into whoever is bothering you."

Jimbo jerked his head up. "You saying hoodoo's involved?"

I shrugged. "I don't know if it's deliberate or if his intent is just so strong that it's manifesting its own little power source." Taking a deep breath, I tried again, this time managing to pick up the box without getting jolted. I cautiously lifted the lid, peering in. Joe looked over my shoulder.

Not good. I reached in, then stopped. "You dusted these for prints?"

Mur shook her head. "No, I touched everything before I realized what I was doing, and Jimmy was all over it the minute he saw what it contained. But I doubt if there were any to begin with. Whoever this is, he's being careful. So far nothing else has had prints, including the bug in the lamp. Go ahead. Maybe you'll be able to pick up something. I'm too nervous to try and White Deer's back in Bellingham for the evening."

I lifted a sleazy red teddy out of the box. Lingerie could be sexy, gorgeous, titillating. Or it could be a hooker's nightmare, soulless and devoid of passion. As I fingered the Lycra teddy, my stomach twisted. I dropped it on the table and hesitantly looked back in the box. A pair of handcuffs—metal, not the soft ones meant for lovers. A bottle of cheap perfume. And a picture of Jimbo that had been slashed.

A swirl of anger and lust coiled around the items, a vortex of sick need. I could almost hear a woman's voice echoing through the room. *Don't touch. Don't look. Don't ask. Don't. Don't. Don't. Good little boys don't.*

"Mur, this isn't just some kid's game. You're dealing with someone who's severely unhinged, and I'm afraid it's going to escalate until you can catch him." The whole energy of the room shifted, as if a bright neon sign had plastered itself on my best friend's chest, a bull's-eye of the most dangerous kind. "Set up a video camera to watch your porch—both back and front. Are you sure none of the neighbors saw the person who left this?"

She shook her head. "Already checked. I live at the end of the street. The park was almost empty—tonight's baseball game is over at the high school. I did call Bonner, but there's only so much that Tad can do. I hate to ask him to assign someone to watch my house. The budget's already overtaxed and we've had to cut down on a lot of the downtown beats."

I chewed on my lip, thinking. "What about the security system? Did they install it yet?"

"Yeah," Jimbo said. "But it won't tell us if somebody's on the porch or in the yard. Good idea on the camera, O'Brien. I'll get one set up tonight. Meanwhile, can you take a peek with your crystal ball? Is there anything you can tell us about this creep?"

Not looking forward to delving into the gutter, I sighed, leaned back in my chair, and picked up the teddy again. "Let me try a little psychometry first."

Closing my eyes, I let my mind drift, let the sounds of quiet breathing from the others lift me up, spiral me out onto the astral. My abilities had grown, or perhaps using them so much simply gave me better control over them, but in either case, trance work had become easier over the months. Slipping into the etheric realm was as simple as stepping into the next room, unless I was tired or sick, or too worried.

As the astral winds buoyed my spirit farther away from the physical realm, I could sense the cord that kept me connected to my body. The others came into view, their energy shimmering around the table. Murray was frightened, her aura danced with sparkles of doubt and worry, throwing off her balance. Jimbo was fierce—a tiger pacing, wanting to protect his mate, but not knowing where the enemy was hiding.

And my sweet Joe was weary and in pain. He should sleep, I thought, but then the thought drifted past and I found myself moving beyond the immediate, following the signature of the lingerie, hunting the source from where it originated.

As I sought my quarry I found myself on a narrow, wooded path, wandering toward the core of a dark forest. The trees echoed with a quiet susurration as a light breeze tickled through their branches, but no breath of fresh air lingered in the wake. The breeze contained voices. Whispers from the past, whispers from the present, whispers of insults long-ago fired without care, of jeers and jabs and taunts from angry women and scornful men.

Wanting to run, to cover my ears, I stumbled as the voices became louder, the laughs more obnoxious. I turned, hoping to backtrack, but the path behind me was blocked with fallen trees. A deep bog appeared, stinking mud and quicksand. Frightened, I whirled to my left, thinking I heard a creature in the undergrowth, but there was nothing there save for a pair of red eyes.

Watching. Glowing. Burning. Desiring.

I tried to pull away, to run and hide, but the steady cacophony of taunts and insults confused me, throwing my sense of direction off. They weren't aimed at me, however, but at someone else, and yet I felt them in my heart as if I were the target. I tried to ignore them, taunts of *stupid* and *sinner* and *if you touch it one more time, I'll cut it off*, but they grew louder, beating a cadence that surrounded me. In the end—there was no place to hide. A whimper startled me, and with growing alarm I realized that it had emerged from my own throat. I dropped to my knees, hands over my ears.

And then, the branches of a huckleberry brush began to part, and I knew some horrendous creature waited on the other side. I scrambled back, but apparently the bog had expanded, because the next thing I knew, I was waist-deep in mud and slime, sinking. I grabbed at the nearest vines, trying to pull myself out, but then the ground shook and I let go, sinking. Chill liquid earth welcomed me, swallowing me down, dragging me under. I opened my mouth to scream and—

"Em! Em! Snap out of it!" An abrupt shake tore me from the scene and I found myself spiraling into my body, slamming with a force that sent me reeling backward in my chair. As I hit the kitchen floor, I blinked. Murray was kneeling over me, with Joe on the other side. Jimbo was crowding them.

"Huh? What happened?" I asked, trying to make sense of where I was.

"That's what I'd like to know," Murray said. "You've been gone for over ten minutes."

As they helped me to my feet, I stared at the red teddy, now sitting in the middle of the floor. The energy seemed familiar, I'd sensed it briefly once before, but couldn't remember where. Whoever was doing this lived in his own little world. And I'd just been privy to some of the paths on which his spirit walked. I wasn't anxious to make a return visit.

Nine

⊰⊱

"SO, TELL US, what happened?" Mur said again, once I was sitting up with a cup of tea and another slice of pizza.

What indeed? I knew right away that I hadn't been remote viewing—seeing through my mind's eye into another actual physical place. Whoever I'd been spying on didn't live in the middle of a forest next to a bog. No, in my gut, I knew that what I'd witnessed was a manifestation of the confusion within his mind. I tried to explain.

"Whoever it is, he's hearing voices. Memories that keep repeating themselves over and over, rather than actual beings talking to him. It's pretty apparent to me that—at least in *his* mind—his parents thought he was worthless. Ten to one he was the kid most picked on in high school. Or most ignored. I don't think he's had any luck with relationships and quite frankly, conjecturing on what I heard and felt, I'm betting that he's a virgin. Or . . ." I didn't want to explore the possibility I was thinking about, but Murray wanted to know my impressions and I didn't want to hold anything back that might help, if even in a small way. "If he's had sex, I doubt if it's been consensual on his partner's part."

Joe sucked in a deep breath. "You mean he's a predator?"

I shrugged. "Maybe. I can't say for sure, of course, but I sense a deep resentment for women, along with a deep desire to touch them. Put two and two together and the picture isn't pretty." I glanced at Murray. "Murray, there's something else. I've sensed this energy before, one time. I can't remember where, but it was last year. If I were you, I'd start checking the whereabouts of any Peeping Toms, rapists, flashers that you might have busted in the past year."

She looked run ragged. "Jeez, that's a tall order. I've arrested a handful of them in the past year and most are back on the streets. The majority were Peeping Toms or flashers. Gross, but for the most part not terribly dangerous."

"I didn't realize we had an epidemic of perverts in Chiqetaw," I said, thinking about Randa and Kip. I wouldn't be so cavalier about where they went from now on.

Murray shook her head. "You'd be surprised how many criminals live here, just like any other town, I guess. Chiqetaw isn't immune." She picked at a piece of pizza crust. "I don't mind telling you that I'm scared. I'll take all this crap into the station and file another report, but there's not much anybody can do until the guy makes a mistake."

A thought sprang to mind. "Mur, I asked you this a day or so ago, but what about that creep Rusty? Have you checked to make sure he really moved to Seattle?"

She frowned. Rusty had made her life a living hell for a while. I knew she didn't like thinking about him, but for some reason, I couldn't let it drop. There was something too nasty about the attacks . . . too personal. And Rusty had been underhanded and way too personal.

"I forgot to check, but I still think you're on the wrong wavelength."

"Just do it, would you?" I paused as a memory surfaced. Snapping my fingers, I said, "Remember when I warned you to watch out for him? That's when I felt this energy. All of this stuff that's been happening has the same feel that all the crap he pulled on you did, only worse."

Jimbo had remained silent, but now he leaned forward and took her hand in his. "She's right. Call Tad now. He'd know for sure, wouldn't he?"

Murray sighed and pulled out her phone. "I hate this." She retreated into the pantry for privacy.

Jimbo looked at me. "If it's Rusty, we'll find him. I have friends who excel in convincing pervs like this to back off. And if they don't back off . . . I have friends of a different nature."

By now, I knew that Jimbo had a soft heart inside that gruff exterior. I also knew that he meant exactly what he said about his cohorts, and that he had no compunctions in putting a stop to the dregs who preyed on women and children. When he was fifteen, Jimbo had lost a little brother to a drifter who liked little boys, and he almost killed the man in the process of tracking him down.

I cleared my throat. "You might want to start with the cameras."

He arched one eyebrow. "Stop your fussing. I'm not going out on a vigilante hunt until I know who I'm looking for. And yeah, I'll start with the video feeds. If I have to wire the whole goddamned house, we'll find out who's doing this."

"We'd better, or this is just going to get worse. The guy's a psycho. I'd bet a year's earnings on it."

I pushed myself away from the table and foraged in the fridge until I found what I was looking for. Joe had made a blueberry crumble for dinner, but with my family leaving town so suddenly, it remained untouched. I popped it in the microwave to nuke it for a few moments.

Murray returned then, flipping her phone shut. "Rusty hasn't been heard from in months. Tad says last he heard, he moved away to live with his brother in Seattle. That's where his last paycheck was sent."

"Seattle's not that far away," I said, wresting a half-gallon container of French vanilla ice cream out of the freezer. Joe removed the now-warm crumble from the microwave.

"Tad's going to check it out, but I'm not holding my breath. What's that?" She sniffed. "Yum. Blueberry. Smells good."

"Joe made it, so you know it's edible," I said, going to the door to call the kids in. As Randa helped me serve dessert, Joe turned the conversation toward his photo shoot the next day. Murray hooted at him and Jimbo whistled. I had almost relaxed when both the phone and doorbell chimed. I grabbed the receiver and motioned for Kip to answer the door.

Rose was on the line. I slipped into the pantry with the phone. "How's Grandma M.?"

"She's doing a little better," she said, "but she's going to need surgery. She needs a double bypass."

Oh shit. Not good! I swallowed my fear and said, "What do Mom and Dad say about it? When's her surgery scheduled?"

"Tomorrow morning at eight. The doctor talked to the folks. He said it's a common procedure nowadays, and he thinks she has a good chance of surviving it and living on to torment us for another twenty years." Her voice trembled, and I could read between the lines. She desperately needed to keep hope alive.

"She'll be okay," I said. "She's a tough old bird."

"Do you really think so? I mean, really? You know— can you tell?"

Well, surprise, surprise. "Hold on, I'll see what I can find out." I took a deep breath. Rose seldom referred to my psychic abilities. For her to ask for my help meant she was truly frightened.

I closed my eyes and reached out to Grandma M. Since she'd been around my house the past few days, there was a chance I could still latch onto her. But instead of Grandma M., I felt a flutter at my elbow and opened my eyes. Nanna stood there, smiling gently, a golden nimbus surrounding her aproned and rosy countenance.

Every once in a while, when I needed her, my beloved Nanna dropped in for a visit. Sometimes she pulled my butt out of the fire, other times she simply let me cry on her ghostly shoulder. Now, she tipped her head, winking at me.

I mouthed, "Grandma M.? Is she going to be okay?" By now I knew that I didn't need to speak aloud. If I focused, she could hear my question.

Nanna gave me a quick nod and I caught a glimpse of Grandma M., resting in a bed. Around her swirled a light, faint, but steady. I knew then that she would live. She wasn't done here yet. I flashed Nanna a bright smile, and she waved and vanished from sight.

"I think she'll be okay," I said into the receiver. "She definitely needs the operation, but her life force is strong, her will stubborn. Unless something unexpected happens, my sense is that she'll pull through just fine."

"Thank you." Rose let out a long sigh and her voice steadied. "I was so worried. Emmy, I'm so sorry we won't be there for your wedding. We'll have a huge party when this is all over and taken care of. Will that be okay?"

I smiled to myself. That was the first time Rose had apologized to me for anything since I was twelve years old. We'd gotten into some argument—silly now, it seemed, but then, of course, it had been momentous. At one point, I'd called her a spoiled little brat and she'd screamed that I was Mom's favorite and she hated me. We got over the fight, but she never again said she loved me so that I really believed her.

"A party will be just perfect," I said. "And thanks again for the necklace, Rose. I'll wear it to my wedding."

"Will it go with Nanna's dress?" she asked.

Gulp. Nanna's dress. What the hell should I say? I bit my lip and stared at the wall, still smarting from the loss of such a precious keepsake. I'd been hoping to save it for Randa, pass it down through generations.

"They would have been lovely together," I finally said. "Except for one hitch. The seamstress who was working on the alterations skipped town and left Nanna's dress in pieces. I'm going to have to find someone who can restore it, if it can be restored. And that certainly won't be in time for my wedding."

She gasped. "What are you going to do? How can you get married without a wedding dress?"

I grinned. A typical Rose reaction. If everything wasn't exactly as she planned it, she couldn't envision another direction. "Everything will be fine. I'll just find another dress. After all, I have the groom," echoing Joe's sentiments earlier. And he was right, I decided. Dress or no dress, I'd be getting married. "That's what really counts, you know."

"I suppose so," she said. "But I'd be dissolved in tears right now."

"Been there, done that. Okay, I have company, honey, and you should go back to the folks. Tell them I love them. And . . . I love you, too, Rosy."

As she hung up, I wandered out of the pantry. Harlow and James were sitting at the table. Joe was rinsing our dinner dishes, and Jimbo was helping him. Murray glanced up, concern on her face.

"Your grandma?" she asked.

I nodded, then called the kids back into the kitchen. "Listen, that was your Aunt Rose. She called about your great-grandma."

"How is she?" Kip looked vaguely worried.

I sighed. "She has to have a double bypass. That's an operation on her heart—"

"We've been learning about the heart in Health,"

Randa said. "That means Great-Grandma has heart disease?"

"Right. She goes into surgery tomorrow. I can't be sure, of course, but I think she'll be okay." I slipped into the chair next to Harlow, who reached out and draped her arm around my shoulder.

"So, are you going on with the wedding?" Harl asked.

I nodded. "To be honest, I'm not that close to Grandma M. I offered to postpone it, but my parents and sister told me no. They'll be taking care of her after she gets out of the hospital and I have the feeling the rest of the summer is shot for all of them."

"Mur was telling me about your dress," she said, tossing her shoulder-length cornrows over her shoulder. She'd stuck with the hairstyle, finding it both preserved those golden curls and yet kept them out of the baby's way. Baby Eileen was almost a year old and growing like a weed. She already promised to reach her mother's height, and she mirrored her father's bronzed skin.

Kip and Randa gave me a quizzical look. "What's wrong with your dress?" Kip asked. "I thought it was pretty."

I inhaled sharply. Regardless of my bravado to Rose, the minute I opened my mouth the pain rushed back. "Nanna's dress was ruined. The seamstress left it in pieces and skipped town. By the way, Mur, any news about her? I'd like to take it out of her hide."

She shook her head. "No, though we found out she booked a flight out of Bellingham, down to Portland. We've contacted the authorities there, but this isn't exactly a high profile case. You may just end up eating the expense."

"If you can't find her, when do I get Nanna's dress back?"

"I'm not sure. I'll talk to Evidence about it."

I groaned and Harlow murmured sympathetically. Kip sidled up and patted my knee. "I'm sorry, Mom."

"Thanks, hon. I'm sorry, too," I said, shrugging. "I'm

just going to have to find a different dress to wear. I hope they catch her thieving ass, though."

Randa looked scandalized. She stood, hands on her hips, and glared at me. "Well, isn't there anything you can do about it? You've got Nanna's book and trunk of charms."

I stared at her. My daughter was advising me to use magic? My daughter who, except in times of extreme emergency, preferred to stay as far on the left-brained side of the world as possible? I snorted. "Hadn't even thought of it, but now that you mention it, I might just do that."

She wrinkled her nose. "Good. You always tell me to do whatever I can to make a situation better. I'm going to stargaze." With a wave, she dashed down the hall and up the stairs.

I looked over at Murray. "Well, I guess I've been told. She's right, though, maybe I can play with things a little. Give good old Janette a case of conscience."

"I dunno," Mur said. "I guess so, but is it really worth the effort?"

I thought of Nanna's dress laying on the shop floor, in pieces. Nanna's dress that she'd carried over from the old country, that had meant the world to her. "Yeah, it's worth it," I said, breathing softly.

James spoke up. "Whatever dress you choose to get married in, I'm still doing the photography for you. Speaking of photos, Harlow and I had an ulterior motive in sneaking out tonight and leaving Eileen with Lily." Lily was their nanny, and a damned good one from what Harlow said.

"Do tell?" I leaned forward, eager to hear about something other than illness, stalkers, or ripped-up wedding dresses.

He cleared his throat. "I got the word today. I have another big photo shoot coming up. I'm going to be gone for four months this time."

I glanced at Harlow. Even though she was beaming, I

knew she wasn't happy. She hated it when James was gone, but she wouldn't interfere. As she'd told me a few months ago, she'd had her time in the sun, and she'd voluntarily given up her career to return to Chiqetaw and marry James.

"I'm happier than I've ever been, Em," she had said. Now on her way to her degree, she'd finally found a new career that meant something to her. Modeling had been a means to an end, providing her with the money to sustain a lifestyle that was comfortable, but not ostentatious. Unlike most of the other supermodels, Harlow had been realistic about the longevity of the career.

"Where are you going?" Joe asked, wiping his hands as he finished cleaning the counter.

James flashed us an impish grin. "Mongolia. A writer for *National Expedition Magazine* is working on a three-part article examining the lives of the reindeer herders. He saw my photos that I took for the eco-safari last year in Africa, and asked *NEM* to commission me to be his photographer. They agreed, so I'll be living with one of the tribes for four months, on the move, photographing them, getting to know their way of life."

His eyes shone with excitement. I also knew James well enough that I knew he hadn't figured out how Harlow really felt about his absences. She kept it well-hidden and had enjoined me to silence.

"When do you leave?" Murray asked, her voice soft. She also knew how Harlow felt.

Harl answered quickly. "He leaves on July fifteenth."

And then I understood her angst. He'd returned from the eco-safari a week after Eileen had been born—late, thanks to some localized trouble over there. And now, he'd be missing her first birthday, which would be in August. I glanced at Harlow and held her gaze. She pressed her lips together and blinked hard. I kept my mouth shut.

Murray wasn't so reticent. "Going to be gone on Eileen's birthday, are you? That must be rough."

James paused in mid-smile, as if it hadn't even

dawned on him. He gave a hurried look at Harlow, then hung his head. "Yeah, I guess I will. I don't like the idea, but she's too young to travel, and Harlow won't go without her."

So, they'd already discussed that option. Sensing tension flaring, I abruptly stood and headed toward the espresso maker. Joe had recently replaced my old one with a new state-of-the-art coffee center. It made espresso, foamed milk, brewed coffee, even heated water for tea, although I still insisted on using my beloved old teakettle. Even though I loved the new machine, I still waxed nostalgic for my old one. We'd shared a lot of good brews together.

"Coffee, anybody?"

"Espresso for me," Murray said, hurrying over to help. She pulled out the grinder. Mur knew my kitchen better than I did.

"Coffee for me," Joe said.

"Me, too—" Jimbo and James spoke as one, then stopped mid-sentence, and laughed.

I glanced at Harlow. "How about you, babe? Decaf?"

She shook her head. "Some chamomile tea would be great. Eileen's been fussing a lot lately. I was up at three last night."

"I told you to let Lily take over at night," James said. "That's what we pay her for."

Harlow's eyes narrowed. "Excuse me, but if our daughter is fussing, I want to know why. Lily takes care of her while I'm working and studying. She needs her sleep, too." As if realizing how sharp she sounded, she stopped abruptly and took a deep breath, letting it trickle out.

Joe jumped in, bringing up his calendar shoot again, asking James for tips on how to pose. As the conversation segued to lighter topics, I relaxed a little. Weddings were always good for a nervous breakdown, I thought, but why did my breakdown have to include all my friends along with me?

*   *   *

THE NEXT MORNING found Joe agonizing over which pair of pants to wear. I handed him his faded jeans that curved nicely around his butt and went back to angsting over the phone. Grandma M. was in surgery, but we'd be at the photo shoot by the time she was out of the operation. I didn't want to make a nuisance of myself by having my cell phone bleat out the tinny rendition of the *Futurama* theme song that I'd downloaded, thereby annoying the photographer and anybody else who might be within hearing distance. So, I settled for calling Rose and telling her I'd phone within the hour after Grandma M. was due out of surgery.

The shoot was taking place in Perry Field, one of Chiqetaw's largest parks. The land had been donated to the town by Wilber Perry, an eccentric and wealthy old man, along with enough money to outfit it fully on the stipulation it must never be sold. As we approached the Larch Street entrance, I forced myself to keep my mouth shut when I saw the gathering of hunks crowded around the photographer and event organizer.

A gaggle of gorgeous men, and a few incredibly endowed women, with all vital parts barely concealed in revealing, steamy outfits. Eye-candy heaven.

Last night, Mur had confided that they'd asked her to be part of the shoot. Of course there was no question that she'd turned them down. She'd worked far too hard to gain the esteem of her coworkers and if she showed up in a cheesecake calendar in a bikini—regardless of the cause—she'd lose the dignity and respect that she'd so carefully built over the years.

It galled me, though. The men involved wouldn't have to worry about their peers. Double standards still ran strong. Joe wouldn't lose any respect for contributing. I had a strong suspicion that the few women involved were in lower-echelon jobs. I just hoped this didn't curtail their chances for advancement. Unfortunately, people seemed to lose track that this was, after all, a *charity* calendar.

Police officers and firemen sunbathed in bikinis and Speedos, and ran around in shorts like everybody else.

As we wandered over to the photographer, I felt eyes turning our way. Mainly from the women, both those waiting to be in front of the camera and those behind the scenes. Their gazes slid over me quickly, then lingered on Joe. I scrunched closer to him, taking his arm in mine. Not that I was worried! Nope, not me. I trusted Joe implicitly. Still, no sense letting him forget I was on the sidelines, cheering him on.

Joe introduced himself to the photographer while the events organizer checked his name off a list. He started to introduce me, but the EO cut him off.

"She can wait over there," the woman said, pointing to me and then to a picnic table. "You said you've been injured? Let's see it. Maybe we can make it work for us." And before I could say a word, she'd slid her arm through Joe's and dragged him away from me, over to the milling group of men and women who were waiting their turn in front of the camera.

Apparently, I'd been dismissed. A little put out, I made my way over to the picnic table where several other women were sitting. One I recognized as Melissa White, Roger's wife. Roger worked with Joe at the station.

"This the place for gawkers and girlfriends?" I asked as she looked up.

"Have a seat and join the rest of the castoffs. It's apparent they didn't expect us to show up. When Roger and I got here, that bitch said, 'What's she doing here?' right in front of me. Whoever hired that bozo is going to hear about it from me." Melissa tapped one long, polished nail on the wooden tabletop, obviously pissed.

"I think it was Eunice Addison," another one of the women spoke up. I glanced over at her. She was wearing a crop top that showed a pair of remarkably large, perky breasts—unnaturally perky—and a low-riding pair of jeans. "I'm Corrie Jackson. I'm Sandy Whitmeyer's girlfriend."

I sat down and held out my hand. "Emerald O'Brien, Joe Files' fiancée." So, this shindig was Eunice Addison's baby? I'd had several dealings with the social maven of Chiqetaw, some good, a few not so good. Overall, she was a nosy old biddy but she did a lot for charity. For that alone, I respected her.

"Oh, we all know who you are," Corrie shot back, a grin spreading across her face. "You've been in the paper so many times that I don't think anybody can live in Chiqetaw without knowing your name."

Once again, my reputation preceded me. I prepared for an onslaught of questions about anything from ghosts to tarot to sparring with murderers, but Corrie surprised me.

"So, is Joe as dreamy in bed as he is to look at?" Her question was innocent, her tone was not.

Startled, I groped for a reply. I considered myself fairly shockproof but this one caught me unprepared. After a moment, I said, "I really don't think our love life is the ideal topic of discussion for this time in the morning."

To take the sting out of my words, I added, "Of course, I think he's wonderful." I spread my fingers, displaying my ring. "Less than a week and we'll be married," I added, just in case she needed a warning. "What about you and Sandy? Been together long?"

She shook her head. "A year, but I'll never see a ring. He can't even commit to where he wants to go for dinner." Her voice sounded like she'd just bit down on something gravelly. "You're older than Joe, aren't you?"

I gazed at her, searching for what might be hidden back behind that wide-eyed innocent act. Corrie was playing with a hidden agenda, but I couldn't quite put my finger on what it was. Out of the corner of my eye, I caught Melissa flashing me a quick look, her face masked but then she gave an almost imperceptible shake of the head and arched one eyebrow.

I cleared my throat. "Yes, I am." Quickly, before she

could say another word, I turned to Melissa. "So, what have you been up to?"

Bless her heart. Even though we'd seldom spoken, she graciously picked up on my desperation to change the subject, and we chatted away as if we were old friends. Grateful for her help, I decided we'd have to invite Roger and Melissa over for dinner some evening. They were coming to the wedding as it was. Roger was one of the groomsmen.

Joe was third in the queue for the camera. Ahead of him, a busty woman in a thong bikini and two triangles of cloth that barely covered her nipples leaned up against a tall, lanky young man with short curly hair. They posed their way through a series of shots.

I held my breath, wondering if the bikini top was going to stay affixed to its target areas, but she must have used a little double-stick tape, a trick I knew about thanks to Harlow, because the cloth didn't budge an inch. The man posed awkwardly and, even from where we were sitting, I could hear the cameraman swear something about "amateurs," but finally he finished and waved the pair off.

Joe's turn was next. As he stepped up to a tree and leaned against it, I gasped. His shirt had disappeared, and his jeans looked a tad bit lower than usual, framing his waist and hips in a delightful way. The bruise on his shoulder looked a bit darker, as if they'd added makeup to make it more symmetrical. As he hooked his thumbs in his belt loops, the cameraman stopped and whispered to the EO, who nodded, a smile spreading across her face.

"Dylan, Dylan, come here!" One of the blond vixens in a bikini wandered over. I immediately felt my hackles go up.

"Who's that?" I asked, keeping my voice low.

Melissa rolled her eyes. "They brought in a couple models to work with the guys. They must think Joe's got it going on if they want to pair him with her." She fought

back a smile—I could see it creeping around the edges of
her lips—and took a quick swig from her Pepsi.

I swung back around to the photo shoot, a knot form-
ing in my stomach. I didn't mind Joe participating for
charity. I'd reconciled myself to the fact that thousands of
women might be looking at him, fantasizing. But having
him pose with some beach-blanket bimbo wasn't part of
the deal! If I said anything, though, I'd sound like a jealous harpy, which wasn't far from the truth. I just didn't
want anybody else to know how I felt but me.

"Put your arm around Dylan and let her drape herself
over you. It'll be a good shot and we can tell people she
helps out in your station house. Or, if it doesn't hurt your
shoulder too much, pick her up like you're carrying her
to safety." The cameraman motioned for Dylan to move
in on Joe. She sauntered over to him, gave him a thorough up-and-down once-over, and then languidly draped
her arm around his shoulder, pushing her boobs against
his chest.

Right then, Joe glanced in my direction. I wasn't
expecting him to look at me and had been focused on
the eye-candy now oozing into his arms. Positive my
jealousy showed like Big Bird at a black-tie formal, I
blushed, tears welling up in my eyes. I fought them back.
I didn't like myself this way, I didn't want to feel threatened.

Immediately, he stepped aside, almost throwing the
girl off balance. "I'm sorry, I pose alone," he said.

The photographer swore. "What are you talking
about?"

"I'm doing this for charity, but no way am I posing
with a half-naked woman splayed out in my arms. At
least, not unless that woman's my fiancée. You let her
pose with me, and we'll do it up hot for you. Otherwise—no go."

"Oh for God's sake," the EO said. "This is just a photo
shoot—"

"That everybody, including my soon-to-be wife and

my dear old aunt, are going to see. Make up your mind.
There are a dozen different places I'd rather be right
now." He crossed his arms, stiffening. No longer exuding
sex appeal, Joe looked downright intimidating.

The EO sputtered but, after a moment, she shrugged.
"Whatever. Just shoot him alone. Dylan, we'll use you
with the cop over there. Go see if *he* has any objections."

As the model headed toward Sandy, I heard a muffled
noise and turned around to see Corrie, blushing brilliant
crimson, glaring in their direction. Sandy, however, welcomed Dylan in, drawing her next to him, oblivious to
Corrie's distress. Corrie jumped up and stomped off.

I glanced at Melissa. "Somehow, this is turning out to
be a little more complicated than they probably thought it
would be."

She nodded. "Nasty business. Roger knows better than
to ever try to get away with anything like that. Actually,
Roger's a lot like Joe. He'd say no even if I wasn't here.
Some men have that internal sense of commitment, some
men don't. Sandy's one of the latter."

As if to prove her point, Sandy leaned down and whispered something in Dylan's ear. She giggled. I could see
Corrie, her shoulders slumped, head down, as she trudged
out of the park.

"She'll never make it in a relationship unless she
learns how to stand her ground," I said, wondering if I'd
been that passive when I'd been with Roy. Hard to tell,
there were times when I looked back and it all seemed a
blur.

Just then, they finished shooting Joe's pics. He
grabbed his shirt and came loping over to me, wincing a
little as he slid his arms into the sleeves. "I'm done. Let's
get the fuck out of here," he said. "And if I ever—*ever*—
get the hare-brained idea to do this again, you are welcome to knock some sense into my head."

"Are you sure? It's for charity."

He ducked his head, laughing. "I'll make a donation
instead. I'm not a model. I'd rather be working, or at

home with you. Speaking of home, what are you doing the rest of the afternoon?"

"I'd better go shopping. I need to find another wedding dress. And I've got to call Rose soon to find out how Grandma M. is."

He pulled me to his side, nuzzling the top of my head. "Whatever you buy, you'll be beautiful in it. You're so gorgeous."

I started to say something about Dylan, but then stopped. There was no need. Joe had shown me just what kind of man he was, as if I didn't already know. I said a quick good-bye to Melissa, and we headed toward the car.

Ten

AS I WALKED through the doors of Joanne's Bridal Boutique, I felt like I'd been swallowed up by the pages of *Modern Bride* magazine. Hundreds of yards of satin and tulle billowed around me, along with brilliant creations in brocade, chiffon, and organza. Mannequins throughout the store dripped with lace—Alençon, Chantilly, Belgian, every pattern I could dream of, all worked into veils, handkerchiefs, and trains.

I faced the racks brimming with dresses, wishing desperately that I'd been able to convince Harlow to come with me. She'd take me in hand, steer me clear of the tacky and ill-fitting, and make sure that I bought a dream dress instead of a nightmare. But she'd had a meeting to attend for the Chiqetaw Arts & Crafts Museum, so we'd agreed to meet for late-afternoon tea at my shop to look over what I'd found. I took a deep breath and forced myself toward the counter.

The clerk glanced at me, smiling. "May I help you?"

Feeling slightly green around the edges, I leaned across the counter and introduced myself. "I took my grandmother's wedding dress in to be altered and just found out that the seamstress skipped town, leaving the dress in tatters. It's far too late to have it repaired for my wedding and I guess . . ." *Never let them know you're desperate; you'll end up paying through the nose.* I could hear Harl's voice echoing in my head. My mouth, however, had a mind of its own. "I need help! I'm getting married on the solstice and that's only a few days away!"

The clerk dropped the pamphlet she was holding—some sort of sales circular—and hurried around the counter. "Oh my dear, you must be just frantic. And so disappointed! We'll find you something that you'll be happy with. I guarantee it." She gathered me up and propelled me toward a the back of the store. "What size are you? Here, let's get you measured."

Before I could say another word, I'd been swept into a large fitting room—far more spacious than any I'd ever before seen—where she hustled me out of my skirt and top and fluttered a tape measure around me.

She clucked as she saw my bra. "You're not wearing the right foundation garments, my dear. You need a bigger cup and a smaller band."

"Oh hell, I forgot my corset. I have a beautiful ivory corset at home. It's been fitted."

"We'll find something to make do," she said and flew out of the room.

I leaned against the wall, wondering what the hell I was doing here. I wanted Nanna's dress, but I couldn't have it. So, why not buy a beautiful dress that wasn't some cookie-cutter gown? Something I loved, that I could wear several times over? All of a sudden I had a glimpse of myself wandering the garden in a white dress, and it all felt so fake. I'd had a formal wedding before and look what had happened. As the clerk buzzed back through the door, her arms full of corsets, I started to protest but then stopped. I was already here and undressed. I might as well have a look at what they had before I left.

She shushed me into sucking in my stomach as she laced the corset in back, tying it with a firm bow. I had to admit, it was almost a perfect fit. Almost too tight, but I could handle it.

"There, that will work." She stood back, assessing me. "Bend over and shimmy your breasts into position."

I did the shimmy—every woman with boobs over a B cup knows about the maneuver that positions the girls properly in the cups. After I stood up, red-faced, she nodded approvingly.

"Now tell me, what style of wedding dress were you going to wear?"

I held out the preliminary sketches I'd kept from my first meeting with Janette. "Here, this is what the dress originally looked like, and this is what we were turning it into."

"Ah . . . very nice. I think we can find something that will be quite suitable for you. I know it won't take the place of a family gown, but we can make you happy. Do you prefer ivory or white? We also have this style in red, and I believe one in a brilliant green. Of course, your dress color will depend on the overall color scheme for your wedding. And you'll probably have to change your veil. Oh, and what are your bridesmaids wearing?"

Feeling awash in a sea of choices I really didn't want to make a second time, I held up my hand. "Nanna's dress was ivory. I have the veil that matches it at home, so there's no need for a new one. My bridesmaids and maid of honor have their dresses already, in a lovely pale violet."

She blinked. "No veil? But you can't get married without a veil—"

"I said, I have one at home." Just then my cell phone rang. "Excuse me. Perhaps you could bring in a couple of dresses for me to try on while I answer this?" I grabbed my cell phone out of my purse as she withdrew from the room. "Hello, and thank you, whoever you are."

Joe's voice burst into my ear. "Em, I don't know what you're talking about, but you've got to get over to the hospital right away."

"My God, again? What happened? Is something wrong with one of the kids?" Frantic, I struggled to reach the ties on the corset while juggling the phone. Please, oh please, don't let it be Kip or Randa. Anything but that.

"The kids are fine. Jimbo's headed in on a stretcher. I'll meet you there."

I could tell he was scurrying around, probably grabbing stuff to head over to the ER. "What the hell happened? Is he okay?"

"He was out at his place, napping. Woke up to find the place engulfed in flames. He managed to call 911, but that's all I know. Roger just called me; he's on the way to the hospital with Jimbo in the back. I'm picking up Murray. She'll be in no condition to drive. See you there." Abruptly, the line went dead.

Hell and high water. I tossed the phone in my purse and again, struggled with the corset ribbons, but couldn't get a good grip on them. Forget it. I yanked on my skirt and top as the salesclerk bustled in, her arms draped with chiffon and organza.

"What—"

"Emergency," I said, tossing her my business card. "Call my shop and Cinnamon will give you my credit card number for the corset. I don't have time to change." I grabbed the purse and stuffed my own bra into it, slipped into my sandals, and raced for the door, leaving one rather astonished and perplexed clerk in my wake.

I skidded to a halt in front of the car. Unlocking the door, I leaped in, flipped open my cell phone, and punched number two on speed dial. When Cinnamon came on, I quickly gave her permission to charge the corset over the phone and hung up. Making sure traffic was with me, I pulled out of the parking space.

All the way to the hospital, I had to force myself to keep my mind on the road. I wanted to pull over, to take a peek to find out whether Jimbo was okay, but didn't dare divert my focus from driving. I made a tight left onto Seventh Avenue, into the hospital's parking lot. Thanks be to

the parking goddess, there were a few spots open next to
the emergency room entrance. I hoisted my purse over my
shoulder and ran for the building.

As I swung through the door, my pulse raced faster
than a hummingbird on speed. Damn it, the last thing
Murray needed was to lose the love of her life. Coming to
a halt in front of the admissions counter, I forced myself
to slow down. Wilma Velcox glanced up at me and smiled.

"Ms. O'Brien—who are we seeing today—" Wilma
started, but I cut her off.

"Not me or my family. A friend is coming in—Jimbo
Warren, James Warren. He's been in a fire. Is he here
yet?" I leaned on the counter, trying to catch my breath.
She took pity on me and reached into one of the drawers,
bringing out an unopened bottle of cold water.

"Drink this, honey. Your face is too red. Your friend
hasn't arrived yet, but we've talked to the EMTs and he's
on his way. Captain Files isn't out there, is he? With that
shoulder wound, he should be resting—"

"No, he's on his way with Jimbo's girlfriend. They'll
be here in a few minutes. He called me and told me that
Roger's on the case." Abruptly, my adrenaline rush decided to exit, stage left, and I slumped, suddenly exhausted. The corset was laced too damned tight and I was
having trouble catching my breath.

"Are you sure you're okay?" Wilma asked, peering intently at me.

Grimacing, I shook my head. "I've got a favor to ask of
you."

"What is it, honey?" She looked ready to call for the
doctor.

Blushing, I said, "Can you unlace this damned corset
I'm done in? I can't get it untied."

Bless her heart, Wilma never said a single word. She
just nodded me into a nearby room and loosened my laces.
As I slipped into my bra, she held up the corset, looked at
me again, then smiled gently. "Honey, you might want to

save this for winter, when it's cooler. And you might want to take the price tag off."

I silently folded the corset and slipped it into a little bag she gave me. Might as well treat it gently. After all, I was paying . . . what was I paying? I glanced at the price tag and almost fainted. Five hundred dollars! Holy hell, that cost more than a month's car payment. I'd have to lose another inch or two, because I sure wasn't going to just tuck it away in my lingerie drawer. For that kind of money, I wanted some use out of the thing. Slipping back into my top, I followed Wilma out to the waiting room.

Joe and Murray arrived ten minutes later. Murray was crying and Joe was trying to calm her down. White Deer was on their heels. She hurried over to me. "Anna's having a rough time. Is there anything you can do? I don't want her to pass out before Jimmy gets here."

Nodding, I slipped off my shoes, crossed my legs on the sofa. I didn't need to be psychic to see that Murray was radiating panic. I sucked in a deep breath, summoning a wave of soothing energy to flow around her, smoothing over the rough edges of fear. Within a few minutes, she was noticeably calmer. Joe led her over to sit between White Deer and me.

The ER doors burst open, then, and Roger rushed in, adjusting an IV drip attached to the stretcher. Two attendants navigated Jimbo down the corridor, past admissions as Wilma yelled out, "Room three."

Murray tried to jump up, but I held her wrist as Joe followed Roger down the hall. If Jimbo was badly hurt, there was no sense in her seeing him before the doctors got started with their treatment. I'd seen burn victims before. The wounds weren't pretty.

Within moments he was back, motioning for Murray to join him. I let go as she sprang to her feet and hit the floor running. White Deer and I caught up just in time to hear Joe telling Murray, "Smoke inhalation. A few burns but he should be okay. Nothing that can't be repaired. He's lucky he's got Roo. That dog saved his life."

Roger strode down the corridor, covered with soot and smelling of smoke. Murray jerked around, wide-eyed. Before she could ask, he said, "The doc is with him. He'll be all right, Detective Murray. Don't panic. He's in good hands. That three-legged dog of his is a wonder, I'll tell you that."

Once again, Roo had come to the rescue of her loving master. I tapped Roger on the arm. "What about Roo? And the other animals? Are they okay?"

"The house was still burning when we left, but it hadn't spread to the outbuildings and I think the boys will be able to confine it. So, the livestock should be okay. The dog got out. A neighbor who came over to see what all the excitement was about said he'd take care of her for now. I'd better get back to the station." He grabbed Joe's hand. "Miss you, man. See you at the wedding! And Emerald"—he turned to me—"Melissa wants to get together soon."

As he exited the building, I led Murray back to the waiting room. Knowing that Jimbo wasn't in life-threatening danger seemed to drain her of momentum and she complied without protest.

Joe had followed Roger out of the building; he could dig up information we might not be privy to. I motioned to White Deer. "Maybe you could rustle up some coffee or tea? And Mur should probably eat something." I handed her thirty dollars and she went in search of the cafeteria.

"Mur, he's going to be okay," I said, tapping her arm. Her face was wet, her expression stricken.

"What's happening, Em? I don't understand. It seems like the past week or two have been so full of troubles that I'm beginning to think there's a curse on us. You sure that dragon is safe?"

I thought of the jade dragon, resting in my étagère at home. "Yeah, it's safe. The curse is long gone. Besides, even with all my troubles, except for my grandma, nothing's been as bad as what you've been going through. If it *were* the dragon, you'd be safe."

"What could have caused the fire? Jimmy's always so

careful." She dabbed at her eyes, her mascara smearing. Murray didn't wear much makeup, but what she did use was effective, making her look polished and pulled together for her job. Now, though, her face was streaked. I dug through my purse and pulled out a couple of the wet wipes I always kept handy.

"Here, use these. Here's my compact. Joe will find out everything he can for us." I left her cleaning her face and wandered over to the window overlooking the parking lot, where I flipped open my cell phone and punched in Harlow's number. As she came on the phone, I dished out the latest news.

"Oh my God," she gasped.

"Jimbo will be fine," I quickly added, "but I don't think I can meet you for lunch today. Murray's going to need me. I don't have time to find a dress, anyway. Instead, I managed to run out of Joanne's Bridal Boutique wearing a corset for which I now owe five hundred dollars."

Harl sighed. "That figures. Listen, give them my love and let me know if there's anything I can do. I'm planning on throwing the dinner for you and Joe Thursday night. Do you think Jimbo will be able to make it?"

I mulled over what Roger had said. "If it's just smoke inhalation and a few minor burns, he should. I'm worried though, Harl. I have a nasty hunch that the fire didn't set itself."

"You thinking arson?" Her voice grew serious. Harl might be all caught up in playing socialite, but when push came to shove, she always came through, and she always put her friends and family first.

An ambulance pulled up outside, lights flashing, and I watched, distracted, as the attendants sprang into action, unloading a stretcher from the back. The patient appeared to be in pain, and her neck was held in a bracelike object. Car wreck, probably. With a sigh, I turned way from the window and settled myself on the vinyl bench below. A

palm frond from one of the potted trees next to me
brushed my shoulder and I pushed it aside.

"My gut tells me so," I said. The moment I saw Jimbo
being wheeled into the ER, I knew that someone had
made a second attempt on his life. "Yeah, I think so, but
don't say anything till we know for sure. The fire marshal
will examine the scene. I'm hoping he finds the cause."

"How's Murray taking it?"

"Like a woman in love, how else?" I glanced back at
her. She'd cleaned herself up and was clutching her purse,
lips pressed together, as White Deer reappeared, tray of
food and coffee in hand. "I'd better go. Thursday night is
fine with me, but if Jimbo's not out of the hospital by
then, I think we'd better postpone it, okay?"

"No problem. Call me later and let me know if he's
going to be stuck there. If he is, James and I will come
down to visit him."

"Speaking of James, what's going on between you
two?" I asked. "I've never seen you two bicker like you
did yesterday."

"Just couple stuff. Don't worry about us. Everything
will be okay. Give Murray my love, and Jimbo, too." As
she hung up, I flipped my phone shut and slid it back into
my purse. With another glance out the window at the now-
departing ambulance, I rejoined Murray and White Deer.

"They have an espresso bar in the cafeteria," White
Deer was saying, handing me an iced mocha. "Triple shot
for you, and one for Anna. I made sure they put in extra
chocolate," she said, smiling.

I accepted the mocha gratefully and saw that she'd
bought sandwiches. As I bit into a turkey and provolone
on sourdough, Joe peeked around the corner, helped himself to half my sandwich, and settled into a chair.

"What did Roger have to say?" Murray leaned forward
so eagerly she almost spilled her drink. I steadied it for
her, setting it on the table next to us.

Joe patted her hand. "The house is gone—totally con-
sumed." He swallowed another bite of the sandwich and

accepted the coffee that White Deer offered him. "From what Jimbo told Roger, he was in the den going over some bills when he dozed off. Roo started barking like crazy, and Jimbo woke up to a room filled with smoke. The flames were just starting to lick the carpet, and he tried to put them out, but once he realized that the whole place was going up, he broke a window in order to escape. Roo jumped out after him. He had his cell phone with him and had enough strength to call 911 before he passed out."

"Oh my God," Murray said, staring at him in horror. "He could have died. Just how okay is he? Do you know how badly he's injured?"

"Roger told me that Jimbo's sustained a few burns on his hands. Nothing major and it's doubtful he'll have much in the way of scars. He got a lungful of smoke and some cuts from the broken window pane, but again, nothing serious. He lucked out, Murray. And thanks to Roo, he's alive. That's one courageous little dog. If it wasn't for her, he might not have woken up in time." Joe leaned back in his chair, a dark look across his face. "Damn it, I wish I'd been there when the call came in."

"He's going to be okay. You being there wouldn't have made things move any faster. Give it a rest," I said, crossing over to sit on his lap. "You'll be back to work soon enough, if you let that shoulder heal up."

He snorted. "Yeah, I guess I will. The doctor should be out in a few minutes, Murray. In fact, I'll bet Jimbo's released today."

Sure enough, within ten minutes, the nurse led Murray to Jimbo's side. I glanced at Joe after she left the room. "Arson?"

His eyes flickered. "What makes you say that?"

"A feeling."

"Hmm . . . Roger didn't say, but I know they're checking it out thoroughly. I told them to notify the fire marshal that there's already been one—if not two—attempts on Jimbo's life, so to be on the lookout for anything suspicious. If this is arson, it pretty much confirms that Jimbo was the sniper's target and not me." He rested his arm around my shoulders and I leaned against his chest.

White Deer leaned forward, clasping her hands between her knees. "Emerald, would you go out there later on with me? To check on the energy? Anna told me about what you picked up before, both when you went to Jimmy's land after Joe was shot, and then again last night. After an incident like this, the energy trails are bound to be stronger."

A peculiar tone rang in her voice and I caught her gaze, holding it. Her eyes were dark, and as I fell into those brilliant chocolate orbs, I found myself terrified. Murray was in danger. And Jimbo was in the way, guarding her from the kook who was focused on worming his way into her life.

"You think her life's in danger," I whispered. "You think someone's trying to kill her?"

She blinked. "There was a raven in the yard this morning. I watched as it waited while a cat stalked a mouse through the garden. The raven screeched and the cat backed off. But then the raven grew distracted by something—I'm not sure what—and flew into a nearby tree. The next moment, the cat was back and the mouse was dead. You take your omens where you find them."

The air thickened as she spoke, and I rubbed my arms. Goose bumps formed a staccato pattern on my skin and I suddenly felt cold. "And you listen to omens, or you pay the price later."

With a nod she said, "Anna trusts in her gun too much. She trusts that the law she upholds will be able to protect her, as if her badge is a magical shield that can ward off all danger."

"I think she's afraid that if she shows fear or vulnerability that her men will think less of her. She had to fight her way tooth and nail into that position, White Deer. She's petrified that she's going to fall off the mountain and that a new king of the hill will usurp her." I studied my nails. They were in dire need of a manicure. "Tomorrow morning we'll head out there and see what we can find. It might be best to leave Murray and Jimbo at home—their fear can shift the readings."

Joe cleared his throat. "I know you're both going to brush this off, but I'm going to ask it anyway. Will it put Emerald in danger to go out there?"

I looked at White Deer, who took a deep breath, letting it out slowly. "Emerald's not in direct danger," she said, "but Joe, you know as well as I do that if we're dealing with a psycho, then anybody who crosses his path is going to be in some sort of peril. Look at your shoulder. And you weren't even aware you were in the way."

Joe's gloom didn't lessen. If anything, her words deepened the shadow on his face. "That's what I'm talking about. I don't want my wife—fiancée—in danger. The last thing I want is for her to be shot or attacked."

I put my hand on his. "Yes, I'm prone to getting myself into scrapes. The universe seems to be determined to put me in the path of some pretty shady characters. But this time, we aren't dealing with ghosts or anything like that."

"All the more to worry about!" He shook me off, standing and pacing the room. "Look, I trust that you can deal with the supernatural beasties, even if they come with 'Beware of the Spook' tags attached. You know how to cope with those matters better than any one of us, except maybe White Deer. But flesh-and-blood crooks . . . you can't tell me that you've had a great track record. You've fielded several of them, yes, but luck has played a big part in your escapes. You can't deny that."

I stared at the floor. He was right, I had to give him that much. I'd escaped by the skin of my teeth several times, through grabbing opportunities rather than making them. "You're right and I won't deny it. But Murray's my best friend. If there's anything I can do to help, then I'll do it, dangerous or not."

He sighed. "I know, and I won't try to stop you. I just want you to be careful. I want you to think before you run into somebody you can't handle. One day, there might not be a way out." With a glance at White Deer, he added, "You know I'm not trying to stand in your way, don't you? That I care about Murray and I'd be out there in a flash if you needed me?"

She nodded. "Don't worry about it, Joe. I know perfectly well how much you care about all of us. Just as you know that you can't cage Emerald to keep her safe. The realities are that each of us could be swept away at any moment. You can step off the curb and get hit by a bus; you can eat the wrong oyster and die of food poisoning. You can get up early one morning to catch a flight and find yourself in the wrong place at the wrong time, like the people who were on the planes that hit the Twin Towers. Life is a gambit, but it's also a gift, not to be squandered in fear. So, you take what precautions you can, and live it to the fullest."

"I know, I see it in action every day at work," Joe said. "All right, go out and check the land, but I want to come along. I won't get in the way, I promise."

"Joe, you need to rest. Our honeymoon's coming up and I refuse to have a husband who can't perform his groomly duties." I leered at him and he laughed, holding up his hands.

"I get it, I get it. Okay, but you promise to look after her?" He waggled a finger at White Deer and she nodded, a rare smile blossoming across her lovely face.

"I promise to do what I can," she said.

"That's all I ask," Joe said.

Murray peeked around the corner. "Guess who gets to go home in an hour?" Relief spread across her face like the sunrise after a long, dark night. She hurried over to us and settled down beside White Deer. "Jimmy's got a few burns, but they'll heal just fine. His lungs were pretty cloudy, but they've been giving him oxygen and they say they don't see any reason to keep him overnight. So, they're going to watch him for another hour and then, if there aren't any problems, they'll discharge him."

White Deer wrapped her arm around Murray's shoulders. "We'll take him back to your place. Tomorrow, Emerald and I are going out to look over Jimmy's land to see what we can find. We'll check on the animals while we're there."

"I'm going, too—" Murray shut up as her aunt shot her a warning look. White Deer was the one person who could still reduce her to silence. "Okay, so I'm not. But will you go over to the neighbor's and bring Roo back to town?"

"Of course we will."

I glanced at my watch. "Oh shit! I was supposed to call Rose about Grandma M. She should be out of surgery by now. And the kids will be wondering if the aliens abducted us—"

Joe stood up and stretched. "If Jimbo's going to be okay, we should get home and make sure everything's okay there. Call us if you need us."

"I'll see you tomorrow," White Deer said. "About ten?"

I hesitated, glancing at Murray. I didn't want to leave until I knew for sure that everything was okay with Jimbo. She seemed to sense my worry and waved me toward the door.

"Go on home and find out how Grandma M. is doing, Em. Now that I've talked to Jimmy, I'm okay. He'll be fine, and so will I." She blew me a kiss, and Joe and I hit the streets. We'd arrived in separate cars, so I asked him to stop and pick up something for dinner while I hurried home to call Rose.

Miranda was watching from the porch when I pulled in. I raced up the stairs. "I'm sorry I'm late, honey. There was an accident out at Jimbo's and we had to go to the hospital. Is everything okay?" I asked, noticing her pale face. My daughter could put Dracula to shame with her fair complexion, but today she looked practically bloodless. She bit her lip, then burst into tears and threw herself into my arms.

"What's wrong? What happened? Oh my God, is Kip okay—?"

"Kip's fine, he's upstairs. But Gunner and Lori are going out! I saw them at the library today."

I blinked. Gunner had broken up with my daughter a few months ago, and she had been upset, but survived without lasting damage. However, the girl Gunner had begun dating at that time had been a relative stranger. Apparently, things hadn't worked out between them, either. I couldn't believe, though, that Randa's best friend would sneak behind her back and date her ex-boyfriend. Her *first* boyfriend.

"Are you sure about this?" Randa jumped to conclusions more often than she liked to admit. Maybe, just maybe, she'd made a mistake.

Randa gave me one of those "God, are you stupid" looks. "I saw them together, talking and laughing."

Betrayal was a harsh mistress, and the only cure for her heartbreak would be time. I still had my doubts that what she really saw was what she thought she saw, but right now she just needed her mother's support.

"Okay, honey. Come on, let's go inside. We'll talk about this more after I've called your Aunt Rose to find out if Grandma M. made it through surgery."

She wiped her eyes. "I'm sorry. I forgot."

"Don't worry about it. Will you bring me a glass of lemonade?" I picked up the phone and dug out Rose's cell number and typed it into my speed dial. As I waited for her to answer, I curled up on the sofa, thinking that there'd been so much chaos lately that home felt like a pit stop. The living room was cluttered with newspapers and magazines, the coffee table was listing under a stack of library books, and to my horror, I noticed a half-eaten sandwich sitting next to the computer. Samantha, our mother calico, was busy gnawing at it. As I started to shoo her away, Rose answered.

"I'm sorry I didn't call earlier. There was another emergency here," I said before she had a chance to speak. "How's Grandma M.?"

"She made it through just fine. She'll be in the ICU for a few days and probably leave the hospital in a week."

Oh, thank God! I couldn't take another shred of bad news. "How are the folks? Dad holding up okay?"

"He's fine. Mother's keeping it together for both of us. You know, I think I understand her a little better now," Rose said, and I could hear the wheels turning in her head. "I always blamed her for being cold and aloof, but between all the emotions running so high in our house, I guess somebody had to be the rock."

I thought about what she'd said. Nanna and I'd been off in our own world. Dad had been yanked around by Grandma M., who was always threatening a heart attack. Grandpa M. just wanted to hide out from Grandma and so gave in without an argument on every issue.

And then there was the infamous War of the Grandmothers, as Rose and I'd dubbed the continuing rivalry between Nanna and Grandma M. Old World Europe versus Irish lace and linens. Yeah, that had been a riot. It had fallen on Klara's shoulders to remain the voice of composure.

"Well, Grandma M. couldn't stand Mom when she married Dad. She was a foreigner. That alone was enough to damn her in Grandma's eyes." I was taking a chance, knowing how much Rose idolized Grandma McGrady, but what I said was the truth. She surprised me, though.

"I guess you're right. Maybe I never gave Mother the credit she deserved. Okay, I've got to go, but I'll call you again tomorrow morning, unless something happens before then. Love you, Emmy."

"Love you, too, Rosy." As I hung up, Joe came through the front door.

"We've got to clean up this mess," I called out, pushing myself to my feet. As I reached for the nearest pile of magazines, I saw his face and stopped. "What's wrong?"

He motioned me into the kitchen. "I need a Coke, and I know you're going to want some of that black death you love so much once you hear what I've got to tell you."

Uh-oh. Not good. Anytime anybody warned me to hit the caffeine, they usually had bad news. "What happened?" I asked, grabbing a soda out of the fridge and handing it to him. I quickly ground beans for a double-shot espresso.

"I just talked to Roger, who talked to the fire investigation team. It's not going to take a detailed examination to figure out why Jimbo's house caught on fire." He popped the top on the Coke and took a long swig.

"Was I right?" I asked, holding the mesh cup full of grounds.

"Yeah, arson. They found gasoline containers outside. It looks like the outside of the house, all around the foundation, had been doused with gasoline. Jimbo must have been sleeping while it happened. His truck and chopper were outside, so it was apparent he was home."

I slowly inserted the cup into the holder and fitted it beneath the espresso spigot. "Then whoever torched his house—"

"Was definitely trying to kill him."

Eleven

⁂

AT PRECISELY TEN A.M. I pulled into Jimbo's driveway. White Deer was already there, leaning against Murray's truck and drinking a latte, and I saw the fire marshal's car pulling onto the road. As I jumped out of my SUV, the smell of smoke and charcoal filled the air, and I gazed silently on the charred remains of what had been Jimbo's house. There was nothing left. Nothing except blackened timbers and heaps of ashes.

I made my way over to White Deer's side, carrying my own iced mocha. "Fire marshal done with his investigation?"

She nodded. "Yeah, but he wouldn't talk to me. Doesn't look like they took much away as evidence."

I glanced around at what was left. The fire had managed to torch one of the sheds, but the big one—where Jimbo worked on his cars and kept his goats—had survived. The vegetable garden had taken a hit, but only in the rows closest to the house. An uneasy silence loomed over the land, and I could feel a creeping malevolence seeping through the air, through the downed timbers of the house. It was as if some shadow had moved through, leaving in its wake wave after wave of flames.

"What the hell?" I asked, looking slowly at White Deer. "Jimbo's land has never, ever felt this angry and unwelcoming before."

She blinked, not taking her eyes off the ruins of the house. "You're right, and I'll tell you another thing. The gasoline may have set off the fire, but something else left this wave of hatred behind. It's almost as if the land's been tainted, saturated with . . ." Pausing, she glanced at me, as if she didn't want to say what she was thinking aloud.

"With jealousy," I said, putting a name to the energy. To name something might draw it out, but it also gave us some measure of control over it. "Envy, jealousy, greed . . . can you feel it?" My skin prickled.

White Deer nodded. "Yes, I can, and it's strong. Emerald, whoever this is, is so focused that his desire has taken on a consciousness of its own."

I thought about Murray's house, her bedroom in particular, and what I'd felt there. White Deer had nailed it on the head. Whoever he was, he left footprints. And if we followed them, maybe we could track him down.

"Perhaps we can trace him," I said, not looking forward to the prospect, but it was the only option we had.

"We'd better get busy, whatever we're going to do. I promised Jimmy and Anna that we'd check on the animals first. I'll go over to the neighbor's and fetch Roo, if you'll check on the goats and chickens." She headed down the road in a light jog.

I looked at the barn, and the chicken coop beside it, not relishing opening those doors and peering into the darkness. With a sudden pang, I wished that I'd agreed to let Joe come with us, but hindsight is twenty-twenty. I pulled a flashlight out of my Mountaineer and slowly approached the chicken coop. Might as well start there—where it would be harder for someone to hide out in the small space.

As I cautiously made my way across the rocky dirt to

the sounds of the breeze rustling through the trees, the thought of coming face-to-face with Murray's stalker began to loom larger in my mind. But he wouldn't be so careless as to be here this morning, would he? And surely the fire marshal and his crew had looked through the out-buildings, so everything should be safe.

Holding on to that thought, I opened the gate to the chicken run and threw open the door to the coop. Silence. What? Shouldn't there be chickens clucking and running around looking for their breakfast? I flashed my light in-side the weathered outbuilding and saw a series of nests, but no chickens. In fact, nothing stirred in the building ex-cept what looked like a mama mouse and three babies. I backed into the fenced-in run and shut the door, then with a final look around, closed and fastened the gate. No chickens. That was odd. Jimbo usually had quite a hand-ful of birds around. He raised them for eggs, as well as meat.

Curious now, paying less attention to the shadow that had cast a pall over the biker's land, I headed over to the big shed. Once a barn, Jimbo had turned it into a multi-purpose outbuilding. It now served as mechanic's garage, goat hotel, tool shed, and storage locker.

I hesitantly pulled on one of the huge doors that opened out and threw it wide so the light could shine in and illu-minate whoever—or whatever—might be inside. As I checked to either side before stepping into the main room, I noticed that like the chicken coop, the barn hung heavy with a shroud of gloom. The scent of goat permeated in the air, along with motor oil and fragrant sweet hay, but save for the scurry of what had to be mice, no sound em-anated from the stalls or loft.

I peered over the first goat stall. Hay, droppings, food bin, water trough, nothing else. The same with the other three. Nada. I flickered my light around to the corners of the room, but nothing. Relieved there was no one there, I headed outside, back into the light, and shut the door

behind me. As I did, I saw White Deer jogging into the
driveway, Roo at her side.

"The goats and chickens are gone—" I started to say.

"I know," she cut in. "The neighbor took them home
last night. He's got them down there for whenever
Jimmy's ready to bring them back." She paused, staring
around the yard. "That may be quite a while, from the
looks of things. So much was destroyed."

"Yeah, so I noticed," I said. "And somehow, I doubt
Jimbo had homeowner's insurance." I leaned down to pet
Roo. The little three-legged dog was panting happily, and
she rolled over onto her back as I patted her tummy. "At
least he got out with his life, and the lives of his animals.
Isn't that right, Roo? You're such a good girl! You saved
your master, didn't you? What a good girl."

White Deer shaded her eyes, looking around the yard.
"Let me put Roo in my truck so she doesn't run off and
get herself in trouble, and then we'll do a check around
the area and see what we can dredge up."

Dredge up. I didn't like the sound of that, but I had the
feeling that's exactly what we were about to do. "Be sure
to crack a window for her. It's going to be warm as the day
goes on."

While she led Roo over to the truck, I took a deep
breath. This wasn't my idea of a fun outing, but I kept
Jimbo and Murray in mind. Their safety was paramount.

I prepared myself by grounding and centering, searching for the earth mana that ran deeper than the malignant
energy hovering around us. I plunged my attention down
past topsoil, past the tendrils of grass and bush, following
the roots of the trees into the depths of terra firma, down
past the shadow that gathered over the land. Reaching out
to the brilliant green light that made up the pure element
of earth, I locked onto the energy that came directly from
the soul of the world. Steadied, I inhaled deeply and
looked up as White Deer returned.

"I'm ready," I said.

She glanced at my eyes and nodded. "Then let's go."

We headed first toward the remains of the house, careful to skirt the sodden lumps of charcoal that had only yesterday made up the walls and roof of Jimbo's home. As we approached what had been the door, I could feel a quiver—a faint discord plucking at the outer strings of my awareness.

"White Deer, I want you to guard me. I'm going to cast out, to see what I can find. I don't think we'll have to go much farther than the house. The energy is focused here—a steady stream of anger."

She took up a spread-legged stance, arms raised to the sky. I could see a rainbow of sparkles flickering faintly around her. White Deer was a powerful medicine woman in her tribe, and even if I hadn't been able to see energy, I would have felt it around her. She was strong enough to make others take notice, and she carried the Lynx within her—the strong, silent teacher who gave up her secrets only when she was ready.

A wave of protection spread out from her, a warding against hatred and anger, against fear. I made sure I was within the boundaries of her guardianship before I settled myself cross-legged on the ground, sitting directly in front of her, and closed my eyes.

Downward, inward . . . I followed the spiral, casting my awareness out of my body, moving onto the astral, letting the world around me fade as I entered the domain of spirit that was forever connected to our own physical realm, but so seldom noticed by the majority of people.

From here, I could no longer see the yard or the remains of the house, but I could see energy. It was as if I looked on the world with alien eyes, my perception picking up the unseen forces running amok. I let out a deep breath. On the astral I could see almost better than on the mundane realm for other senses strengthened my sight— a gut *knowing* as to what certain forces had in mind.

The area that had been Jimbo's house was oozing with sludge—mottled brown and sickly. I shivered. It was as if the residue left by whoever torched the place had morphed into a mindless jelly that was seeping through the yard. The energy didn't notice me. It couldn't notice anyone. It simply *was*—without thought, without form. And it devoured joy, and light, and peace of mind.

I sought for a clue on how to neutralize it. There was no way anyone—animal or human—should stay here until the place had been cleansed and purified. Sage and Florida water wouldn't be enough, that much was clear. Just like the Will o' the Wisps that had inhabited the lot next door to my house, this was bigger than a simple warding could take care of. The ooze might be mindless, but that didn't mean it was safe, and it could only be residue of a troubled and twisted mind. Murray's stalker was one sick puppy.

White Deer stiffened behind me. From my vantage, her energy spread over us like an invisible umbrella, a shield to keep out the danger that might lie within this leechlike amoeba. I reached out, touched her lightly with my mind.

"I'm going in. I'm going to follow the trail," I whispered to her without speaking a word, but she caught my intention and I felt her nod as she strengthened her focus.

I inhaled deeply, let it out slowly and renewed my connection with the glowing earth, then used the energy to propel me toward the massive blob. I skirted the edges, looking for anything that might link it to its originator. Finally, near the place where the fire marshal had found the gasoline cans, I saw a cord leading off into the mists that continually rolled through the astral plane. Steeling myself, I plunged into the roiling clouds, following the trail.

As I drifted along, buoyed by a gust of etheric wind, I suddenly stumbled and, once again, I found myself in the dark forest, filled with bog and quicksand. Shit! I didn't like this place. Perhaps it was only a metaphor for the chaos that existed within his mind; nevertheless, it had developed a life of its own, creating a massive shadow that followed him wherever he went.

I carefully sidestepped a puddle of bog water. Maybe I should have a closer look at these woods. They might give me a hint as to who lived in this little world, and right now we needed every clue we could find. The more I saw of what was going on, the more frightened I was that Murray would end up on the wrong side of this guy's psychosis.

The trees were tall timber, Douglas fir and tamarack, but many of them were snags—widow-makers that had been struck by lightning, burned and charred along the sides. The undergrowth contained the usual fare for our area: huckleberries and junipers, ferns and salmonberries, but when I examined several of them closely, I saw that they were infested with caterpillars and aphids. I pulled my hand away as a bloated spider crawled out from beneath one of the leaves and raced toward my fingers.

Shit. Enough. I didn't want to be here any longer. I turned, ready to head back toward the area where I'd first entered the astral when I saw a movement to my right, behind a moss-covered trunk.

I paused, waiting, watching. There—it moved again. I didn't want to follow, but I felt compelled to find out what was creeping around in this man's mind. Maybe he was possessed, or maybe this was just one of his inner demons, lurking in the corners.

As I took a step in the direction of the movement, a man emerged from behind the trees. Of indeterminable age—he could have been twenty-five, he could have been sixty—he had brilliant red hair and was taller than Murray but not as tall as Jimbo. Lean but muscled, he wore a camouflage uniform and combat boots. But it was his eyes that drew my attention. They were the color of glacier water, pools of frozen ice just starting to melt.

I sucked in a deep breath. I'd found him—Murray's stalker—and I had a bird's-eye view. Fortunately, he couldn't see me, but as I watched him, I began to sense that he was searching for something, as if he could feel my touch on the edge of his consciousness but couldn't quite figure out what was going on.

I began to back away. He didn't need to think that I was another voice in his head. Slowly, so as not to catch his attention, when I was far enough away I turned and jogged back toward the edge of the forest.

I could feel him standing there, behind me, staring mindlessly into the jungle that comprised his thoughts. His energy filled the forest like a rolling vortex, a mingling of anger and pleasure. As I skirted a patch of quicksand, leaping over a fern that blocked my path, I realized that he was enjoying the chase. He was a predator, out hunting, and Murray was his quarry.

I thought about turning, trying to throw a scare into him, but a feeling in my gut told me that would only do more harm than good.

Up ahead, I saw the end of the woods and I narrowed my focus, zeroing in on the area in which I'd entered this realm. As I reached the edge, I gave one last look over my shoulder. He was playing with a bowie knife, still staring, and the feral smile on his face told me that he was contemplating something too horrible to even think about. I closed my eyes and leaped, spiraling back into my body, slamming so hard that I pulled a muscle in my neck.

Behind me, White Deer embraced me in her shield, evicting any hidden goop that might be clinging to my aura. I moaned and unfolded my legs and she offered me her hand. I staggered to my feet. Shivering, I wanted nothing more than to run to my SUV and get the hell out of there, but logic took over. He didn't know who I was, or that I was spying on him.

I draped an arm over White Deer's shoulder and she helped me over to a picnic table set to one side. I dropped to the bench, wincing. "Damn, I hurt. I feel like I've been pummeled."

White Deer slid in opposite me and waited, pushing a water bottle across the table. Taking a long swig, I wiped my mouth and told her what had happened. "Whoever he is, he's far more dangerous than we thought. He's totally in his own world, and he views himself as a hunter, out to capture his prey. I think he likes . . . I *know* he enjoys inflicting pain."

"You saw his face." It was statement, not a question.

I nodded. "Yeah, and I'm going to ask Murray to let me look through her mug books. If I can pinpoint him . . ." I glanced around at the rubble. "I think we've found all we're going to find. I want to get back to town so I can talk to Harlow. I've got a hunch, and she's the person to help me. I'll drop over to Mur's house tonight, unless she's busy. Have her give me a call if she doesn't want company."

We headed toward our vehicles.

"I paid the neighbor fifty dollars. He'll keep the goats and chickens until Jimmy decides what to do about them. Obviously he can't come back here to live," she said.

Roo barked from her front seat and I opened the door, scratching her behind the ears. "You're a brave dog, you know that? And a lucky one," I murmured. The man I'd encountered would have no compunction about killing a dog. In fact, I was positive he lacked any sort of conscience. Perhaps he'd been abused as a child, but he'd made a choice to hurt, rather than help, others. Now, he lived in a world where he was king and where his rules prevailed. And when a man fancied himself emperor of the world, trouble usually ensued.

I turned back to White Deer. "Keep an eye on Jimbo and Murray for me? Tell them what happened. You guys are coming to Harlow's dinner party on Thursday, aren't you?"

She nodded. "We'll be there. I'm so sorry, Emerald. You deserve a better wedding week than you're getting. I still feel there's some discord around you that's drawing in the chaos with your family. You shouldn't have to worry about all this, considering you're already dealing with your grandma's heart attack and Joe's injuries."

"Listen, I wanted to talk to you about that. I've been sensing something off with my crystal necklace. I can't pinpoint it, though, and every time I start to check, something else intervenes."

She pursed her lips, staring beyond me at the woods.

After a moment, she shook her head. "You might be right. Or it might be nerves making you jumpy. Sometimes things happen in cycles—a lot of people will die in a short time, or a series of natural disasters will happen."

I let out a long sigh. She was probably right. Coincidence existed and sometimes it was all bad. "Well, I'll bring it with me when I come over tonight and maybe we can check it out?"

"Of course, I'd be happy to take a look at it. Perhaps I can sense whatever you aren't able to pin down."

Giving her a quick hug, I said, "Thanks, White Deer. I appreciate it. Okay, I'm heading for Harlow's. I'll talk to you tomorrow night, if not before."

As I climbed into my SUV, I glanced back at the blackened remains of Jimbo's house. Suddenly overwhelmed with sadness, I wished, not for the first time, for breathing space. Without worry, without fear.

BEFORE I HIT the highway, I dialed Harlow's number on my cell phone. She agreed to meet me for coffee. I'd suggested coming out to her house because I wanted her expertise with the Net, but she promised to bring her laptop with her. We decided to meet at Starbucks, where she could get Wi-Fi access.

By the time I swung into the parking lot and pushed through the doors, she was waiting. She'd left Eileen at home with Lily. As much as she loved her baby, I knew that Harlow wasn't cut out for mothering 24/7 and was happier with a nanny than she'd be without one.

She'd already set up her laptop. I stopped at the counter and ordered a triple-shot grande raspberry mocha, no whip. Drink in hand, I joined her, taking a long sip before leaning back and relaxing.

"You look wiped," she said.

"Wiped ain't the word for it." I told her what had happened. "What I want to do is look up this dude who was bothering her last autumn at the station and see if I can find a picture of him. I'll never forget that face from my vision."

She opened a browser. "What's his name and where is he located?"

"His name is Rusty Jones and he lived here in Chiqetaw until he was fired. Bonner told Murray that Rusty was supposed to have moved to Seattle to live with his brother."

She tapped away on her keyboard and sat back, waiting for the results to tabulate on the page. "So, how's your dress hunt?"

I snorted. "At this rate, I'll be walking up the garden path naked. Joe might not object, but I don't think that's the best way to start a marriage. At least not ours. I don't know, Harl . . . I can't help but wonder if I'm being given a sign."

Narrowing her eyes, she typed rapidly. "What are you talking about?"

The whir of the coffee grinder interrupted us and I waited until it fell silent, rubbing my temples. I had barely let myself think about my fears, let alone say anything aloud, but now that she'd asked me I found myself spilling my guts.

"Am I supposed to marry Joe? Things keep happening, so many that I wonder if this isn't a sign warning us to wait. Maybe getting married again is a mistake. Maybe things won't work out. Maybe . . ."

"Maybe you're just getting cold feet. Or maybe you've been spooked so many times that you can't help but looks for signs and omens in everything that happens." She grabbed my hand. "Remember when I found out I was pregnant? How I was afraid I'd never be able to raise a child? You convinced me that everything would work out, and it has. Yeah, James and I are snippy lately over his latest assignment, but that will blow over. You and Joe are meant for each other. I've never seen you so happy, Em, nor so confident. Joe adores you, he worships the ground you walk on. Don't break his heart over a little bad luck."

I stared at the table, at her hand holding mine. Maybe I'd gotten so used to things not being what they seemed that I was borrowing trouble. Letting out a long sigh, I gave her an affirmative nod.

"You're right. A lot of people go through far worse than me and they don't break their engagements over it. I guess I'm just scared. I know I love Joe, and I know he loves me. We mesh so well and he adores the kids. What more could I want?" And as I spoke, I knew it was true.

She pushed my drink toward me. "Good! Get some caffeine in your system and let's see what we have here."

We peered at the list of sites on the screen. Harlow had a top-of-the-line laptop, and it occurred to me that she'd become quite a computer whiz over the past two years. Her fingers flew over the keys with a dexterity that I couldn't possibly ever match.

"Here we go . . ." She clicked on the first link and a group photo came up. The caption said it had been taken a couple years ago, and it was a picture of the men and women of Chiqetaw's police department. An alarm started going off in my head as Harlow pushed the laptop toward me. "See anybody that looks familiar?"

I leaned in and glanced over the rows of men and women, some in uniform, others in civilian garb. A flash of brilliant red hair caught my eye and I gasped. "Is there any way to enlarge this?"

She frowned. "It's not a thumbnail so unless I save it and work on it in a photo program, no. I can do that, if you want, but the quality won't be very good. Let's try another site."

The second revealed nothing of use, nor did the third, but the fourth was a college alumni site and under Rusty's name was a photo and biography. Bingo. The same man I'd met on the astral. As I stared into those glacial eyes, I could almost swear he knew what I was up to. I glanced at the bio and read that he'd gone on to join the Chiqetaw Police Department, but it hadn't been updated since he'd been fired.

"That's him, Harlow. That's the man who's chasing Murray. And he's far more dangerous than we thought."

Harlow took a close look at him. "Hmm . . . he does have a freaky look about him. Let me bookmark this and then we'll see if we can find out anything else." She added the link to her bookmarks and then went back to the search. After a handful of fruitless leads, a sly smile spread across her face. "Oh Lordy, looky here, Em. Rusty's been a busy man since he got fired."

The site was a forum board, and as I glanced at the topic of discussion, I shuddered. I'd seen some freaky things, but this was a group touting not only survivalist mentality, but also misogyny. And Rusty had been a busy bee, posting all over the boards. I skimmed until I came to a thread of rants about being spurned by one's object of affection.

"Holy hell, look at this." As we read, both Harl and I instinctively pulled back from the laptop. The post was full of obscenities, describing a woman Rusty accused of teasing him. He called her a cock-tease and had posted a vivid and explicit description of what he'd like to do to her. Though he never mentioned her by name, I knew he was talking about Mur.

Harlow paled beneath her exquisitely airbrushed tan. "We need to show this to Murray. She can take it to her boss and maybe they can pull him in for questioning."

"If they can find him. He was supposedly staying with his brother, but that could have been a smoke screen. If he's into survivalist mentality, he could easily exist on very little out in the woods." I chewed on one nail until Harlow slapped my hand.

"Stop biting—you'll regret it on your wedding day. If he is living out in the woods, he's got to be getting Internet access from somewhere. These posts are recent." She contemplated the screen.

"A friend in town . . . library access. Tad Bonner can take Rusty's picture to the library and ask if they recognize him." I glanced at the clock and swallowed the last of my mocha. "I'm calling Mur. We need to go over there right now and show her all of this. Rusty's twisted, Harl. Very twisted. He's strong and he's crazy and he's after Murray. And anybody who stands in his way is toast."

Twelve

✢

I STOPPED IN at home on the way so I could get my necklace. By the time I got to Murray's, Harlow had already arrived but she hadn't said anything about what we'd found out. Murray ushered us into the kitchen.

"Jimmy's upstairs asleep. What's going on?"

"Do you have wireless service, or is there someplace I can plug into the Net with this baby?" Harl asked, holding up her laptop.

Murray pointed to a small writing desk that already had a laptop sitting on it. "I have DSL. You can sit over there," she said. "Go ahead and use my computer if you want, though yours looks top-of-the-line."

While Murray booted up her laptop, I asked her if White Deer had given her the rundown on what had happened out at Jimbo's.

"No, actually, she's not home yet. She called to say she was stopping by the Crystal Pyramid for a new smudge stick." The Crystal Pyramid was a new metaphysical shop in Chiqetaw. They sold the usual array of crystals, smudge sticks, candles, and books. The owner seemed very nice, not at all flaky. His name was Ryan Neilson and he seemed both down-to-earth and to possess no small amount of talent himself.

"Mur, did Tad ever find out if Rusty is actually in Seattle?"

"Yeah, he found out, all right." She shook her head, turning the laptop over to Harlow. "Apparently, Rusty's brother knows nothing about Rusty's whereabouts. He stayed there a little while, then disappeared after his brother threw him out for being rude to his wife. We haven't been able to pinpoint him through a DMV search, so I guess he really is a potential suspect. But would he come back after all this time? Yeah, I got him fired but . . ."

"Brace yourself, Mur. We found some pretty damning evidence against him." I poked through the cupboard where I knew Murray kept her goodies. Sure enough, three packages of Oreos and—*What did we have here?* A box of Thin Mints. "Can I open these?" I asked, holding them up.

Mur shrugged, smiling faintly. "Sure. Now, what happened out there?"

I broke open the cookies and slid them onto the table. "I met your stalker on the astral," I said.

"What?" She was out of the chair, leaning across the table before I could open the fridge to find milk for the cookies. "And keep your voice down. If Jimmy wakes up, I don't want him hearing any of this. The last thing I need is to worry that he's going to run off hunting some elusive pervert."

"He might not be that elusive," I said, and proceeded to give her the rundown on what had happened. When I described the man I'd seen, she closed her eyes and let out a deep breath.

"It's Rusty, isn't it?" I asked.

"Sounds like it," she said, shaking her head. "How do you know?"

"Harlow will show you," I said, poking through her fridge. A gallon of chocolate milk rested on the top shelf and I poured two glasses—I knew Harlow wouldn't want any. But Diet Coke would catch her eye. I snagged a can and carried it over to the desk, where she was engrossed in working her magic on the keyboard.

She glanced up at me. "Here it is. The first site."

Murray leaned over her shoulder. Rusty's picture came up and she frowned. "That's him all right. You sure that's who you saw?"

"Plain as day. I know that's not proof that you can use in court, but it gives you a direction in which to look. Plus . . . Harl, show her that message board." I took a step back. I might not be the most diplomatic person in the world but when Murray got angry, she blew. And I didn't want to be in the way.

Harlow vacated the chair, allowing Murray to sit down. As she scanned the page, I could see her shoulders tense up. "I'll kill him. I swear, I'm going to hunt the dog down and tear him apart." She whirled. "I have to show this to Tad. Maybe he can trace the IP address to get an idea of where that little worm's been hiding out."

I bit into a second cookie. Murray could bring a grown man to the ground in a whimpering mess. She was a warrior, in the truest sense of the word, and had found law enforcement a good channel for her talents.

Harlow raised one eyebrow. "So, call him. Or shoot him an email with the URLs. We'll wait."

Mur forced herself back into the chair and tersely typed out a message, copying and pasting the URLs of the two sites. She didn't divulge what she told Bonner about why she thought it was Rusty following her, and I didn't ask. After a few minutes she cleared the screen, cleaned out the cache and history.

"I don't want Jimmy stumbling onto those sites. He'd figure it out right away." She grimaced as she joined me at the table and absently bit into a cookie. "Damn, I hate this. That little perv is out there somewhere, and he's got his eyes on me. And if what you say is right, he's dangerous enough to cause serious damage."

"Yeah, and you can bet he's not going to hesitate. My guess is that his psychosis has been building for years," I said, thinking about what I'd felt from him on the astral. "He's probably hiding out in the mountains near here, or with a friend. Do you remember anybody he might have palled around with?"

She shook her head. "Not right off hand, but let me think for a while. I do remember a couple of guys hanging around his desk, but it will take a moment for me to put names to the faces. Most of the time, I barely noticed him. I was polite, I said hello when I saw him in the halls, and I said good-bye at the end of the day. Apparently that wasn't enough. And you can bet that he blames me for his getting fired, even though he was the one caught sneaking into my computer and hacking my password."

A thought stopped me. "Computer? Murray, have you checked your computer for something called spyware? Kip was talking about it the other day."

Harlow smacked her head. "Why didn't I think of that? I'm not an expert at it, by any means, but Em's right. You need to make sure he's not tapping into your computer files. Since he was in your house long enough to both plant a bug and trash the place, he might have been able to break into your computer and set up some Trojan program."

Murray groaned. "Oh great. Are you sure? I mean, I know it's possible . . ."

"There are kids Kip's age who could break into your machine," I said. "Do you have your computer password protected?"

Again, a groan. "Yeah, but it's so simple I bet he could figure it out within a few minutes."

I closed my eyes. What mattered to Murray more than anything in the world? Jimbo? Too simple. "I'll bet it's either Sid or Nancy," I said, naming her snakes. She flashed me a nasty look and I knew I'd hit it right.

Just then, my cell phone rang. It was the booking agent for the Barry Boys.

"Ms. O'Brien? I'm sorry to drop this on you so suddenly, but the Barry Boys won't be able to play at your wedding. There's been a change of circumstances and the band won't be playing any more gigs for the rest of the year. Of course, we'll refund your deposit. I'll cut a check and get it sent off to you today." *Click.*

I stared at the phone and flipped it shut. "I'm about ready to scream. The Barry Boys can't make it for my wedding, so not only am I out a dress and my family, I'm also out a band." Suddenly angry, I smacked my hand on Murray's hundred-year-old oak table. "Jeezus, what the hell is going on?"

Harl and Mur stared at me. I avoided their eyes. Seldom given to temper tantrums, I felt like my entire wedding was falling apart before my eyes. Of course, I considered, compared to being stalked by a psychic wacko, perhaps it wasn't quite so bad. I shook my head, trying to clear my thoughts, but everything still seemed so bleak.

Shrugging, I said, "Sorry, just feeling the pressure."

"Pressure from what?" White Deer came popping through the back door.

We made room for her at the table and filled her in on what we'd been talking about. "So, we know who's after Murray. And, on the side, my wedding is more and more resembling something from a minimalist painting."

She narrowed her eyes. "Emerald, your aura is flaring up in a most peculiar way. What's different about you than this morning?"

I frowned, then snapped my fingers and dug into my purse. "Here, this is the necklace. Maybe just carrying it around causes havoc?"

She took the necklace in hand and closed her eyes, running the faceted crystals through her hands. "Em, I think these are . . . if I had to give it a word, I'd say they were hexed." Her voice was soft, and she had an odd, faraway look in her eyes.

"Hexed? You mean cursed?" Oh God, I thought I was

done with curses. But as the events of the past few days ran through my mind, the idea seemed less far-fetched.

"No," she said. "I'm trying to puzzle out the energy here. It's not like the dragon—not that sort of curse. I'm picking up a sense of sorrow . . . almost despair. And chaos." She laid the necklace out on the table. "You said this is an antique?"

I nodded. "Yeah, Rose bought it at a shop in Seattle. She said . . . what did she call it?" I thought for a moment. "Oh, yes. The dealer called it the Bride's Circlet."

Harlow immediately returned to Murray's computer and started tapping away at the keys. "Let's see if we can find out anything about it. If it's an antique, maybe there's something on the Web about it."

I picked up the string of crystals and ran it through my fingers. Rose would never deliberately give me anything to hurt me; that much I knew. So, if there was some hex associated with the necklace, I was betting that the shop-keeper hadn't mentioned it to her. Chances were if some spell or charm was attached to the necklace, the shop-keeper wouldn't even know about it.

White Deer poured herself a glass of lemonade from the fridge and pulled out a loaf of bread. "Anybody want to share a sandwich with me? I didn't eat lunch and I'm starving."

I shook my head, having filled up on cookies.

Murray glanced at the clock. "I thought I'd toss a few steaks on the grill for dinner after Jimmy wakes up, but I could go for half a sandwich. Turkey and Swiss, please. With mustard."

While White Deer slathered bread with mustard and mayo, Harlow steadily clicked through several links she'd pulled up on her browser.

"Got it!" she called after a few minutes. I slipped out of my chair and leaned over her shoulder. Sure enough, there in a grainy and faded photograph, was my necklace. Either that or a carbon copy.

Harlow skimmed the article. "This is a site that specializes in paranormal happenings, ghosts, hexes, etc. The entry is written by the descendant of someone named Thomas Carter. Let's see . . ." She began to read aloud:

> *In 1805, the Bride's Circlet was commissioned for Sally, the daughter of Thomas Carter, a British subject who settled his family in Jamaica. Sally was engaged to her cousin Niles, who lived in Port Royal at the time. The necklace was handcrafted by a jeweler back in Ireland and shipped to Jamaica for Sally's wedding. Unbeknownst to the bride-to-be, Niles had been having an affair with one of the family's slaves, Betsy, but he broke it off shortly before the nuptials.*

"Well, that's a fortuitous start to a marriage." Mur snorted. "Nothing like a pre-wedding affair to spice up a marriage."

"Yeah," Harl said. "And it gets better." She shook her head. "Em, I don't think I'd wear that necklace anymore, if I were you."

I held the necklace up so the light shining through the kitchen window reflected on it, sending little prisms every which way. Rose had been right about one thing—it was definitely an antique. Two hundred years old. "Why? Spill it. What happened?"

> *When Niles told Betsy that the affair was over, the slave girl flew into a jealous rage. Niles threatened to have her sold. Angry at his betrayal and fearful over being sold away from her family, Betsy poisoned Niles and tried to make it look like an accident.*
>
> *Fortunately for Niles, she gave him a less-than-lethal dose of poison. When Betsy learned he was going to survive, she stole the necklace and ran, thinking she might be able to sell it for enough money to escape and hide. But Thomas Carter tracked her down and Betsy found herself on the wrong end of the rope.*
>
> *Sally refused to marry Niles, who shortly thereafter*

fell from his horse and died of head injuries. The Bride's Circlet was never worn—Sally gave it to her cousin.

   Ever since then, every bride-to-be in the Carter family who possessed the necklace found their marriages doomed before the wedding. Eventually, rumors sprang up that Betsy had hexed the crystals when she ran for her life and that any bride who owns it will find misfortune dogging her heels all the way to the altar. Eventually, Charles Carter, an immigrant to the United States, sold it outside of the family and it disappeared into the mainstream public.

Harlow stopped, grimacing. "Sounds like your necklace has quite the history, Em."

"No kidding." I balanced the string of cut crystals in my hand. Such a beautiful necklace and so much grief associated with it. While I doubted that the slave had actually hexed the choker, her fear and anger could easily have penetrated the crystals, amplifying over the years.

"I don't think this necklace was actually cursed to begin with," I said. "But all it takes is a number of people believing that there's a hex in order to create one. The mind is an incredibly powerful thing."

"What are you going to do with it?" asked White Deer.

I shrugged. "Dunno. I guess I can try to cleanse it. It's so lovely that I hate to give it away, and Rose gave it to me so I really don't want to have to tell her I got rid of it. Maybe I can smudge it or something. It's had almost two hundred years of concentrated focus on it as a bearer of bad luck, so I'm not sure how effective my charms will be. Maybe Nanna can help me." I glanced up at White Deer. "Do you have any ideas?"

The moment the words were out of my mouth, I wanted to retract them. Right now, White Deer's focus should be on protecting Murray. "Never mind," I said before she could speak. "You have your hands full already. I'll just see what I can do. If I can't cleanse it, then I'll put it in a safe-deposit box until later. Maybe if it's out of the house, it won't be able to affect me. By the way, does it say how much this thing is worth?"

Harlow clicked away, then looked over at me. "Em, your sister paid in the neighborhood of five thousand dollars for that."

I almost choked on my cookie. I knew it was expensive, but that was beyond any guess I might have made.

"One thing's for sure," she added, "you need a new necklace to go with the new wedding dress, which you have yet to buy."

I grimaced. "Two corsets and no dress. Maybe I should go show-girl style. Corset, garter belt, a thong, and a pair of stiletto platforms. Think Joe would like that?"

Harlow cracked up, and Murray and White Deer joined her.

After they'd managed to stop laughing, Harl said, "Yeah, but this isn't Reno, Em. And Joe isn't Elvis. Hell, if I have to drive to Seattle and buy you a dress myself, I'll do it."

On that note, I stood up, pocketing the necklace. "Okay, I guess we've gone as far as we can today. At least we know who we're looking for, Murray. That's a lot more than we could say this morning."

Harl nodded. "You can be on the alert now that you know who's after you. And surely the Chief will be able to help once he sees those sites." She closed Murray's laptop and stood up. "What about the dinner party tomorrow night? Murray, you think Jimbo's up to coming?"

Mur nodded. "Sounds good. I need something to take my mind off this creep, and I refuse to let him put a dent in Em's wedding. Jimbo will be fine. He just needs a little rest today. Seven at your place, right?"

Harlow wrinkled her nose. "Yes, and dress up. I'm going formal."

We were headed toward the door when the bell rang. Mur answered. It was a florist, carrying a long, narrow box. She signed for it and carried it over to the coffee table. As she unwrapped it, I could see how worried she

was—and her instincts were right on key. The flowers
were beautiful, deep crimson roses, thirteen of them,
shrouded in baby's breath and fern. But there was something off. They weren't diseased, in fact they were almost
perfect. But their beauty seemed contrived rather than natural. Mur opened her briefcase and pulled out a pair of
latex gloves, snapping them on. Then, and only then, did
she slide the card out from the envelope.

"Oh hell."

"What?" White Deer asked, approaching slowly. Murray held up the card for all of us to see.

> *I've lost my patience. I told you to get rid of him,
> and he's still with you. And I saw your witch-woman
> friend poking around out at the lake this morning. Tell
> her to back off because your boyfriend's not the only
> one with a house that can catch on fire. Nobody's
> standing in our way. You spurned me before, but I know
> it was only because we worked together. But now it's
> time for you to stop playing hard to get. I know how
> you really feel about me. I know that you want me. ~R*

"Shit, you've got to show these to Bonner," I said.

She slumped in a chair. "Yeah. White Deer, will you
stay here while Jimmy sleeps? I don't want to leave him
alone."

I watched Mur for a moment, trying to think of something to say to make everything all right, but I knew there
wasn't a thing I could do. Suddenly, she perked up and
snapped her fingers.

"I remember! I've been racking my brain and I remember a couple of guys that showed up at the station a
few times to pick him up. They were outcasts and mis-
fits." She jumped up and looked around the kitchen.
"Ladies, I think I'll pay a little visit to Rusty's friends and
see what they might know about his whereabouts."

"Why not let the Chief take care of it?" I asked.

"Em, don't you get it?" She paced the length of her

kitchen, stopping to stare out the window into the backyard before turning and leaning against the counter. "Tad
will run prints on the flowers and card. He'll check on
Rusty's last known residence, but he *has* to go through
channels if we're to make any charges stick. That could
take several days. I have a nasty feeling that Rusty's not
going to wait days before making his next move. He's already tried to kill Jimmy three times. Next time, he might
not miss. I'm not going to rush in with my gun out or anything like that, but I need to start investigating on my
own."

"Then I'm coming with you." I pulled out my cell
phone. "Let me call Joe and tell him I won't be home till
later."

Mur pressed her lips together and shook her head.

"Let her go," White Deer interjected. "You need help,
and Emerald's always been your backup, Anna. You two
look after each other, you're soul mates. Don't let your
stubborn streak rule on this matter. I want you in one piece
and that means someone is going with you."

I crossed my arms and planted myself in front of Murray. "If you are simply going to ask a few well-placed
questions, then there's no reason I shouldn't come along.
You've taken me on interviews before, so why should this
be any different? Jimbo's life is at stake, woman. Get with
the program."

"Just cave on this, Mur, or you're going to regret it,"
Harlow chimed in with her two cents. "You aren't con-
ducting official business, you're simply going to knock on
a few doors and ask a few questions."

I knew Mur was irritated but she simply nodded and
grabbed a light jacket to wear over her tank top. First,
however, she strapped on her shoulder holster. At my
look, she said, "I never go unprepared."

"As well you shouldn't," White Deer said. "Never take
chances when you know there's an enemy nearby."

Murray sat down with the phone book to look up the
addresses of all of Rusty's friends whom she could remem-

ber. Harlow used the time to jot a shopping list for the dinner party, while I called Joe and told him that I'd be later
than I'd thought. "I'm helping Murray ferret out a few
clues. Will you feed the kids if they come in before
I do?"

He wasn't at all happy with my news. "Does this have
something to do with your little jaunt out to Jimbo's this
morning?"

I sighed. When I thought about it, I owed him an explanation. We were practically married, and I expected
nothing less than honesty from him. I couldn't hide my
actions if they might be dangerous in any way.

"Yeah, it does." Quickly, I filled him in on what had
happened there, and what Harlow and I'd discovered on
the Net. "So, we know who it is. Murray and I are just
going to drop in on a few old buddies of his, see if he's
been hanging around—"

"What? Are you both insane? What if this pervert is
staying with one of them? What if he's there when you get
there? What are you going to do then?" Joe wasn't exactly
shouting, but Murray, White Deer, and Harl all turned and
stared at both me and the phone.

I smiled at them weakly and tried to calm him down.
"Honey, you know as well as I do that Murray carries a
gun. White Deer thinks it will be safe enough—" Here,
White Deer glared at me, but I turned away. She had en-
couraged me to go with Murray; I was going to use her en-
couragement in the most beneficial way possible.

"Yeah, Murray does carry a gun. So does this Rusty
guy. I know—I was on the receiving end of one of his
bullets, if you haven't forgotten. I have no intention of letting you end up in the same position. Or worse." He was
so pissed off that I could practically feel the steam racing
through the wire.

I'd known that one day it would come to this. An argument over one of the dubious activities I'd been called
upon by the universe to do. Even though he said he was

okay with it, when push came to shove, most men didn't want their women stepping into danger.

With a sigh, I said, "Listen to me, Joe. Murray's my best friend. She needs help and I'm going to help her. She's been there for me when my life was on the line and she's saved my butt before. If I can help by simply going to a few houses with her, standing outside on the porch, and asking a few questions, then I'm going to do it."

He paused long enough for me to add, "We've talked about this before. You know that sometimes I end up in danger, that sometimes the universe just picks me up and dumps me into the middle of murder and mayhem. Joe, I can't escape my destiny, and I can't turn my back on a friend. I'll be careful. I promise you that. But I can't promise to walk away when I'm needed."

"Damn it," he said, and I knew I'd won. If, indeed, there could be a winner in a situation like this. "Go ahead, but please, Em, I love you. For God's sake, be careful, and don't do—"

"Anything stupid," I finished for him. "I'll call you in a little bit and give you the addresses of where we're going if you promise not to show up and blow things."

He promised, and as I hung up, I realized how good it felt to have someone care so much about me. It made me want to run home and throw myself into his arms, into our bed, to ride him with that wild passion that erupts with the realization of just how deep love can root itself in our hearts.

Instead, I flipped my phone shut, slid it back into my purse, and turned to find Murray, ready and waiting. Harlow was holding the door open. White Deer waved at us, promising to keep watch over the house and Jimbo.

"I'll keep the home fires burning," she said. "And I'm going to double-check the outside cameras to make sure they're wired right. Jimmy has a knack for all things mechanical, but I think I'm a little better with electricity than he is." She grinned.

Murray laughed then, a real laugh—not forced or

clouded with worry. "Yeah, I'll agree with you there." As we headed out the back door, she said to Harl and me, "Jimmy was rewiring a lamp that got busted during the break-in. White Deer was trying to help him but he kept insisting he knew what to do and he got so caught up in proving his prowess that he ended up crossing a couple of wires and zapping himself a good one."

Harlow stopped by her car. "Tomorrow night at seven, then. And make sure you call me if anything important happens before then." She paused, then put her hand on my arm. "Babe, don't wear the necklace until you've cleansed it. Please?"

I gave her my promise. "Yeah, though I think just owning it is putting a crimp in my wedding. Great, some ancient Jamaican love affair is tainting my own. I wonder . . ." So many mishaps. My dress, Roy showing up at the party, Joe getting shot, now the band . . . but then, sometimes coincidences happened, and sometimes bad luck was just what it seemed. Still, no sense in taking chances. "I'll put it away for now and deal with it later."

Murray and I took my SUV. I'd drop her off at home before I headed back to my house. As we buckled up, I called Joe to give him the names and addresses, then turned to Murray. "So, where to first?"

She consulted her notebook. "Bernard Dresser, 1690 East Columbine Lane. The street intersects with Olive, right after Suzette's Used Books."

"Columbine Lane coming up." I put the car into gear, and we headed out to try and trap ourselves a rat.

Thirteen

꠵

THE HOUSE WAS overgrown and rundown. Paint peeled off the weathered siding, while a few scattered shingle tiles lay around the yard. The lawn had been cut in the recent past, but the weeds along the borders of the sidewalk were knee-high, and a worn sprinkler gave off a tired spray of water. A cloud hung over the rambler, as if the house and grounds were just a pit stop, ignored and unappreciated.

Murray knocked on the door while I stood to the side. After a moment, we could hear a shuffling inside and then the door opened a few inches. I could see that it was still chained, but if that was the only lock it wouldn't guard against anyone who truly wanted in. A woman peeked out. She might have been thirty, she might have been sixty. I was betting on the former even though the deep creases in her face showed a lot of wear and tear.

"What do you want?" she asked, eyeing us up and down. "You here about the rent?"

Murray glanced at me, then shook her head. "No, ma'am. I'm a detective and I'm just here to ask a few questions—"

The minute the word *detective* left Murray's mouth, the woman's face went blank and she began shaking her head.

"I don't know anything. I've got kids to tend here—"

Smoothly, as if she'd fielded situations like this time and again, Murray put her hand on the door to prevent it from closing. "If you'll just give us a moment, I'll ask my questions and be out of here."

The woman squinted at her, hesitating. "What you want to know?"

"What's your name, please?"

"Jolene Johnson," came the sullen answer.

"Ms. Johnson, do you happen to know a man named Bernard Dresser?"

A flicker raced through Jolene's eyes. "Yeah, what about him?"

"This is the address I found for him. Do you happen to know where he is?" Murray seemed accustomed to one sentence answers. I patiently kept my mouth shut.

This time, there was more than a flicker of acknowledgment. "No, but if you find him, you tell him to get his butt home. Damned idiot hasn't paid the rent and the kids are hungry." Jolene opened the door a little wider. "You want to come in?"

We accepted, though I noticed as we entered Murray's gaze swung from side to side. I knew she was scoping out the place, checking for any potential dangers. The room into which Jolene led us was neat as a pin, but the teeth of poverty had gnawed on the edges. The furniture was used, the television a good twenty years out-of-date. A sickly-looking fern graced one window, and an oil painting—a still life of flowers in a vase—overlooked the fireplace. I could see three pairs of eyes peeking out from one of the other rooms.

"Have a seat," Jolene said. "Would you like some coffee?"

Murray shook her head. "No, thank you, we won't take up much of your time. Ms. Johnson, what's your relationship to Bernard?"

The woman sighed and dropped into an orange recliner. "Bernard and me was dating. I let him stay here 'cause he paid rent. But two nights ago, he went on a drinking binge and I haven't seen him since. Rent's due and I don't have it."

I was getting a good lesson in diplomacy by watching Murray. She nodded, her face blank. "Do you know if Bernard has a friend named Rusty Jones?"

Jolene snorted. "Yeah, he knows that creep. I told him no way was he letting that little pervert come around my kids. That guy's crazy-eyed and I don't want him in my house or anywhere near it."

Murray tossed a glance my way. So, we weren't the only ones who had problems with Rusty. "Can you tell me why you think he's such a creep?"

"I'll tell you why," Jolene said. "I went over to his place last year with Bernard and I found pictures of naked women tied up. They were in his bathroom. I don't want anybody like that near my kids."

"When's the last time you saw Rusty?"

"Mommy, Mommy, I'm hungry!" A little girl, no more than four years old, came running out of the bedroom. She was neatly dressed, though her clothes looked like hand-me-downs a step lower than out of a thrift shop, and her black hair was caught back in a ponytail.

"I know, baby," Jolene caught her up in her arms, settling her on her lap. "This is Destiny, my youngest daughter. I apologize—she don't mean to interrupt. We just don't have much in the kitchen and I got to watch what money I have."

I was struggling to avoid reaching in my purse for my wallet. Murray must have been thinking the same thing. "Mrs. Johnson, do you know about the Bread and Butter House?"

Jolene looked puzzled. "No, what is it?"

"Families can get a good meal there, and they give out food vouchers. Are you on AFDC?" She flipped a page in her notebook and jotted down the address, handing the paper to the woman.

"No, 'cause I had Bernard living with me. They wouldn't give us any money or food stamps. I usually get child support, but my ex-husband's in jail and can't pay none this month. My mother's supposed to be sending me a check, but it hasn't come yet." She wiped a loose strand of hair away from her eyes and I could see the resignation and weariness eating away at her.

Murray nodded. "I suggest you kick Bernard out so you can apply for food stamps and AFDC. If you go to the Bread and Butter House tonight before eight-thirty, you'll be able to get a good meal for you and the children. If you don't have a car, I can call them and they'll bring food and a voucher to your house. Now, when was the last time you saw Rusty?"

Tears in her eyes—looking grateful and relieved, Jolene bit her lip. She squinted. "I'd say end of March. That's the last time Bernard took me over to where he was staying."

"And do you remember where that was?" Murray asked.

"Oh, that one's easy," Jolene said. "He was staying in a van out at Cadillac Bob's."

BEFORE WE LEFT, I asked if I could get a drink of water. While I was in the kitchen, I slipped a twenty out of my purse and folded it, sliding it into a clean mug that was sitting on the counter.

Back in the car, Murray let out a huge sigh. "God, sometimes I hate my job. I see this time and again. It's no different in Chiqetaw than in any other city or town. People too poor to eat, women with a handful of children who never managed to get their high school diploma, let alone a college education. Guys skipping out when they don't want to deal with the children they fathered. It's enough to make me cry."

I nodded, adjusting my mirrors and fastening my seat-belt. "Yeah. To be honest, I left a twenty in her kitchen. I can't stand to see kids go hungry."

Mur gave me a wide grin. "I left one on the coffee table when you were in the kitchen. Well, at least they'll eat for a few days. I didn't see any sign of booze or neglect—the Johnsons are just a poor family struggling to make ends meet. I'll call the Bread and Butter House when we're through and make certain Jolene got in touch with them. If not, I'll ask them to go out and check on her and the kids. They've got counselors there who can help her apply for the assistance she needs."

"Where to next? Cadillac Bob's?" I asked, starting the ignition.

"Ugh . . . yeah, that's the next logical stop. Let's go."

I eased the Mountaineer away from the curb. Cadillac Bob's had to be the eighth wonder of the world, though definitely a man-made wonder. Bob Cappinalo was a fix-ture in Chiqetaw. He'd purchased a ten-acre plot just out-side the town limits so the town didn't have jurisdiction over him. He rented out space on the land to bus people, trailers, anybody with a tent who wanted to camp out for a bit. The county had slapped him with violation after vi-olation, mostly health concerns. Each time, he cleaned up the mess just enough to squeak by a follow-up investiga-tion. Until the next time.

Cadillac Bob's was on Ridge Rock Drive, a winding road that led out into the country past several old farms. Developers hadn't discovered the Ridge Rock area yet, so the houses still retained an individual flavor, with wide old oaks towering in the front yards and natural ponds that still provided a haven for the geese who flew in every spring.

Five miles down the road, a few yards past the borders of Chiqetaw, a driveway to the left led into Cadillac Bob's. I turned onto the dirt drive, skirting the numerous potholes that dented the path leading up to the main house—a sprawling jungle of add-ons. Jimbo's house had been a mansion compared to this place. The surrounding acreage was devoid of grass, probably from oil spills and the numerous vehicles passing through. Buses of every size and shape were scattered around the land, along with campers, a couple VW vans that looked directly out of some '70s movie, and one RV that had seen better days. A dozen Cadillacs in varying stages of disrepair filled in the empty spots.

"Jeez, this reminds me of some hippie compound," I said, pulling into a spot near the house.

Murray laughed. "Well, it's certainly more ragged than the biker's enclave, but somehow I doubt if any old hippies would hang out with Cadillac Bob, the way he pollutes the land. Last time they got him, he'd dumped hazardous chemicals on the property. He paid the fine and that was that."

We slipped out of the SUV and headed up the stairs, taking care to skirt the broken boards that looked like they might splinter beneath our feet. Murray knocked on the door and after a few minutes a man yanked it open. Somewhere in his fifties, he was sporting a muscle shirt that barely covered his beer belly and pair of low-riding jeans filled with holes and splattered with old paint. He squinted behind his pair of pink wraparound sunglasses.

"Yeah?"

He was succinct, that I'd give him.

Murray held up her badge. "Are you Bob Cappinalo?"

"What's it to you?" he asked.

"I'm Detective Murray," she said. "Are you familiar with a man named Rusty Jones?"

Good ol' Bob shrugged. "Maybe. What's he look like?"

Murray held up a picture of Rusty. She must have had it in her car, which told me she'd suspected the little perv for longer than she wanted to admit.

Cadillac Bob leaned in closer and peered at the picture, then straightened up and nodded. "Yeah, he was here earlier this year. I kicked him out around the beginning of April."

"Can you tell me what kind of vehicle he was driving? And did he live in it?" Murray pulled out her notebook.

Bob leaned against the door arch. The sounds of a ball game in the background told me that he was probably anxious to get back to his beer and chips. "He had a green van—wasn't a Volkswagen. Think it was an old Ford or something like that. I don't pay much attention. All I care about is getting my rent money."

"Is that why you evicted him?" Mur asked.

"Yeah. The S.O.B. stiffed me for a month's rent. Two hundred bucks. Told him to clear out or I'd take a baseball bat to his van."

I glanced at Murray. Two hundred dollars for parking a van on somebody's property for a month? No wonder Bob could afford to pay all of those fines.

Murray kept her eyes on him. "Have you seen Rusty since that time?"

He shook his head. "Nah, or he'd be in the hospital . . . unless he coughed up the money plus interest. Now, you got any more questions? My game's on and, frankly, you're a good looking woman, Detective, but I'd rather be watching b-ball."

Murray cleared her throat. "One more question. Do you keep records of the license plate numbers of people who stay here? I can't believe you don't take out some form of insurance on somebody who might pull out in the middle of the night. You have their license number, you can trace them."

Bob winked at her. "Sure, have to have some guarantee. But I cut a deal with folks who ask. Up-front fee to remain nameless, no questions asked."

"And I suppose that Rusty wanted to cut a deal?" Murray sighed, flipping her notebook shut and sliding it back into her pocket.

"You got it, sister." The door slammed shut in our faces.

"Well," I said, "that was abrupt." We turned and eased our way down the stairs. As we headed back to the SUV,

I glanced around the area. The energy here was muddled, confused. Shivering, suddenly wanting to get the hell out of here, I crawled into the driver's seat and fastened my seat belt. Murray followed suit and neither of us spoke until we were back on Ridge Rock Drive.

"Well, you have a vehicle description. Can't you run his name through the DMV's records and find out exactly what he's driving?"

She nodded. "Yeah, I'll do that after you drop me off. Well, at least we know he's been in the area within the past few months. Tad will want to hear this. Can you let me out at the station? I'll have one of the guys drive me home."

"Do you really feel up to Harlow's dinner party tomorrow night?" I asked. "If not, you don't have to come."

"Are you kidding? Em, you're getting married. I wouldn't miss it for the world." She paused. "I know this whole mess has interfered with your focus on your wedding, and I'm sorry. I can tell you're stressed."

"Yeah, well, Grandma M. didn't have a heart attack because of you, and Roy didn't show up because of you, and it wasn't your fault that Janette ruined Nanna's dress. Apparently I have Rose's crystal necklace to thank for that. Or maybe just the wedding disaster faerie. How come this always happens, Mur? Am I just a magnet for trouble?"

A long future suddenly unfolded before me, one filled with chaos and trouble and broken limbs and tripping over dead bodies. "I try not to whine or complain, but once in a while I'd like to take a break from all this crap. I hoped my wedding would be that break, but apparently life has other ideas."

"I know Harlow's already said this, but, Em, you're getting married to a wonderful man who adores you and the children. I know all of that other stuff would be nice, but doesn't having Joe make up for not having your grandmother's dress or the Barry Boys playing at the reception?"

I pulled up in front of the station and she jumped out.

Before she shut the door, I said, "Yeah, I know you're right. But sometimes the props matter, you know? It's okay. I'll find a dress, and we can use canned music . . . but . . . you know."

"I know, Em. I know." She slammed the door and waved.

As I pulled into traffic, I wished I could be more nonchalant. Murray had her priorities, but ceremony and pomp weren't among them. Harlow, however, would understand. Maybe I'd give her a call and cry on her shoulder again.

WHEN I WALKED through the door, I could smell the aroma of KFC floating out from the kitchen. I grinned. Apparently Joe hadn't been up to making dinner.

"I'm home!" I headed into the kitchen, ready to tear into a drumstick. Instead, I found Kip with his mouth full, and Randa weeping hysterically as Joe tried to calm her down. He looked up at me, helplessly.

"What on earth happened? What's wrong?" I rushed to the table. Joe stepped into the pantry, motioning to me to follow him. Nothing appeared to be wrong with Randa, so I followed him. We sidestepped Samantha and her brood, who were happily stuffing their faces. I frowned as I watched the four swelling bellies. They'd grown a little plump on their indoor-only lifestyle. It was about time we found a way to give them more exercise.

"What's going on? Why is she crying?"

He lowered his voice. "Apparently, Randa got into a fight today."

"Randa? A fight?" Incredulous, I peeked around the corner. She did look a little rough for the wear, now that I thought about it. "With who?"

Joe rolled his eyes. "Lori. I don't have the whole story but I got a call ten minutes ago. Lori's parents are on their way over. They don't sound happy."

Oh God. The Thomases were a rich-bitch couple displaced from Bellevue, the richest city in Washington

State. Both lawyers. Natalie—Lori's mother—had succumbed to a nervous breakdown and not even the promise
of a new fur coat could bring her out of it. When an old
friend of the family offered Luke a job at his firm in
Chiqetaw, the Thomases made the move, with Natalie
kicking and screaming.

"Wonderful, Natalie already considers our family hoi
polloi, and she torments that poor girl of hers all over a
few extra pounds." My dislike of the woman was hard to
hide.

Joe pulled me into his arms. "Before we go any further,
give me a kiss." He placed warm lips against mine and I
melted into the embrace, realizing that I wanted nothing
more than to forget all our worries and lose myself in a hot
frenzied sexcapade. I moaned gently, pushing my breasts
against his chest, sensing his arousal as my own flared.

"Shit," he whispered. "I want you. Now."

"That's what it's like, having kids. Their schedule, not
ours." I pulled away, but pressed one finger to his lips.
"Later, tonight. When the world is quiet and we have only
ourselves to think about."

He nodded. "Our time. It's a promise."

"Now, let me go talk to Randa before Natalie and Luke
get here." We rejoined the kids and I sat down next to my
daughter, who was still sniffling. She'd rarely ever cried
before hitting her teens, but puberty had struck hard on the
hormones.

"What happened, honey?"

She wiped her eyes and sullenly stared at the table. "I
got in a fight with Lori."

I tipped her head back, checking her for bruises. She
looked relatively unscathed. "Tell me what happened—
and remember, I know when you're lying." It was an ability I'd had since they were small and they knew it wasn't
a bluff.

With a swallow, she rubbed her nose and said, "I was
in the park across from the library when I saw Lori. She
came over to talk to me and I told her to leave me alone.

She kept saying that she and Gunner weren't dating, but I know they are—I saw them together! Lori wouldn't shut up and I got mad. I told her again to go away and when she wouldn't, I pushed her. She started to cry and . . . and . . ."

She was blushing. Whatever she'd done next was bad. I could see it in her eyes. "And what?"

Randa gulped. "I called her a fat hippo and told her that everybody laughed at her. I told her that—that—"

Speechless, I stared at my daughter. "You told her *what*?"

In a very small voice, she said, "I told her that everybody at school laughed at her and called her names behind her back, and that Gunner thought she was a pig. And then she hit me and I hit her back and the next thing I knew, Officer Wilson was holding us apart."

Joe spoke up. "Deacon brought her home. He took Lori home, too."

Unable to comprehend how nasty my daughter had been, I leaned back in my chair, my gaze fastened on her. She blinked, trying to look away but couldn't. I knew she was upset about Gunner and Lori, but the fact was she had no proof that the two were actually dating, and even if she did, her behavior had gone so far beyond acceptable that it took all my control not to slap her face.

"Kip, you listen to this, too. I want you to both remember what I'm about to tell you, because I'm going to say it once—and that's all it better take. Understand?"

Kip's eyes were wide. Randa seldom ever got into trouble like this, and I couldn't decide whether he was more impressed by her level of infraction or by my tone of voice. He nodded, his mouth full of jojos and chicken.

Randa's eyes fluttered and she bobbed her head. Barely.

"Randa? I said, *do you understand me*? I want an answer."

"Yes, ma'am," she said quietly.

"Okay, here it is. This sort of behavior, whether it be

toward a friend, a fellow student, or an adult—especially Joe, your father, or myself—is off limits. If it happens again, I won't hesitate to drag you to the bathroom and wash your mouth out with soap. And you'd better believe that I can—and will—do it. I didn't raise you to be trash-talking, snot-nose delinquents. I don't care how upset you are, there's no excuse for you to attack somebody else. Especially when you *don't even know the truth of a situation.*"

Randa blew her bangs away from her face, rolling her eyes, and I lost it. I grabbed her wrist and pulled her to her feet. "You have everything—a good home, pretty clothes, a mother who lets you follow your passion. You know what you want to do, and your teachers back you one-hundred percent. Have I ever once complained about outfitting you with six-hundred-dollar telescopes and that trip to space camp? Have I?" I leaned into her face, forcing her to look at me.

She swallowed hard and shook her head. "No, ma'am."

"Then why the hell have you turned into such a little drama queen? Lori's parents make her life hell. The poor kid has to work twice as hard for her grades as you do. She's not popular, she doesn't fit in at school, and you go and call her a *hippo* and make fun of her? I'm ashamed to be your mother right now."

"Em! Em—" Joe's voice was neutral, but I glanced in his eyes and realized that I'd broken my own boundaries. I meant everything I'd said, but I could have found a better way to approach the situation.

Randa sank into her chair. She began to shake and threw herself on the table, her head in her arms. Kip slowly put down his chicken and wiped his hands. He nervously glanced up at me, then patted her shoulder.

I slumped in the chair next to her. Why did I have to apologize when she'd been in the wrong? "Randa, listen to me. I'm sorry. I shouldn't have grabbed you like that. But you have to acknowledge your behavior and take responsibility for it."

She grunted something I couldn't catch. I reached out, probing her energy. Yes, she was upset at me, but I had the feeling that she more upset at herself. That cheered me a little. Maybe it wasn't too late to bring her to her senses.

"Randa, Lori's been your best friend for quite a while. You'll have a lot of boyfriends through the years, but a best buddy . . . you just can't replace them that easily. You haven't even listened to her side of the story, have you?" I gently but firmly rubbed her back. She stiffened at first, but then I felt her take a deep breath and let it out slowly.

I frowned. What was it going to take to bring her around? "Randa, you know what you did was wrong. The Thomases are coming over and they want to talk about the fight. I think they're bringing Lori."

Slowly, Randa raised her head. "They're coming here?"

"You'd better believe it. Can you imagine what happened when Deacon took Lori home? You know the way Mrs. Thomas acts toward her." Guilt. I didn't like using it, but if it jogged her conscience, I'd willingly play that game.

Her mouth twisted in a little *o* and she reached for a paper towel, blowing her nose. "I guess it was pretty bad."

I took the opportunity to put my arm around her shoulders. "Randa, listen to me. Lori and you have your differences, but do you really, truly believe that she'd do something like date Gunner when she knows how much it would hurt you?"

Randa contemplated her nails. After a few minutes, she shook her head. "Maybe I'm wrong. Maybe she was telling the truth."

"Why didn't you give her the chance to explain?" But I already knew. Randa's ego had been so hurt by Gunner's rejection that she was ready to believe anything and everything bad about him. She pretended to be okay, but under the surface, she'd probably been seething for months.

Taking a deep breath, she let it out slowly. "I don't

know. I guess I just wasn't thinking straight. Maybe I didn't want to believe her. Even if they were just studying together, it hurt to see him talk to her rather than to me."

The doorbell rang. I looked up at Joe. "Can you show them into the living room. And, honey—"

He flashed me a worried smile. "Yeah?"

"Welcome to my world."

Joe laughed then, gently. "I have news for you, Ms. O'Brien. I've been a part of your world since the day we met." With that, he ducked down the hallway to go answer the door.

I told Randa to wash her face and wait in the kitchen until I called her, then joined Joe. The Thomases, Lori in tow, were sitting in the living room. Natalie and Luke were so stiff that I wondered if they were wearing matching corsets. Lori was curled in the rocking chair, her face puffy and red.

My heart went out to the child—not only did her parents deride her, but her best friend had turned on her. On a whim, I closed my eyes and made a quick scan of her aura. Not a deceptive bone in her body. She was telling my daughter the truth.

I let out a long sigh. "I think Randa has something she wants to tell you, Lori. If you go in the kitchen, she's waiting." In my experience, once children truly realized that they'd done wrong, they'd work things out amongst themselves, if you left them alone.

Lori hesitated, but Randa must have been listening at the door because she pushed her way into the living room.

"I'm sorry. I believe you about Gunner. I know I hurt your feelings, and I'm sorry." My daughter's face was as blotchy as Lori's, and I knew how hard it was for her to admit she was wrong. "Will you come in the kitchen so we can talk?"

Lori glanced back at her parents, who gave her a stiff nod. The two girls slowly walked into the kitchen and I prayed that the truce would turn into a tearful reunion. I turned back to Natalie and Luke. Joe slid into place by my side.

"Well, this is awkward," Luke said. He looked bored and I had the feeling his wife had dragged him here over strenuous objections.

I shrugged. "It's not the best way to spend an evening, but I think the girls will resolve it. Randa realizes that her behavior was unacceptable and she will be punished for it."

"Well, having my daughter brought home by the police for brawling was certainly embarrassing. I was entertaining and my guests heard everything." Natalie pulled out a cigarette and prepared to light it.

"I'm sorry, you can't smoke in here. You'll have to go out to the driveway for that," I said.

"Oh for . . . I'll wait." She gave me a disgusted look and tucked it back in the engraved silver holder. "Now, I'll be the first to admit that Lori needs to lose weight, but really, a brawl? In a public park? That, I cannot forgive."

"Oh for God's sake, Natalie. They're kids. Kids fight." Luke stood up, stuffing his hands in his pockets. "I was carted home by the cops more than once and it never amounted to anything serious."

"You were a boy, and you didn't suffer from social in-eptitude. I'm afraid this is just going to make Lori clum-sier and more apt to lock herself in her room with a book when she should be out doing things and making friends."

Though she didn't exactly say it, I could tell that Natalie meant "other friends"—other than my Randa. I jumped to my feet. "I don't presume to tell you how to raise your daughter, but a little more kindness at home might give her the self-confidence she needs to reach out to others."

Luke glanced at his watch. "This is ridiculous. I have a business meeting in Seattle at six A.M. and I don't have time for bullshit like this. If the kids are good, then we're out of here." He glanced at me. "Tell your daughter she'd better get a hold of that temper," he said, heading for the door.

Natalie let out an indignant squeak but she gathered her purse. "I'm not going to stop Lori from visiting Randa. Lord knows she needs more friends, but, Emerald, if this happens again, I'll sue your butt off for damages, regardless of whether the girls make up. Tell Lori to be home in an hour." She stomped out, fluttering all the way to the door.

Joe and I followed them, waiting on the porch as they spun out of the driveway in their Jag, zooming off up the street.

"Good God, I feel sorry for that kid." I stared at the sky. The evening was clear and drowsy. Joe slid his arm around my waist and I rested my head against his arm. "It's been such a rough week. You getting shot and then my grandma, and Murray and the fire at Jimbo's. Now Randa . . ." With a sigh, I pulled the velvet pouch holding Rose's necklace out of my pocket. "Joe, I need to cleanse this. It's hexed."

He did a double take. "What?"

I told him what we'd found out about the Bride's Circlet. "So, I either find a way to cleanse it, or I'm getting rid of it."

He started to laugh. "Leave it to you, babe, to be given a jinxed necklace as a wedding gift. That's too perfect. Come on, let's go see how the girls are doing." Holding the door open, he guided me inside. We slipped down the hall, peeking around the corner. Lori and Randa were sitting at the table, talking intently. Randa glanced up and waved us in.

"Mom, you were so right. Lori was telling the truth and I acted like a total jerk." She reached out and grasped Lori's hand in hers, squeezing tightly. Lori's eyes were shining and I gathered that—whatever she'd said—Randa had managed to take the sting out of her insults.

"Good. I'm so glad you're friends again," I said. "Lemonade okay?" Randa nodded. As I poured three glasses and carried them to the table, Joe retreated to the living room, stating that girl talk wasn't his forte. I sat down next to Randa and she gave me a guilty smile.

"So, what really happened?" I asked, hoping I wasn't treading into thorny territory.

Lori blushed. "Gunner wants to get back together with her and was asking me if I'd talk to her for him."

Whoa. Talk about irony. I glanced at Miranda. "So, are you interested?"

She shrugged. "I don't know. I like Gunner, and I was really upset when he dumped me, but now I'm not sure how I feel. I'll think about it. Right now, I want to spend time with Lori. I've been a total ass."

I tapped her on the head. "Yes, you have been. And I'm glad you girls are friends again—very glad. But Randa, I have to punish you for your behavior."

Her face clouded over. "I know. How long am I grounded?"

I contemplated the situation. I could ground her, but I wanted her and Lori to actually spend time mending their friendship. Then it hit me. Something that she'd agonize over, something that might actually stick.

"I'm not going to ground you this time." Her face lit up but I held up my hand. "Not so fast. I want a two-thousand-word essay. It's to be well-thought-out, with no typos. I want a heartfelt analysis telling me why what you did was wrong."

Bingo. The look of panic on her face told me I'd hit pay dirt. She hated English with a passion, and this would both make her think about what she did and force her to use her brain on something else besides stars. She was starting high school in the fall, and she'd be subject to a lot of pressure. I wanted her to face her inner demons before she was called on by her peers to unleash them, though a little voice in the back of my mind warned me she might be on the receiving end of the taunts rather than dishing them out.

"Mom—"

"No whining, miss. You're getting off easy. Your essay is due in two weeks, and it better be good or I'll make you write it again. And Lori can tell you how she felt so you can use it in the essay, but you're not to let her help you write it. Got it?"

With a nod, she said, "Yes, ma'am. And . . . I really am sorry for what I did. It won't ever happen again."

"Okay then, off with you."

"Can Lori spend the night?"

I glanced at the plump, pretty young woman and once again wished that I could make life easier for her. "Would you like to stay, hon?" She nodded. "Okay, go call your folks and if they say it's all right, then it's fine with me."

As they took off for the living room, I slowly dragged myself up the stairs, wondering where Joe had gone to. I was exhausted, too tired to even think straight. When I opened the door to my bedroom, I heard running water and peeked in the bathroom. Joe had drawn me a tub full of bubbles, and he'd lit a dozen pale pink candles that formed a brilliant line along the vanity.

"Your bath awaits, madam." He bowed as I broke into a goofy grin.

"You always know just what I need." I pulled him to me and slid my arms around his waist.

He rubbed my back. "And I intend to go right on knowing just what you need. Take your bath. I checked on Kip and told him everything's okay. He's fine, so don't worry about him."

"I love you," I said, mumbling into his chest. "I love you so much."

Joe leaned down and planted a kiss on the top of my head. "That's all I want, Emerald. That's all I want."

Fourteen

⁎

EARLY THE NEXT morning, I headed out to look for a dress. Before I hit the shops, I decided to stop in and see how Cinnamon was doing. I pulled into my parking space by the Chintz 'n China and bustled into the shop.

Cinnamon's face lit up. "Emerald! You just here for a moment, or you planning on sticking around for a while?"

"Why?" I asked, glancing around. As usual, the shop looked checkerboard cheerful—clean, quiet, calm. Just the way I wanted it to be. "Anything happen I should know about?"

She shook her head. "No, but business picked up yesterday and we were run ragged. I haven't had a chance to do any restocking on the shelves." She put down the dust rag she was carrying and finished adjusting one of the teapots in our Summer Delights display—a colorful medley of fruit-shaped teacups surrounded by herbal tisanes and citrus-flavored teas. A pyramid of various marmalades rounded out the display.

"Well, I hate to disappoint you," I told her, adjusting one of the jars of marmalade, "but I'm just here for a few minutes. A couple more weeks and I'll be back for the long haul."

The shop bells rang and I looked up to find a woman in her mid-fifties, wearing black rectangular reading glasses on a chain, headed my way. Her hair was piled on her head in brilliant orange curls, and her blush and lipstick stood out against her overly tanned skin.

"Thank heavens I caught you!" She thrust out her hand.

"I'm Emerald O'Brien. May I help you?"

She ran her eyes over me and shook her head. "No, this won't do at all. You'll simply have to go home to change."

What the hell? "Excuse me? Who are you and what are you talking about?" Diplomacy was overrated.

She stopped short. "I thought you knew I'd be coming. I was sure I called ahead. Oh dear, I probably forgot!" Her laughter cascaded over me, leaving me even more confused. Had I somehow managed to wander into the wrong shop—one that looked like mine but wasn't? Was Rod Serling just around the corner, waiting to give his opening spiel?

"Again, you are—?" I tried again, letting the question dangle in my voice.

"I'm Ingrid Lindstrom, with the *Chiqetaw Town Crier*. I've come to interview you for the article and photo shoot about your upcoming nuptials with your handsome young hunk." She winked and I suddenly understood.

Ingrid Lindstrom, the gossipmonger from hell. More than once she'd insinuated bizarre things about me, all in an attempt to turn a clever phrase, but the woman couldn't write her way out of a paper box. Randa and I'd spent many a Saturday morning groaning over the latest installment in Ingrid's column.

I shook my head. "Thanks, Ingrid, but I'm not interested and I have no idea why you thought I would be."

Ingrid's face fell. "But Cathy said you might."

Cathy? Oh no! Please, oh please, I silently begged, don't let Ingrid Lindstrom and Cathy Sutton be in cahoots. One media hound was bad enough, but two? Unthinkable.

Cathy owed me a big one, and she'd stayed off my case for a while but I had a feeling debts of gratitude ran short with her.

"Well, Cathy was wrong."

After an awkward pause, Ingrid said, "How's Mr. Files doing? Has he recovered from the shooting? Rumor has it that your ex-husband left town—"

"My ex had nothing to do with the shooting," I said shortly. "And Joe is fine."

"Do the police have any idea of who shot him?" The woman was a pit bull. She wouldn't let up.

"I can't make any comments while the investigation is ongoing." I crossed my arms. Why had she picked today of all days to wander into the shop? Why not yesterday, when I wasn't around?

"Well, the whole town is interested in your wedding. Are you having a public reception?" Ingrid looked over the top of her glasses at me, as if she expected a personally engraved invitation.

The vision of several hundred bored townsfolk crashing my wedding scared the hell out of me. "No! It's private. Only friends and family allowed. I'm sorry, but I have to go," I said, as Maeve entered the shop.

Ingrid gaped at me as I pushed past her and overwhelmed Maeve with a hail of *hellos* and *come right with mes*.

At first bewildered, Maeve caught sight of Ingrid and her expression changed. She looped her arm through mine and veered toward the tearoom. Grateful for her quick pick-up, I let out a long sigh.

"Caught you in the nick of time, I see," Maeve whispered, strolling toward an empty table. The tearoom usually filled up around noon and stayed busy until about one, then business picked up in the late afternoon when shoppers were on their way home.

"Saved by the bell . . . the shop bells," I whispered back. As we settled at the table, I began to breathe a bit easier. "Thank you. I thought it was bad with Cathy, but Ingrid is dumber than a fence post."

Maeve grinned. "My dear, you haven't yet met some of my relatives, have you? Ah well, how are you this fine morning? And what are you doing at the shop? I thought you were taking a break before your wedding."

I buried my face in my hands. "I think I'm just going to just ask White Deer to marry us in the backyard, nekkid under the full moon."

"What's going on?" Maeve asked, rising to fetch herself a glass of iced limeade and a lemon bar.

Cinnamon had chosen a decidedly citrus theme for the day's goodies. "Lemonade Days" was chalked on the menu board, and almost everything for sale had something to do with the sunshine flavor. Lemon gazpacho, lemon bars, limeade, lemon-lime tea. I was relieved to see that she'd wisely included raspberry sparkling water and chocolate peanut butter chip cookies for those whose tastes prefer sweet instead of tart.

I poured myself a glass of sparkling water and chose a tuna on rye sandwich. My shop was one of the few places where I could eat fish. Randa had a life-threatening allergy, and having seafood in the house could be dangerous, so I only ate it when I was out at a restaurant. Even then, I brushed my teeth and rinsed my mouth before kissing her.

Once we were back at the table, I filled Maeve in on everything that had happened, starting with the crystal necklace and ending with the lack of a dress.

"I'm supposed to go shopping today but I'm overwhelmed. By now, all the dresses look the same to me." I sipped my drink.

Maeve gave me a soft smile. "All weddings are stressful, but you seem to be under assault." Her eyes lit up. "I know! Let me play faerie godmother. Go home and get your necklace and corset, then come over to my house."

I cocked my head to the side. "You wouldn't happen to have a dress for that corset, would you?"

She broke into a grin. "I might at that. My mother was about your size, and I have her dress. She wore it when she and my father were married on a faerie mound. I've kept it all these years—my sister didn't want anything to do with it since it wasn't the latest fashion, and I certainly couldn't wear it at my own wedding. I'm quite a bit taller and broader in the shoulders than Mother was. But I think it might fit you. If so, I'd like to see it used by someone truly in love, rather than let it molder away in my heirloom trunk."

A wedding dress worn on a faerie mound in Ireland? Couldn't ask for anything much more magical than that. And I trusted Maeve not to offer me something hideous— she had, after all, given me her mother's crystal ball.

"Maeve, you're a lifesaver. How about one-fifteen? Will that work?"

She nodded and glanced at her watch. "And now, I must be about my shopping. I've just finished shearing my llamas and I need a new part for my spinning wheel. I think this may be my last season with the creatures, though. I'm thinking of opening up a little herb shop. I'd sell plants in the spring and fall, as well as a variety of dried products during the rest of the year. Also, hand-woven wreaths and holiday boughs during Christmas."

"Running a shop is hard work," I said, thinking of how many hours I usually put in at the Chintz 'n China.

"Oh, I know. I'd limit my shop hours to three or four days a week, so it wouldn't be overtaxing. I've money enough not to worry about turning a wide profit. It just sounds like fun."

We agreed to meet at her house at one-thirty and she left with a quick TTFN and a wave. I bussed our dishes, then relieved Cinnamon at the counter for an hour or so, to give her time to restock the shelves. Thankfully, Ingrid was nowhere in sight. By twelve-thirty, the shelves were stocked and dusted, and I handed the reins back to Cinnamon. I brushed my teeth, then gathered my purse and keys. The scent of tea and spice and pastries spiraled up to fill my lungs and I longed to be back at work, following my simple routine that made me so happy.

MAEVE LIVED NEAR the southern border of Chiqetaw. She'd put hundreds of hours into landscaping her land, and her gardens burgeoned into an array of brilliantly colored plots. But there was something else, besides the roses and hydrangeas and rhododendrons that gave such life to the land here.

It was as if Maeve had tapped into the perfect place to nurture her spirit. She had the magic touch, every plant thrived here, and even the rock garden seemed to hum with life. Somehow, she'd forged a connection with the land that ran as deep as the tree roots. A sovereign bond existed between the soil and the woman, and the verdant foliage springing forth from the land stood as silent testimony to her dedication.

As I parked next to her modest pickup and slipped out from the driver's seat, the sharp tang of freshly mowed grass hit my nose and I breathed deep, letting the smell soothe my senses. Maeve's garden smelled *green*.

She met me at the front door. A strikingly tall woman, she would have been called "handsome" a hundred years ago. She had changed out of her linen pantsuit into a pair of tidy jeans, a button-down short-sleeved striped shirt, and a pair of gardening gloves.

"I was just finishing up with the nasturtiums. Come in."

I'd been to visit several times, but the custom-renovated rambler never ceased to amaze me, with its loft-high ceilings and multiple skylights that let through the brilliant blue of the afternoon sky. Maeve's decor tended toward minimalist Scandinavian. The first time I entered her living room, I'd expected to find old walnut antiques and lace curtains, but instead, found light birch furniture free of frills or carving, and sheer panels covering sleek blinds. The floors were hardwood, not a speck of carpeting entered her house, although each room contained a Persian rug.

I glanced at her dining table and saw a large white box sitting on it. She saw me looking at it and nodded.

"Come. Let me see your necklace while you examine the dress. If you like it, try it on for size."

I handed her the necklace and approached the box. It was old, but obviously well-cared for. I would expect nothing less from Maeve. I hesitantly reached out and touched the bow, then slowly pulled the ribbon away. At first I'd been excited about the possibility of wearing a wedding dress that had history to it. Now, I felt a sort of reverence.

"Maeve, do you think your mother would mind a stranger wearing her dress?" I asked as I lifted the top off the box.

"Not at all. Mother was a lot like me, and since she entrusted her gown to me, she obviously trusted my judgment." She held up the string of crystals. "You said these were made in Ireland?"

"Yes, though they ended up in Jamaica."

As she turned away, still holding the necklace, I carefully unfolded the acid-free paper in which the gown had been stored. A wash of ivory satin met my gaze, a sparkle of light flickered in the corner of my eye. Slowly, making certain my hands were clean, I lifted the gown from the box, gasping as it fell open to reveal its full beauty.

A vision in lace and satin, the dress was formfitting, with a low sweetheart-cut neckline. The ruched bodice had lace inserts across the waist and down the sides, framing the breasts, while pearl buttons fastened the dress in back. The sleeves were mildly poofy at the shoulder, tapering into points that would cover the top of the hand. The back of the skirt flowed into a rounded train that trailed a good yard behind the hemline.

No visible stains or tears marred the gown, and I found myself entranced, hoping with all my might that it would fit me. "Oh, Maeve, this is so beautiful Are you sure you want me trying it on? I just love it."

Maeve bustled over to me. She had placed my necklace into a vase. I couldn't see what else was in there, but right now my focus was on the vision in satin before me. "Of course I want you to try it on. You may use the guest room. There's a mirror in there. Let me help you; I don't think you'll be able to fasten those buttons by yourself."

She escorted me into the bedroom. I pulled my corset—the original one—out of my tote bag. "I hate to ask this, but can you help me lace this up?"

Maeve laughed. "Oh, dear. I remember the days when we were expected to wear girdles as a matter of course. My mother used to get so mad at me because I'd run off to school before she could make sure I had my proper foundation garments on."

I grinned at her. "My Nanna didn't believe in corsets or girdles. She said they restricted the rib cage." I slipped out of my skirt and top, suddenly wondering if I was making Maeve uncomfortable, but she just smiled with her usual nonplussed demeanor. "I have to take my bra off for this," I warned her.

"My dear, I am over sixty years old. I am a woman. Every day of my life, I see my own breasts. I doubt seeing yours will be much of a shock. Now, let's get you cinched into this thing."

Laughing, I slipped out of my bra and fit the corset around my waist. Maeve stood behind me and cinched the ribbons snug, but not so tight I couldn't breathe. I bent over and shuffled my boobs into place, and then arched my back. Unlike my five-hundred-dollar fiasco from the bridal shop, this corset actually fit. Of course, I'd paid good money to have it custom designed from a store in Seattle.

Maeve held up her mother's dress, unfastening the pearl buttons one by one. "My mother commissioned this from a seamstress in Dublin. The lace is Carrickmacross lace, which originated in Italy but developed a distinctive

Irish flavor as the lace weavers adapted it. The buttons are mother-of-pearl."

I rested my fingers on the material, shaking my head. "It's incredible. I can feel the love that went into this, and there's something else." I raised my head. "A wildness . . . ?"

She nodded, smiling. "You felt it, then. Faerie energy. I have pictures from my parents' wedding. The barrow was ringed by mushrooms and wildflowers—all natural. My mother's family has a long history with the Sidhe and she laid down the law with my father. They would marry on the mounds, or not at all."

"Wasn't that rather unusual?"

"Oh yes," Maeve said. "The priest was scandalized but my mother's family was so well-placed that the wedding proceeded without a hitch. That morning, Mother walked out by the mounds alone, her last day as a single woman. She told me, when I was a little girl and again when I was grown, that she heard a faint music playing from below her feet, but saw nothing. When they were married later that day, a doe followed by a buck raced past."

She held out the dress. "There now, slip this on and let's see if it fits."

I stepped into it and held my breath as I slid my arms into the sleeves. At first, I thought it would be too tight but suddenly, there seemed to be plenty of room. I felt like a princess as she began to button me up.

"Oh, Maeve," I whispered, smoothing the satin skirt. The dress accentuated every curve of my body in all the right ways. As she turned me around to face the mirror, I gasped. A shimmer seemed to hover around me, whether it was the satin glowing in the afternoon light or just a trick of my eyes, I couldn't tell.

"Don't forget the veil," she said, lifting out a length of matching lace that was attached to a golden barrette. I thought briefly of Nanna's veil, but this one matched the dress. Inhaling deeply, I let go of the old vision and accepted the new. Maeve fastened the veil on my head and I froze, unable to believe that the woman in the mirror was truly me. "There now, that's better than a store-bought gown, don't you think?"

I could only nod, unable to speak. After a few minutes, I stammered out, "Please tell me you mean it, that I can wear this dress. I love it."

"It might have been made for you, my dear. And I'm sure Miranda will look just as lovely in it when her wedding day arrives." Maeve arranged the train as I realized what she'd said.

"Miranda? But you can't mean—"

Maeve gently grasped me by the shoulders. "Emerald, what am I going to do with this dress? I've already had the only wedding I'll ever have and I could never fit into this even if I were to remarry. When my husband died, I knew that he was the only man I could ever tie my heart to. My sister and her family don't care about heirlooms. If I keep this, it will sit in the closet until the day I die and then be carted off to some vintage thrift store to be bought by strangers."

I saw her point. What was the use of keeping heirlooms if they sat in the closet, gathering dust and shadows?

"And you fill it out so beautifully," she continued. "I couldn't think of asking for it back. You have a daughter who—and I guarantee this—will want to wear it when she gets married. I know these things sometimes," she added. "So, consider this my wedding gift to you."

Stunned, I searched for the proper words, but "thank you" seemed so inadequate. "Maeve, I don't know how—"

"Then don't try. I already know what you're trying to say, so there's no need. Now then, since this fits, let's get this off you." She bustled around back, unbuttoning the dress and untying my corset. While I changed back into my regular clothes, she shook out the gown and gently placed it on a padded hanger. "There, if there are any wrinkles they'll release by the day of your wedding."

As we returned to the living room, I felt a renewed sense of optimism. Everything would work itself out. I wandered over to the plate-glass window that overlooked Maeve's backyard. A bevy of jays had taken over one of the fir trees and their shrieks echoed through the golden light of afternoon.

Maeve reached in the vase that I now saw was filled with water. She pulled out the crystal necklace and carefully wiped it off with a soft cotton cloth. "Here now, this should be cleansed."

I peeked in the vase. The water looked clear. "What's that?"

She gave me a secretive smile. "Holy water with a little lavender and lemon essence added."

Holy water? She had to be kidding. "Where on earth did you get hold of holy water?"

"Oh dear, not from a church. I have one of my cousins send me water from a sacred well near Kildare. They live a few kilometers away from it, and twice a year I ask them to nip down and snooker me a few gallons, then carefully pack them and send them air express. I keep a fountain out back and each day, I add a quarter cup of the well water to it. I think it does the birds good," she added, touching her finger to her temple.

I held the necklace lightly, closing my eyes, keying in on its energy. For some reason, I hadn't picked up on the chaos attached to it, but now I could sense a clarity in the crystals that hadn't been there before. It felt almost . . . blessed.

"Maeve, what would I do without you? You're like some guardian angel. In some ways, you remind me of a younger version of my Nanna."

"Well, that's a compliment, but if I weren't here, someone else would be. Sometimes, the powers that be find it in their heart to throw us a safety net." She glanced at the clock. "And now, my dear, I have work to do. I don't want to rush you out but, I promised a flat of peppermint seedlings to my neighbor and I've barely started on them." As she walked me to the door, she asked, "Would you rather leave the dress here, or take it with you?"

I thought about it. No sense tempting fate. The dress felt safe at Maeve's. "Leave it here for now," I said, stepping out into the late afternoon. I gave her a hug and slipped into my SUV. Maeve was right. The universe could be a tough taskmistress, but sometimes she came through.

WE DRESSED FOR dinner with care. Harlow was going to a lot of trouble and when she said formal, she meant it. Joe wore a lightweight suit jacket and a pair of khakis. Randa had chosen a sky blue sundress, and Kip looked spiffy in his dress shorts and new polo shirt. I gazed at them. My family. My comforters, and my responsibility.

I showered and dressed in a little black number that was formal enough for dinner, yet cool enough for a summer evening. I hesitated for a moment but, trusting in Maeve's sacred well water, fastened Rose's necklace around my throat. Sometimes, the universe required a leap of faith.

As I changed out my purse to a velvet clutch bag, I felt someone in the room next to me. I looked up to find Nanna watching me. She walked over and laid a gentle hand on my shoulder. It was only a whisper—a shift in the air currents, but it was enough to make me tear up.

"I miss you, Nanna," I said. "I wish you could be at my wedding. I'm so happy with Joe."

She beamed, then crooked her finger and glided over to the closet in which I kept her trunk and pointed to it.

"There's something in there you want me to see?" I pulled out the trunk and, sitting on the floor, lifted the lid. I couldn't imagine what she wanted me to look at, I'd been through the trunk time and again. And yet, something called to me. I sifted through the charms until I came to a pair of matching Algiz runes.

The rune of protection, Algiz looked similar to a three-pronged fork. I had several of the runes throughout the house, guarding the doors alongside the security system and locks, but I didn't recall ever seeing these. They were about two inches long, marcasite, with tiny garnets inlaid at the base. Jewelry hooks on the top indicated they were intended to be used as pendants.

I looked up at Nanna. "Do you want me to wear one of these?" Did I need protection? Was she worried about me?

She nodded, then gently lifted her fingers to brush the center of my forehead. I closed my eyes as the breeze of her ghostly fingers ruffled through my hair. The image of Murray flooded my mind.

"Murray! You want me to give the other to Murray?"

Nanna stepped back, nodding gently. And then, lifting her fingers to her lips, she blew me a kiss and vanished.

I stared at the charms in my hand. I knew that I hadn't seen them in the trunk before and yet . . . and yet . . . perhaps I had. Stranger things in my life had happened, and I'd learned to pay attention when they did. I slid both charms onto black ribbons and dropped one in my purse. The other I slipped around my neck, after taking off the crystal choker.

Joe's voice echoed up the stairs. "Get your buns in gear, babe. We have to put gas in the car before we head out for Harlow's."

One last look in the mirror. Something about my eyes caught my attention. They were almost glowing. Emerald to match my name, they glimmered in the evening light that filtered in through the window. Puzzled, and feeling oddly aware, I headed down the stairs.

WE TOOK THE shortcut to Harlow's through Birchwood Ravine. The blackberries were tiny green nubs on the bushes, but in a couple months, the ravine would be overgrown with plump, ripe fruit, as well as the occasional bear or cougar that wandered through the area. As we turned onto Wildflower Drive, leading to Harlow's house, I closed my eyes and leaned my head against the

seat. This was how it was going to be from now on. Joe
and me and the kids. A complete family. My life felt fuller,
less my own and yet somehow expanded.

Harlow met us at the door. "You look so nice," she
said. She was wearing a short pink sundress and a pair of
silver strappy sandals. I wondered what it would be like to
have legs that went on forever.

Horvald and Ida were there, as well as Jimbo and
Murray, and White Deer and Maeve. Joe and the kids
and I completed the guest list. While Kip and Miranda
went with Lily, the nanny, to visit Eileen, the rest of us
settled in the living room with cocktails. James was
playing bartender.

I accepted a wine spritzer and motioned Murray to one
side. "I have something for you. Nanna told me to give it
to you. I wouldn't have even known it was in the trunk if
she hadn't led me to it." I pulled out the Algiz rune pendant and handed it to her.

She weighed it in her hand, then looked at me. "You
think I'm in danger."

"I know it," I said, my heart sinking. I'd been able to
forestall my worry for a while with the joy over actually
knowing I had a wedding dress, but now it hit full force
again.

Murray slipped it over her head. "I have two pieces of
news—one good, and one not so good."

"Give me the good news first," I said, wanting to for-
tify myself.

"We caught Janette. She tried to slip back into town
and another irate bride-to-be who lost her dress saw her
and called the cops. You'll be able to pick up your dress
next week from Evidence."

A tingle of satisfaction ran through me. It wasn't nice
to be happy at others' misfortunes, but Janette earned it.
"Great, I won't have to throw a hex on her. What's the bad
news?"

"Tad officially found out that Rusty's in the area, but
we can't pinpoint his location. He's been seen in a few

shops, but nobody seems to know where he's staying. We've put out an APB on him. Who knows if it will do any good?"

"Hey, what are you two talking about? Get over here," James called out from the bar.

We drifted back to join the others. The rest of the evening went smoothly and it was such comfort to be in the company of friends without some tragedy intervening. We had rack of lamb and asparagus, sorbet, fruit and cheese for dessert, and I told everyone about Maeve coming to my rescue with the dress and necklace. We were gearing up to leave when Murray's cell phone rang. She moved off to the side for a moment, then hurried back.

"That was dispatch. I'm needed on a call. There's been more trouble out at the old Catlan house."

"Are you going alone?" Jimbo asked.

She shook her head. "Dispatch said one of the guys will meet me there. Probably just teenagers partying again. Jimmy, can you grab a ride home with someone?"

He gave her a quick peck on the cheek. "Sure thing. Be careful. Call if you're going to be late."

As she wheeled out of the drive, I felt a flicker of apprehension, but she was wearing the necklace. It should give her some measure of protection. The evening wound down around shortly thereafter and we headed for home.

Fifteen

❧

THE GROUND WAS soggy beneath my feet and I was having a hard time keeping my balance as I jogged through the dark woods. Overhead, the moon was dark, in her secretive place where she went each month to hide and grow strong and full again. Stars glistened in the cloudless tapestry, and the soft hooting of owls signaled the beginning of the night's hunt.

I wasn't sure where I was going or how I had gotten here, but I knew that I couldn't stop. I had to keep running, to find what had been stolen from me. Vines coiled menacingly from the forest, and tree roots crept to trip me. I fell, rose to my feet, then fell again. Bruised and aching from the dampness of the night, I paused, trying to catch my breath.

Something tugged at the back of my mind and I fought to recall it. I knew it was important but no matter how I tried, the memory disappeared before I could grasp onto it. If I could just catch a glimpse of what it concerned . . .

The kids? I reached out, trying to find them in the forest, but they weren't there and the sense that they were snug in their beds reassured me. Joe? This time I sensed a restlessness, but no threat of danger. He was tossing and turning in his sleep. Likewise, when I searched for Samantha and her kittens, the threads came back—feline contentment, full stomachs and a warm soft spot in which to slumber.

Reassured that my family wasn't in danger, I turned back to the forest. How had I gotten here? I couldn't remember. Had I come with someone? Had I driven here in my sleep?

Asleep . . . that rang a bell. I quickly scanned my surroundings. While the woods surrounding me looked like the typical Northwest forest should, there were little things . . . I squinted, staring at the trees, and then realized that I could see faces in them. Swirls in the bark, eyes gleaming from dark hollows. I was seeing their true nature, their spirit and essence that eluded most mortals during waking consciousness.

Which meant . . .

. . . I was asleep. Bingo! A bell chimed in the back of my mind. I was sleeping, but this dream wasn't just any run-of-the-mill dream. No, I knew instantly that I was lucid dreaming, that I was aware and out on the astral while my body remained safely at home.

So, why had I come here? I'd occasionally found myself wandering the astral, out for a stroll, during my dreams, but this time felt different. A sense of urgency plagued me, as if there were something I must discover.

As I turned, looking for some sign to guide me, a noise to my right startled me. The foliage pulled back, revealing a path opening up through the trees and I followed it, winding through a place of long moss and towering firs. And then as the trail grew rougher, I began to see webs stringing from branch to branch, a canopy of silk overhead. I paused, listening. The rustle of scurrying insects sent a shiver up my back. No longer neutral, the forest had suddenly become ominous and threatening.

A closer look at the webs revealed spiders, thousands of them—with great bloated bellies and stiffly jointed legs, scuttling along the silken strands. I was standing beneath a colony of arachnids, and terror kicked in as I broke into a frenzied run. Dodging branch and bough, I prayed they wouldn't fall on me, that I wouldn't trip and land in one of their webs.

Panting, I skirted root and rock, as the woods broke open into a meadow. I came to a screeching halt as, once again, I saw the quicksand and bog that I'd come to recognize as the twisted labyrinth of Rusty's mind.

Hell! Had I somehow linked with him in my sleep? I wanted to wake up, to break the connection, but something inside whispered, "No, go on."

I slowed my pace, carefully navigating the treacherous terrain. And there, under the darkening moon, I saw them. Rusty and Murray. He had chained her to a tree and was standing guard over her, a large knife in his hand. I stumbled forward as he gazed at Murray, his eyes shining like glacial floes reflecting in the starlight.

"Let her go. She doesn't love you," I pleaded, but he didn't seem to hear me. Mur was crying silently; but as she looked up, our eyes met and she gasped. A warmth burned at my chest and at first I thought Rusty had attacked me with some sort of psychic blast, but then I saw that the garnet in my rune pendant was glowing. I glanced back at Mur. Her pendant was doing the same. We were linked by the runes.

"Help me. Emerald, please help me." Murray's scream echoed through the night.

"I'll save you. I promise I'll find you," I cried out, but my words were like a whisper on the wind.

Rusty laughed aloud as he reached out to stroke her cheek. "How can she help you when she doesn't even know you're gone?" And then, in the blink of an eye, they vanished and I was alone in the silent woods.

"EM, EM! WAKE up. You're having a nightmare."

I slammed back into my body as Joe woke me out of

my slumber. At first I couldn't remember what I'd been dreaming about and then everything flooded back. I scrambled out of bed.

"What's going on?" Joe asked, switching on the light and sitting up. "You look freaked."

Panicking, I looked down at the rune hanging around my neck. The garnet was glowing. I grabbed the phone, punching 1 on the speed dial. "I have to call Jimbo!"

"Why? What's wrong?" Joe looked thoroughly confused by now.

"Murray's in danger," I said, waiting impatiently as Murray's line rang.

"Anna, is that you?" Jimbo's breathless voice came over the phone and my heart sunk. It hadn't been a dream.

"It's me, Emerald. Murray's in danger. I just had a nightmare about her."

"She never came home. I just got off the phone with the cops and they said that Dispatch never called her. They never logged a complaint about the Catlan house. He got her, Em. That damned bastard got her."

"Are the cops out at Catlan's? If he told her to meet him there, then you can bet that's where he grabbed her." I was already motioning for Joe to hand me a pair of jeans and a sweater.

"Yeah, I'm headed out to meet Deacon. I was grabbing my keys when you called."

"I'm going with you. I gave her a necklace and I have one that matches it. The runes link us. In my dreams, my pendant led me to her."

Joe had already slid into his jeans, and he looked ready to come with us, but I shook my head and mouthed, "You have to stay with the kids."

"I'll pick you up in ten minutes," Jimbo said. "Wear thick clothing. We may need it."

The phone went dead and I dropped it on the bed and turned to Joe. "Rusty tricked Murray. He's got her. I saw them in my dream. This can only lead to bad, Joe. Once he realizes that she won't stay with him willingly, once he sees that she really, truly wants nothing to do with him, he'll kill her. I'm going with Jimbo. We're meeting Deacon, though, so the cops will be there."

Joe stared at me for a moment, then nodded without putting up a fight. "You think you can find her using that, right?" He pointed to the necklace. "I know you have to go. I'll watch the kids, but promise me you'll be careful. And take your cell."

"I will, but don't you dare call me. If we find him, I don't want the phone alerting him that we're there." That had happened before to me and almost cost me my life.

"What do you need to take with you?" Joe pulled on a T-shirt.

I layered my clothing, pulling on a light tank, then a flannel camping shirt, and, lastly, a warm hooded sweatshirt. "Flashlight, spare batteries, the switchblade Jimbo gave me, cell phone, some water, and a couple candy bars." To be honest, I had no idea what I'd need, but that seemed like a logical list.

Joe raced downstairs to pull it together while I jammed my feet into my Keds and tied them in a double knot. No tripping over untied shoelaces for me. By the time I made it downstairs, he had a lightweight fanny pack waiting for me. It even had a place to clip on the water bottle. I fastened it around my waist as Jimbo pulled into the driveway, his truck rumbling like a freight train.

He ran up on the porch. "Damn it, now's when I need my chopper. My truck's so loud it'll wake the dead."

I grabbed my keys from the desk. "The boys at the enclave gave me a bike—we can use that," I said, handing them to him. Joe grabbed the helmets out of the closet for us.

"You got it, babe," Jimbo said, heading back down the steps.

Turning to Joe, I paused. This was my love, my other half, the key to my heart. "I'll be safe. I know I will. Please don't worry. Just watch the kids and pray that we find her in time. Rusty is mad, Joe. He's totally, utterly mad."

Joe pulled me to him and kissed me so long and deep that I couldn't breathe. "You'd better keep your promise. Get moving. Go save her."

I raced down the stairs and climbed on back of the bike, jamming on my helmet. Jimbo started the bike and it purred to life. Within moments, we were headed into the darkening night.

THE OLD CATLAN place was about four miles outside of town on a back road leading toward Mount Baker. The Catlans had owned a substantial property but most of it had been subdivided through the years as the family dwindled. What was left was an abandoned house, a couple of barns, and about two acres of scrub. Local teenagers used it for parties, and the fire department was constantly worried that they'd torch the place someday, but so far, the remaining Catlans hadn't seen fit to remedy the problem.

Jimbo barreled along at sixty miles an hour over roads so bumpy that I braced myself against his back in order to ward off whiplash. Holding tight to his waist, I leaned into the turn as we swerved into the driveway. Deacon and Sandy were already there. As we climbed off the bike, they motioned us over.

"They've been here!" Deacon led us to an area where they'd set up a spotlight. It was cordoned off with crime tape. Murray's car was there, the driver's door still open. A few feet away, Murray's purse lay on the ground, its contents scattered across the hardened dirt. Her gun was there, gleaming under the stars.

"Was it Rusty?" I asked, my hand on Jimbo's arm to steady him. He'd seen the purse and gun, and now his face had drained of color and he looked almost ready to faint.

Deacon glanced at Jimbo, as if assessing his state of

mind. "We already found a print on the purse. Yeah, it's him. You guys nailed it on the head."

"I'll kill him," Jimbo said, so softly I almost didn't catch it at first. "I'll kill him and feed his heart to the buzzards."

Ignoring him, I turned back to Deacon. "Do you know where he took her?"

Deacon shook his head. "Not yet. This was the perfect place for a setup. He lured her out here and somehow managed to take her off guard. The place is abandoned and isolated. There have been several reports over the past few weeks of trouble here that didn't pan out, so I can see why the detective would have believed that it was just another crank call but she had to check it out. I wonder if Rusty made the others to build up a pattern."

"What the fuck are you doing standing around here? We have to find her before that S.O.B. hurts her!" Jimbo's rage shook the air. He was hopeless and helpless and terrified. I tried to calm him down, but he was having none of that. "Can't you even keep your own people safe? The cops in this town are a joke. No wonder Anna bitches so much about the department."

"We know he's driving a green van—an older model. Ford. We've got APBs out all over the county, and the state patrol has set up roadblocks on all the main arterials between here and Bellingham. He won't slip past us," Deacon said, but I could hear the uncertainty in his voice.

"Where's Bonner?" I asked.

"He's fielding operations from the station. I've got search teams combing the property, and we're going through all this evidence to see if there are any leads." Deacon glanced over at Murray's purse and back at Jimbo. "Hey, man, I'm sorry. We're doing everything we can. Detective Murray's resourceful. You know she's going to be fighting him."

Jimbo stared at him, then stomped away without a word. Deacon glanced over at me. "Take him home, Emerald. Somebody should be waiting by the phone in case he calls with a ransom demand."

"He's not a kidnapper in the traditional sense of the word and you know it, Deacon. He wanted Murray and now he's got her. He's not going to be asking for money." I stared him down until he ducked his head.

"I know, I know, but there's nothing you can do here, and I don't want Jimbo going off the handle and interrupting our investigation. You know perfectly well it's not a good idea to have the family on hand during times like this. What if . . ." He paused, then lowered his voice. "What if we find . . . her? What if we find her and she's not in good shape? He doesn't need to be here to see it. Do you understand?"

And then I did understand. Deacon didn't hold a lot of hope. He knew what they were up against, and he didn't have a clue as to where Rusty had taken her. In a flash, I knew what he was thinking.

"You think he's going to kill her, don't you?" I said, whispering.

Deacon shrugged, but the look on his face told me everything I was afraid to hear. "Take Jimbo home, Emerald. For both your sakes."

There was nothing else for me to say. I knew she was alive, knew there was a chance to save her, but first we had to know where to look. I walked over to Jimbo. "They want us to go home and wait, in case she calls."

"White Deer's already waiting by the phone. And just how is Anna going to call? Her fucking cell is over there on the ground!" Jimbo let out a low growl. "O'Brien, I need you to find her. I know you can do it. White Deer keeps saying you and Anna have linked souls. Can't you use that connection to find out where he took her?" He sounded desperate.

I stared at the moonless sky. Murray was more than my best friend. She was family. She and I were sisters in so many ways and no matter how close Rose and I ever became, there was no way we'd ever connect on the same level that Mur and I did.

"Come on, let's get away from here and I'll do my best. I can't promise, but maybe . . ." I didn't want to tell him that Deacon's pessimism might interfere with my search. The last thing Jimbo needed was to know that Murray's coworkers thought she might be dead. I turned back to Deacon. "Give me your number. We're heading out."

I punched his cell number into my phone and then jogged over to the bike. Deacon waved, one short shake of the hand.

BEFORE WE HIT the road, I knelt on the ground to link to the earth mana. When I felt steady enough, I clasped my rune pendant in my hand and closed my eyes. I focused my thoughts on Murray, on her regal countenance, her unquestionable sense of honor.

As I reached deep into my mind for the threads that connected us, I made the leap onto the astral. There—in front of me—a golden cord of friendship and an oath that bound us together, that had stood the test of time. I reached down to pick it up and felt the energy flowing through it. Both ways.

Murray was still alive.

Feeling reassured, I began to trace the cord. I followed it through the mist, through the fog to the edge of a tall wood. This time, I knew the forest wasn't a metaphor. She was trapped in the woods with Rusty. But where? Every which way we turned, trees surrounded us. We weren't in a city, Chiqetaw existed on the edge of the wilderness. Rusty could have her tied up anywhere.

And then, the lines of a poem skittered through my thoughts.

> *Every time I think of you, I lose another night of*
> *   sleep,*
> *I pray that you will come to me and be my own to*
> *   keep.*
> *I would bring you to my home, to my side to stay,*
> *In the mountains by a lake, we will find our way.*

*I wish on every falling star, though my heart, it
    breaks,
I will have you for my own, or life itself forsake.*

Holy hell, the card! The card he'd sent her with the ring! The picture on the front told me everything I needed to know.

"I know where he took her," I shouted, breaking out of trance. "I know where they are."

Jimbo grabbed my arm—gently—and looked deep into my eyes. "Where?"

"Icicle Lake Falls. The campground next to the lake. That's where he took her." As I looked down at the pendant, the garnet began to glow red. "We've got to go in by way of the bridge," I said.

Jimbo jumped on the bike. "Get on," he said, flooring it.

"What about the cops? Shouldn't we tell them?"

"We'll call them when we get there—they won't go out there just because you tell them your necklace told you where she's at."

He had a point. Deacon was good about listening to my hunches, but even he might balk at following advice from a piece of jewelry. If we went out there and found nothing, we'd be wasting their time—and possibly putting Murray in danger by diverting their attention. On the other hand, I knew I was right. She had to be at the lake. Once we found her, we'd call Deacon. I climbed on behind Jimbo and wrapped my arms around his waist.

"I'm ready."

As we headed into the darkness, I did my best to hold on tight to that golden cord that connected Murray to me. Please, I thought. Please know that we're coming to get you. Please be strong. Please, don't die before we can find you. But the only answer I received was a drowsy flicker, and in the depths of my heart, I wasn't sure whether we'd make it in time.

Sixteen

❖

WE HEADED FOR Icicle Lake Falls campground. Jimbo focused on the road, while I continued to focus on that thin thread through which I might be able to save my best friend. Over the months, my abilities had grown and strengthened, but that was no guarantee I'd be able to take on Rusty. He knew the woods like the back of his hand. Perhaps I could call upon the the energy of the woods to give us an advantage.

"Stop the bike for a second," I shouted. Unquestioning, Jimbo pulled over to the side and turned off the engine. "I'll be right back. Wait here for me."

The night air was chilly, just on the edge of damp. Less than three yards away from the road, the trees took over, and I cautiously hopped across the shallow culvert separating the forest from the highway. As soon as I stepped into the boundary of the forest, I could feel the heartbeat of the land rise to meet my own.

I grounded myself firmly, anchoring myself in the earth mana that spiraled up to embrace me. A greenish glow emanated from the trees, from the bushes, from the grass beneath my feet. I reached out with my hand, lightly

touching the edge of the light. It gently flickered at my
fingers and I sucked it into my body, absorbing it like a
sponge, letting it permeate my soul.

The energy buoyed me up, blending with my own life
force as the essence of crystal and rock, of stone and bone
woven together to form a foundation from which I could
work. This was the strength and core of the earth, of all
that was tangible. Heady with the life-sustaining shimmer,
I stepped onto the astral, content that my body was safe
where I stood.

Once again standing amidst the etheric fog, I took hold
of the energy and began to create a shield that would
strengthen and protect me. A thought occurred to me and
I reached out to include Jimbo in the shelter of my charm.
When I was satisfied that it would hold strong, I broke out
of trance and glanced around me. My sight seemed to be
heightened. I could see shapes in the darkness where before there had only been murky shadow. A titter of laughter startled me, but it was fleeting, like the chime of bells
on the wind.

Jimbo watched me closely as I climbed back on the
bike. "You look different," he said.

"I know. I've done what I can to prevent Rusty from
sensing our approach."

Jimbo grunted, but said nothing as we sped along the
road leading to the campground. When we were near
the bridge, he eased the bike off the road and killed the
ignition.

"How do we find them?" he asked.

"If my intuition is right, they'll be near the bridge," I
said. "We'd better go on foot from here. We don't want
the noise of the engine to warn him that we're on his
trail."

"Good thinking," Jimbo said. "I know the basic layout
of this campground, I come here to fish now and then. The
campsites start on the other side of the bridge."

I glanced at my pendant. The garnet was shining just
enough to tell me we were near. "Let's get going."

As we hoofed it up the road, I thought about the last time Jimbo and I'd crept through the woods. He'd helped me rescue my son, and in doing so, we'd forged a bond. Now, once again, we were plowing through the darkness together, in pursuit of someone *he* loved.

A roaring sound alerted me to the fact that we were near the water. Icicle Falls thundered into the lake, feeding several streams that filtered out from the icy flow. The bridge ran over the mouth of the largest fork. As we approached the covered overpass, my chest grew warmer. The garnet was gleaming.

"We're getting closer," I whispered to Jimbo.

He slowly stepped up on the bridge and then paused, motioning for me to join him. As I peered over the side, the starlight illuminated the foaming water below. On a spit next to the stream, I was able to make out the shape of a van. *Rusty.*

"How did he get down there?" I said in a low voice.

Jimbo leaned down and cupped his hand around my ear. "Ten to one he's been staying out here. I bet he scoped out all the access roads and fire roads in the campground. We don't have time to go hunting for the trail, though, and I've never taken a vehicle down to a spit like that. I usually just wade over from one of the official campsites or climb down the side of the ravine."

"Do you think he knows we're here?"

Jimbo watched him for a moment. "No, I think the roar of the falls covered up the sound of the bike."

I bit my lip. Jimbo was right. The thunder of the falls and gurgling currents of the lake and streams would easily swallow up any noise from the bike. The real trick lay in getting down the hill unnoticed.

"Well, we don't have much of a choice," I said after a moment. As much as I didn't want to think about it, we were going to have to go over the edge and hope we didn't trip or lose our footing. "We have to go down that ravine."

Jimbo gave me a short nod, then began searching along the rim of the road on the other side of the bridge. I moved back away from the bridge and flipped open my cell phone. After three rings, Deacon picked up.

"We found them. We're out at Icicle Lake Falls campground. Rusty's got his van down by the stream that flows under the covered bridge. Get out here, and bring an ambulance just in case."

"Don't do anything—wait for us to get there," Deacon said. But he knew we were already committed because before he hung up, he added, "Emerald, if you insist on going after them, don't let Jimbo kill the guy. And be careful."

I flipped my phone shut and jogged over to Jimbo's side. "Police are on the way, but it's going to take them a little while to get out here."

He pointed out a slope that dipped over the bank and I peeked over the side. If we were going to make it down the hill in one piece, this would be our safest bet. From what I could tell, the gradient was at its easiest decline here—at least we'd have a chance. My stomach lurched at the thought, but I knew that this was our only option.

Jimbo slowly stepped over the lip, motioning for me to swing in behind him. Trusting on faith, I followed. Slowly we worked our way down, moving sideways to prevent vertigo, bracing each step as we leaned in toward the side of the hill. Thick stands of huckleberry and fern covered the grade, and I prayed that we wouldn't run into any stinging nettle or I'd be out of commission and on my way to the hospital.

Jimbo stopped abruptly, holding up his hand. I waited as he tested his footing in several directions. After a moment, he made up his mind and we shifted to the right about two yards and continued our descent.

By now, my calves were screaming from the tension that ricocheted through my body. I shifted, trying to ease the muscles, but must have set my foot down wrong because the rocky incline on which I stood started to slide. Managing to keep from shouting, I flailed, teetering as my balance suddenly took exit, stage left. Jimbo caught me just before I went rolling down the hill.

"Sorry . . . sorry." I tried to keep my voice low.

"Jeezus, be careful, woman. You okay?"

"Yeah, I just lost my balance."

"Fine. Now put a lid on it. We're almost to the bottom."

A few more yards and we were peering out onto a gentle rocky slope leading down to the edge of the stream. We were within running distance of the van, and now we could see that the man standing beside it was staring at the stream as if he were lost in thought.

A sudden movement broke my concentration. Some little animal raced out of the bushes and across my Keds, but it was enough to startle me and my carefully woven shield crumbled, leaving me open and clear. Rusty whirled around and I could hear his laughter echoing through the campground.

That was all it took. Jimbo broke into a dead run, straight for Rusty, who hesitated for a fraction of a second, then took off the other way. I could feel Rusty's confusion. He hadn't been prepared for our appearance.

I scrambled up and skidded my way down the last of the slope, racing over to the van, where I yanked open the back door. The interior light went on, flooding the area and blinding me. I blinked. There, bound and gagged on the floor, lay Murray.

I fumbled in my fanny pack and pulled out my switchblade, slicing through the ropes that bound her. "Murray! Murray? Can you hear me?"

I tried to pull her into a sitting position but it was obvious that she'd been drugged. Making sure she was lying on her side so that she didn't choke, I jumped back out of the van and looked around for Jimbo and Rusty. They were a few yards away, near the water, in a fight to the death.

Light on his feet, Rusty danced around Jimbo, managing to knock him to the ground. Standing over the biker's body, knife in hand, Rusty raised the blade. Jimbo tried to scramble up, but I could see he wasn't going to make it in time. If I didn't do something *now*, Jimbo was toast.

I raced toward them, closing the distance with only a few steps. Focused on Jimbo, Rusty didn't notice me until I was right behind him and then it was too late. I lunged, throwing my weight against him. Rusty shouted as we tipped forward with me clinging to his back.

Jimbo rolled out of the way and came up in a crouch. Rusty still had hold of his knife as we hit the dirt and I let out a loud "oomph" and pushed myself into a sitting position, straddling Rusty's butt. He tried to twist around but Jimbo stomped on his wrist with one booted heel and Rusty screamed and let go of the knife. The blade thudded to the ground.

"Get out of the way, O'Brien. He's mine," Jimbo said, his voice a thunder of threat and fury.

"Jimbo, listen—you can't kill him. They'll put you in jail. We have him down. You can't plead self-defense if he's already down!"

"Not if you don't say . . ." Jimbo stopped, looked first at me and then at Rusty, and slowly shook his head. "Never mind what I was gonna ask you to do." His voice broke, and I knew exactly what he wanted to do, because I wasn't far from the thought myself. Luckily, I had more self-control than the biker.

"Go see to Murray. I can keep this guy down," I said. Jimbo headed toward the van and I leaned hard on Rusty's back. "You owe me one," I told him. "You owe me your life and you'd better remember it."

Even as I spoke, Rusty reared back. I grabbed a fistful of his hair and shoved his face into the dirt as hard as I could. "Down, boy."

"Bitch!" He struggled, trying to twist away.

"Shuddup!" I pushed a little harder on the back of his head and he stopped his struggling and lay silent. Just then, the high-pitched whine of sirens sounded from above, and flashing lights flickered at the top of the bridge. Jimbo shouted, waving his arms, and a spotlight glared down, illuminating the campsite. Deacon was there.

THE EMT CREW loaded Murray onto a stretcher as they discussed the best way to get her out. "She's in no immediate danger," Larry Davidson said. Joe and Larry seldom had the same shifts, but I knew who he was. "But going up that ravine is going to be rough. On the other hand, it will take a good hour to get an ambulance here via the access road."

"How's Murray doing?" I asked.

"She's stable, her vital signs are all good. She's been drugged, but there's no sign of an overdose. We're monitoring her. I think we'll take her up the hill, though. I don't want to wait."

"What do you think he gave her?"

"We found a bottle in the back of the van—GHB." Larry glanced over at Rusty, who was being loaded onto a stretcher as well. "He had to get it from the streets, because it isn't legal for him to have otherwise."

"What's GHB?" I asked, fearing the worst.

"Gamma hydroxybutyrate. Used as a date-rape drug, for one thing. He gave her quite a jolt from what we can tell. The dose was high enough to knock any fight out of her. Easy enough to get from any dealer."

Oh God. I looked at Murray's limp figure on the stretcher. She was awake, but barely. I wondered how he'd gotten the drug into her. "Will she be okay? Was she . . . did he . . . never mind," I finally said. It was up to Murray to tell me whatever she needed to tell me, whenever she was ready.

Larry scowled. "She should be okay, no thanks to that scumball."

"What about him?" I nodded in Rusty's direction.

"Shattered wrist, twisted ankle. He'll live." Will shot a look over at Jimbo, who was with the paramedics who were assessing how to get Murray up the hill. "I know your buddy wanted to hurt him. You did a good thing, even though it doesn't seem like it."

He had me there. As for me, I took no pleasure in sparing Rusty's life. While not a violent person by nature, when my loved ones were threatened, I turned into Mama Bear. Big, mean, nasty Mama Bear.

I dusted off my jeans and wandered over to the edge of the stream flowing out from the lake. Under the starlight the water glistened, and I knelt down by the edge, wiggling my fingers in the bubbling froth that flowed over the river rocks that were as big as my head. Icy cold, the water was born high in the mountains from the glaciers that cloaked Mount Baker. In daylight, it would be milky gray, thick with minerals.

The mountains and forests here were wild—as pristine as any forest could be in this day of logging and deforestation. The land was old and carried with it memories from the past, the footfalls of prospectors and miners, the soft whisper as tribal members passed through, the echo of explorers new to the untouched wilderness. And before that walked legends that came from out of the very earth herself.

This was no place for men like Rusty. They were anathema to the soil, tainting everything they touched. I glanced up at the stars and breathed a silent wish that the world could be a safer place for everyone I loved.

THE CLIMB UP was easier than the struggle down the mountain. Deacon helped me, even managing to steer me away from a thicket of stinging nettle. I almost lost my balance again, but Deacon caught me and I finished the climb with no further problems.

At the top of the hill, I turned to him. "Deacon, how do you think he drugged Murray? From the scene at the Catlan place, she sure didn't go along willingly."

He stared at me, his long lashes fluttering over his dark chocolate eyes. "I found a gun under the driver's seat of the van probably, the one he shot Joe with. You and Jimbo were very lucky he didn't have it with him when you snuck up on him. Probably didn't have a clue you were there, or he would have shot you dead. I know his type."

Leaning against the side of the patrol car, he added, "My guess is that he was waiting for her. He snuck up on her before she could get her gun out, forced her to take the pills at gunpoint, then just waited until they hit. The effects are pretty quick, and it looks like he gave her quite a hefty dose. I'll bet she was unconscious within ten to fifteen minutes, if not sooner. They'll have to monitor her at the hospital overnight. GHB can be a dangerous drug and the side effects aren't pretty."

It made sense, and yet imagining the scene set my stomach churning. Murray, held at gunpoint, forced to drug herself into the hands of a predator. I shivered. "Make sure they throw the book at him, Deacon. I'd rather see them shovel dirt over him . . . but please, at least make sure he's put away for good."

Deacon sighed. "We'll do our best, Emerald. Trust me, the boys on the force will call in every favor we have to convince the judge that this nutcase needs to be tossed into a deep hole, without a ladder."

Jimbo wanted to go in the ambulance with Murray, and I told him go ahead. I called AAA and asked them to come pick up the bike and haul it to my house, and then climbed in Deacon's patrol car. Rusty was already on his way to the hospital under armed guard.

"I'll drop you off at home. You can file a report tomorrow," Deacon said.

"Thanks. I'm exhausted." I leaned my head against the back of the seat and took one last look at the bridge, knowing it would be a long time before we came back out to Icicle Lake Falls.

Seventeen

⁂

TWO DAYS LATER, I woke to sunshine and a sense of excitement. It was the summer solstice. My wedding day. I sat up, grinning at Samantha, who had sprawled out on Joe's side of the bed, taking advantage of his absence. While I didn't pay much attention to old wives' tales, I had made him sleep at Murray's house. I didn't want him seeing me in my dress until we were walking up the garden path to the altar. Samantha stretched and blinked.

"Do you think Harlow's managed to pull it all together?" I asked the purring cat, rubbing her belly. Harl had jumped in, making me promise to let her take care of the finishing details. For the first time in days I felt like we might actually make it through the ceremony.

I rolled out of bed and looked out the window.

The morning light was peeking over the skyline, and all signs pointed toward a brilliant day. I pushed open the window and let the fresh air stream in, filling the room with the promise of new beginnings. Joyful in every sense of the word, I danced around the room until a knock on the door startled me. Kip and Miranda usually weren't up so early.

I quickly slipped into my satin robe and called out, "Come in."

Murray peered around the corner. "So, is there a bride in the house?" She ducked into the room.

"Murray!" I skipped over to give her a long hug. "Lordy, I thought this day would never get here. Look! Maeve dropped off my dress last night." I pulled her over to the closet, flinging open the door, but something in her eyes stopped me cold. "Mur? You okay?"

She shrugged, then forced a smile. "Yeah, I'm okay. It's just going to take a while before everything seems normal again. I think I'm fine and then . . . I just flash back."

I sat down on the bed and yanked at her hand until she joined me. "Mur, is there anything you didn't tell us? Did Rusty . . . did he . . ."

Murray was good at reading between the lines. She shook her head. "I don't know, Em. After I took those pills, the world could have ended and I'd have been oblivious. The doctor said she doesn't think so—my exam showed no evidence that I'd been raped but there are ways . . . He wanted to, though. And he said . . . the things he said while waiting for the drug to take effect. I can't get them out of my head."

I knew that it would take months for her to cope with the aftermath of the abduction. Feeling subdued, I hung my head. "I'm so sorry. I'm so sorry that this all happened. I wish we could have found him earlier."

"If wishes were pennies, we'd all be rich. No, Em." She laid a soft hand on my own. "You and Jimmy saved my life. I'll never forget that. Don't you let me spoil today. I'm fine, it's just going to take some time to process all of this. White Deer will help me, and I have you and Harlow and Jimmy."

"What's going to happen to Rusty?" The thought of him roaming the streets gave me the creeps.

"Stalking and kidnapping a police officer isn't exactly the smartest thing to do. He'll get sent away for a long,

long time. Deacon was right, by the way. I pulled into the old Catlan place, but there didn't seem to be a soul around. I got out of the car, gun drawn for trouble, but nada—as with the other calls. So, I slid my weapon back into the holster and was heading back to my car when Rusty sprang out from behind a thicket of Scotch broom with his gun. I couldn't do anything except follow orders. If I'd resisted, he would have killed me right there."

She paused, then added, "Jimmy told me you stopped him from permanently exorcising Rusty from the gene pool. Thanks. I couldn't bear to lose him to prison and that's what would have happened."

"Yeah, I know." I gave her a long look, wondering whether to say what I was really thinking. Finally, because Mur and I didn't keep secrets, I added, "Murray, you have to know something. The *only* reason I stopped Jimbo was because of you—because you need him in your life. People like Rusty don't get better, they don't learn, and the courts go and release these twisted bastards every day to go out and do it all over again. For Jimbo's own welfare, I had to make him back off. But I didn't want to," I whispered.

"I know," Mur said. "I want him dead, too. Now, on to happier things. Please show me your dress. You and Joe have gone through hell for today, and you deserve to be the most blushing and beautiful bride there's ever been."

I looked deep into my best friend's eyes. "You know you've always been my best buddy. We'll grow old together—crazy old ladies, drinking tea, watching the sunset from our porches with Joe and Jimbo at our sides . . ."

She spluttered. "You know as well as I do that our old age will probably still be a mess of ghosts and ghouls and malcontents. I can just hear our theme song. 'Still ghost-busting after all these years!' Now haul out that dress and show me what Maeve scared up for you."

I carefully lifted the gown out of the closet. Murray gasped. "Oh Em, it's you. It's absolutely perfect. I know you wanted Nanna's dress but—"

"But this dress seems made for me, doesn't it? I love it. And Randa will wear it on her wedding day, I hope. Or if she doesn't want to, then maybe Kip's bride." At the thought of my children getting married, I flopped down on the bed. "Life is changing, Murray. Things never stay the same. Today Randa's fourteen. Tomorrow, she's going to be in college and gone. And then Kip. I don't know what I'll do when they leave."

"Yes, you do," she said firmly. "You and Joe will go gallivanting around, living your lives together. And you'll be perfectly happy. Now, let's get some breakfast in you. You're getting married this evening, woman!"

THE WEDDING WAS set for eight P.M. Randa and Harlow helped me into my dress. They were dressed in lavender—not some poofy-sleeved bridesmaid's night-mare, but simple sheaths that they could wear again and again. Randa's eyes gleamed as she helped Harlow pin the veil to my hair and then crowned it with a wreath of ivory and pink roses.

"Mom, you're so beautiful." Randa stood back, assessing me.

Harlow turned me toward the mirror and gave a little shove. I slowly approached. Suddenly nervous, I finally found the courage to look at my reflection. Maeve's dress fit like a glove, hugging every curve in just the right way. Harlow had curled my hair into a chignon, leaving a strand to coil down either side of my face. She'd also helped me with my makeup, and my eyes smoldered, sexy and seductive and mysterious. As green as my name, I thought. As green as the woods on a summer's afternoon.

One day I'd remember this. I'd look back and remember how beautiful I felt, and how loved, and how lucky. But today—today I was living through it, butterflies and all.

"I'm ready," I said, quietly, stepping into the low-heeled ivory pumps that Harl picked out for me.

"Not quite," she said, holding up her hand. "Give me a

couple minutes before you come downstairs. I've got a surprise for you. Two, actually."

As she ran out the door, I turned to Randa. "Where's your brother?"

"Jimbo helped Kip dress. They should be out in the garden by now." She paused. "Mom, you're happy, aren't you?"

The hitch in her voice surprised me. "Honey, yes, very much so. Why? Are you worried that things aren't going to work out?"

She shook her head. "No, not that. It's just . . . I want to know you're doing this for you—not just to give Kip and me a dad. You've been a great mom. *We* don't need anybody else."

I gazed at her. My daughter was growing up all right. "Randa, I'm marrying Joe because I love him and he loves me. We fit together. I wouldn't even think of marrying him if he didn't treat you and Kip right, but that's not why I said yes. Joe and I are . . ."

"Soul mates?" she asked.

Grinning, I shook my head. "Not exactly. But we're right for each other."

"How do you know when it's right?" she asked, smoothing out my train.

"You just know, honey. There comes a point where you look at the person and you realize that you want to spend the rest of your life with them. Sometimes it doesn't work out, like with your dad and me. Sometimes it does." I pulled her to me and gave her a long hug. "Okay, let's go get me married off before I'm an old lady."

As I descended the stairs, Miranda held my train so it wouldn't get tangled up on anything. When I reached the bottom of the staircase, I saw a huge bouquet sitting on the bench in the foyer. Harl peeked around the corner from the living room.

"There's your first surprise."

"Who's it from?" I asked, staring at the assortment of

roses, carnations, and baby's breath. It must have cost the sender a pretty penny, that's for sure.

"I didn't look—that would be snooping."

I picked up the envelope sitting beside the vase. It wasn't the standard gift card, but rather a full-sized greeting card. As I slid it out of the envelope, the picture of two bells chiming—wedding bells—appeared. When I opened it, I almost fainted. The flowers were from Roy.

> *Emerald, I know this isn't enough to mend fences, but I thought a lot about what you said. The kids deserve better than me for a father. I don't know if I can ever be what they need—what they want—but by the time you get this, I'll have checked myself into a rehab clinic to dry out and try to get a handle on the booze. It's a step in the right direction. Have a wonderful wedding and give the kids a hug from me. Check for child support for the next six months enclosed, and a check for your wedding. Buy yourself something nice. Roy.*

Dumbfounded, I stared at the two checks in my hand. He'd given Joe and me a thousand dollars. Part of me wanted to send it back. I didn't like accepting gifts from Roy and I knew Joe wouldn't like it. Then I stopped myself. It made Roy feel better, and if he truly was in rehab, it would help him for me to accept it. But I wouldn't spend it. I'd put it in the kids' college funds.

"Em, who was it—good Lord, was it bad news?" Harl asked, staring at me.

I wiped the shocked expression off my face. "No, actually it wasn't. Now, what's the second surprise you promised me?"

"It's me!" a voice called from behind Harlow.

"Rose? Rosy?" I started to run but stopped myself. I could do some serious damage if I tripped over my train.

Rose popped out from behind Harlow, dressed in her lavender sheath. "I couldn't pass up the chance to be a bridesmaid, not with a dress this pretty." When I started to question her, she held up one hand, stopping me. "Grandma's going to recover, and the folks are with her. They told me to come to your wedding and give you their love. In fact, Grandma M. was the one who suggested it." She stopped short, looking me up and down as if I were a statue or painting. "Oh, Emmy, you're so pretty."

I barely had time to give her a kiss when Murray chimed in. "Everybody's waiting. Get a move on, woman. Don't give Joe a chance to rethink getting hitched." She winked.

"Fat chance," I said, laughing.

As we headed out the door, Harl stuffed my bridal bouquet into my hands. It was a mixture of pink and ivory roses, with long fronds of maidenhair fern tucked in.

Crossing the yard to the garden, I glanced back at my house. I'd come a long way in the past few years—a lot farther than I'd ever expected. I'd seen things that convinced me of the presence of absolute evil, and of brilliant and pure good. I'd stumbled over death and legends come to life. And now, love had come sweeping back into my life, this time to stay.

"Oh!" I let out a little shout as I saw that Harlow had managed to scrounge up the arched trellises we'd planned on having. They were bedecked with roses and ivy, with grapevines and silk ribbons, with flowing drapes of sheer lace and bells that tinkled playfully on the faint breeze.

One arch stood at the beginning of the spiral walk, another at the end, leading into the center of the garden. As we approached the first trellis, I caught a glimpse of the wedding party that waited in the center of the labyrinth.

White Deer stood, strong and regal in a periwinkle blue dress that kissed the ground. A deerskin cloak graced her shoulders, and a beaded headband held back her waist-length hair. She gazed at me, silent and patient. Facing her, Joe was wearing a black tux, and beside him, Kip— his best man—beamed.

All our friends were there, on benches and folding chairs. Lana and Cinnamon, Jimbo and James, Horvald and Ida, Maeve and Aunt Maggie—clutching tissues aplenty. Deacon and his wife had come, along with Greg, Sandy, and Roger and Melissa. And Gunner and Lori were there, too.

Harlow, Rose, and Randa took their places in front of me, followed by Murray. I waited expectantly. Then, in a hushed pause, floating through the air like a single feather, came the sound of the flutist who stood to the side of the wedding party. High, thin tinkling notes, so winsome that I caught my breath, drifted toward me from the garden. Faerie songs, the flutter of wings on the wind.

As we followed the labyrinth to the center where I would stand beside Joe to pledge my love and devotion, I glanced to my right. There, peeking from behind a hydrangea bush, stood Nanna. She blew me a kiss as I walked by, and I knew that whatever may come, the constants in my life—my children, my friends, Nanna, and Joe—would always be there to shore me up. I took one long, slow deep breath and headed for the altar.

Full Moon Bridal Ritual

❖

WEDDINGS ARE MAJOR transitions in life. As with every big shift, it can be helpful to perform a simple ritual to mark the rite of passage and prepare ourselves for the new journey on which we are about to embark.

On the eve of the full moon before your wedding, gather with a group of close girlfriends near a body of water—a lake, a stream, a river, or the ocean. A pool will do if you live in the desert.

Ask each guest to bring a white votive candle in a heat-proof holder. The bride-to-be should dress in a simple shift (make sure the material can withstand getting wet). Guests should dress festively.

When everyone is present, invoke sacred space by having everyone join hands as you stand in a circle. Take three deep breaths and let them out slowly. The bride's best friend should say:

> By wind and water, by flame and earth, I ask that this space be blessed and sacred, be touched by heart and by love, by joy and by protection, by friendship and by allegiance.

Let the energy settle. Everyone should sit in a circle with the bride-to-be in the center. One by one, each guest should light her votive candle and set it in front of her, while giving the bride a heartfelt blessing and wish for the impending marriage. Make certain to avoid bringing sarcasm or negativity into the circle. This is not the time for man-bashing jokes.

When everyone has offered her blessing, the bride's best friend should hold up a chalice of wine (or grape juice, if there are objections to alcohol), and say, "To (insert name of bride), may your wedding and marriage be blessed!" Sip the wine, then pass the chalice clockwise around the circle. Each woman should follow suit.

After the toast, lead the bride to the water's edge, where she will wade in up to her chest. If she doesn't swim, have someone who does swim go with her for safety.

The bride-to-be should focus on the water, feeling it wash away any lingering worries and doubts. Feel the mantle of being single make way, opening up space for the new life to come—a life shared with someone else. When finished, exit the water, dry off, and then feast on a wonderful buffet of fruits, cheeses, and breads.

For me, my second marriage has been a brilliant and wonderful ride. Oh, there are tearful times, and worrying about someone you love isn't easy, but it's been worth every minute of it. To all those looking toward marriage in their near future—I wish you blessings on your life to come.

~the Painted Panther
Yasmine Galenorn

Emerald O'Brien owns a teashop, reads
tarot cards, communicates with the other
side and, on occasion, is called on by the
living—and the dead—to solve a mystery.

The Chintz 'n China Mysteries
with charm recipes included!

by Yasmine Galenorn

Ghost of a Chance
0-425-19128-1

Legend of the Jade Dragon
0-425-19621-6

Murder Under a Mystic Moon
0-425-20002-7

A Harvest of Bones
0-425-20726-9

"GALENORN IS A BRIGHT NEW STAR IN THE
MYSTERY HORIZON."
—MIDWEST BOOK REVIEW

Available wherever books are sold or at
penguin.com